IN LOVE
WITH
THE NIGHT

a novel

by

Liz Torlée

blue denim press

Library and Archives Canada Cataloguing in Publication

Title: In love with the night : a novel / Liz Torlée.
Names: Torlée, Liz, 1950- author.
Identifiers: Canadiana (print) 20220263574 | Canadiana (ebook) 20220263590 | ISBN 9781927882764 (softcover) | ISBN 9781927882771 (Kindle) | ISBN 9781927882788 (EPUB)
Classification: LCC PS8639.O78 I5 2022 | DDC C813/.6—dc23

The night
Hath been to me a more familiar face
Than that of man; and in her starry shade
Of dim and solitary loveliness
I learned the language of another world

from **Manfred** — Lord Byron

Other Books by Liz Torlée

The Way Things Fall

Dedication

To Louise, friend and comrade

Contents

PROLOGUE

Amina had never seen so much money. She could scarcely believe it was real. Just one of the notes in the bag would have bought them enough food for days.

She was fifteen years old, crouching by the side of the road with her father, eating *beghrir* bread, the only food they could afford with the few odd jobs he managed to secure. She fiddled with the sandal on her right foot. It was torn at the side. Her father had tried to mend it, but the tape was coming loose. A long squeal of brakes and the angry blast of a car's horn made her look up. Everything was bright and still. The noise of the market jarred to a halt. A well-dressed man hung suspended in the air, arms raised above his head, red tie flapping across his face. The leather bag he was carrying flew from his hands and money began to spill from it. It was American money. People yelled, loud and frantic. They leapt in the air, pushed and elbowed each other, scrambling for the notes, stuffing them into pockets and bags, and waistbands. The man fell in slow motion, hitting the hood of the car and rising again before slamming into the ground. His legs buckled beneath him. Amina remembered the look of panic on the face of the driver as he leapt from the car, yelling at everyone, pushing people out of his way. He knelt by the fallen man. A woman brought water, and they held the man's head so he could sip from the bottle. A small crowd gathered around them. "Ah, he's wealthy," someone said. "He will live, *Insha'Allah*. He will get good care." The ambulance came, and the medics shouted gruffly, shooing everyone away.

Amina watched her father searching with others for fallen notes among the barrels of onions, cucumbers, and tomatoes. When he returned to her side, she showed him the bag hidden beneath her skirt. It had landed right beside her. It was still half full.

PART I — THE TOWER

Chapter 1

Five years later, Amina stood before the large, ruined monument at the Merenid tombs in Fez, Morocco and looked down over the walled city of her home. It was magical at dusk when the lights of the medina came on and the muezzins' calls echoed around the valley. This was where she liked to come to think about her father. It was two years since he died, two years of grief she sometimes feared would tear her apart. She gazed at the sky and whispered to him, told him about the good life she lived now, and all because of him—the best father a girl could wish for.

The tombs were popular with tourists, and there were many here today, posing under the famous arch, taking selfies, or ambling along the trails. Amina watched a young couple scramble over a low crumbling wall, clutching and sliding their way round to a narrow shelf of rock. They sat with their feet dangling over the edge, arms around each other, and gazed across the valley, waiting for the sun to set. She hoped they would not linger too long. The slopes were dry with loose pebbles, and in the fading light it was easy to lose one's footing and take a serious fall. Amina would like to have stayed for the sunset too, but it was a good half hour walk back along the Avenue des Mérenides, and she wanted to reach the Blue Gate when her friends at one of the hotels came off duty. They would sit for a while on the terrace and enjoy a mint tea before continuing the journey home.

"Look at you. A proper hotel employee. Full-time," these friends had said, clearly impressed with the new status she had assumed after her father's death. "Not like us seasonal workers. Maybe one day *you* can hire us." She dismissed all this as friendly banter and laughed along with them but, deep inside, felt again the thrill of incredulity when the owners of the hotel had wanted her to stay, promising to finance training and education so she could take on her father's responsibilities. To this day, she marvelled at this good fortune…that they would trust and depend on her…she who had no qualifications and had been swept, literally, out of the gutter and into their lives.

Amina's father had worked as the Front Desk Supervisor and helped with general administration. She believed that if the owners, Hadir and his brother Dominic, thought of her at all, it was as the daughter of a member of their staff, several steps removed from their rich, colourful world; a young girl who loved to run errands or tag along with the maintenance staff, helping to sweep floors, empty ashtrays or pick up lemons that had fallen from trees in the open courtyard. She knew every nook and cranny of the wonderful building and had learned how things were run.

When Hadir called her to his office a few days after her father, Ahmed's funeral, his wife Sophie was sitting beside him, a sheaf of papers in front of her. Amina went cold and clammy with the thought of the life she would now have to lead.

"Ahmed's office will be yours, of course. And we thought we could turn one of the older suites over to you," Sophie said. "It needs renovating, and you can decide how you'd like it done. There is an excellent introductory course on hotel management we'd like you to take when you feel ready. I have information on it here."

What was she saying? Something about one of the suites, and a course? Amina must have gone pale because Hadir looked at her with consternation. "You don't need to answer right away," he said. "But will you think about it?"

"Do you mean I can stay and work here?" Her voice broke with a stifled sob.

Sophie leapt from her chair and drew her into a tight embrace. "*Mon Dieu*, Amina. That you should ask this. That you should ever for a moment have *questioned it.*" She turned, still clutching Amina, with a remonstrative look at her husband.

Hadir winced. "Forgive me Amina. I assumed you knew how much we need you, how much we appreciate what you do." He coughed. "How much we love you."

Amina felt detached from her body, hearing the words Hadir spoke but unable to believe in their sincerity. She could no longer fight the tears and turned away, red with embarrassment.

Sophie drew her to the couch by the window. "Don't stand there looking helpless," she barked at her husband. "Get us some mint tea and *ghriba bahla* cookies…the ones Amina likes."

Hadir left quickly, clearly happy to get away from these emotional women.

"Life is strange, Amina," Sophie said. "That you and your father should have been at the side of the road on the day of that terrible accident…he was destitute but walked all the way to the hospital with you, to find Hadir, to give him that money. When I think about how he was treated all those years ago in Cairo…well, the sheer goodness of the man prevailed and sent our lives on a different course. You can stay here forever if you wish. We are your family now."

As the sun sank lower behind the Merenid Tombs, the jumbled rooftops and tiny alleyways of the medina looked like a golden honeycomb.

"We are your family now." Amina doubted she would ever hear sweeter words. A slight breeze picked up. She drew her scarf closely around her shoulders and turned for home.

Chapter 2

The Riad Capella was a classic Moroccan boutique hotel, tucked away in a narrow alleyway in the Fez Medina. An oasis of luxury in the noisy chaos of the souks, it was popular with wealthy tourists and foreign business executives. No cars could drive in the Fez el Bali district, so guests were dropped at the Blue Gate and met by one of the local boys, always eager to be recruited for a few *dirhams*. The boys put the luggage in large wooden carts that they wheeled back to the hotel, weaving crazily through narrow, cobbled streets, and taking a mischievous delight at the consternation of guests running behind. Amina had to apologize to the visitors when they crowded into the lobby gasping for breath. But once they were safely inside, most thought of it as a big adventure. They talked about their growing concern as the alleyways got narrower and darker, their incredulity when they saw the huge wooden door in the wall, the simple brass plaque with the hotel's name. Their eyes widened when the door opened to an inner courtyard and they saw the fountain, the lemon trees, the intricate mosaic patterns on every wall.

Amina took charge at this point, shepherding them to one of the velvet-draped "conversation rooms" off the courtyard, aptly named for the intimate talks and friendly chatter they inspired. She would urge the guests to help themselves to cool drinks, fruits, nuts, and sugared candies laid out on the large mahogany coffee tables. Other members of staff materialized from the shadows to complete the check-in, take care of luggage, answer questions, and get the honoured guests whatever they could possibly want or need. Amina always felt a swell of pride as the visitors visibly relaxed before her eyes, sinking back into plush cushions, breathing in rich smells of musk and citrous and sandalwood.

***

"A most excellent meal and such a beautiful restaurant." The man opposite Amina leaned back, patted his large stomach, and nodded appreciatively. He and his two colleagues represented a travel organization currently considering the hotel as part of a tour package for small groups. The family had invited them for dinner. "Your chef is French, I believe."

"Henri trained in Paris and worked for a while in Nice," said Sophie. "We are fortunate to have him."

Amina explained the different meal options available for groups and offered to introduce them to Henri who would answer any specific questions they might have.

"My brother Dominic is sorry he couldn't join us tonight," said Hadir, offering more wine. "He is off to North America soon to pursue our interests there. Well, that's what he tells us. Maybe there are women across the Atlantic we don't know about."

There was general laughter at this, but Amina saw Hadir flinch and guessed that his wife had given him a sharp kick under the table.

"Our twin boys are in New York," she said. "They are doing a year in the States as part of their course at the International School. Dominic will be dropping by to check in on them."

Amina noted the impressed looks of the visitors and wondered again how rich the family was. The money her father had returned to Hadir after the accident had saved them from ruin. Hadir and Dominic's parents had died several years ago within months of each other without settling the debt from a risky financial scheme to shore up their other hotel in Casablanca. Certain people were expecting a big payment, people who accepted only cash. Hadir had been so stressed about the meeting, so anxious to get there on time, that he did not see the car and walked right in front of it. A lot of money was lost that day, and they had to scramble to make up the difference. "Thank God we got back what we did." Sophie made that dismissive wave of her hand. "All done with, *balayé.*" In the end, it seemed the Casablanca hotel was destined to fail. They eventually sold it and used those funds to gain a foothold in North America.

"I'm hoping Alex and Rafik will run the new hotel over there," said Hadir.

Sophie shook her head. "My husband is getting ahead of himself. Our boys are only fifteen. But it's a nice thought."

They all clinked glasses to that.

When the visitors finally departed, Amina joined Hadir and Sophie on the roof. It was late; guests who enjoyed a nightcap at the rooftop bar had already headed for bed. Emerging from the last flight of stone steps, she watched Sophie take a deep drag of the shisha pipe. Her wide silver bangle glinted in the light from the candles on the table at her side. It looked singular and special on Sophie's tanned arm. "Never wear more than one piece of jewelry," Amina once heard her tell a friend.

Amina looked with envy at this elegant woman, her hair pulled back severely and wound into a clip on the back of her head, her long elegant fingers cradling the tip of the hose. "What a klutz you are, *mon cheri*," she said to her husband, squeezing his arm. "People don't want to think one of the owners is off chasing North American pu—Amina, there you are. Come on over here. Tell us how impressed they were."

The three of them chatted idly, passing the pipe around. A loud banging of doors and high-pitched swearing stopped them mid-sentence. A female voice yelled in French. *"Merde! Il est fou, fou. Fils de pute."*

"Aiieee," said Hadir, his hand to his throat. "She'll wake the entire neighbourhood with that racket."

All three ran down the stone steps to the top floor of the hotel where the family's quarters were. The door was open to Dominic's room. A young woman was inside, screaming, tossing her clothes from the wardrobe onto the bed, opening and slamming drawers and closet doors. She stared at the three of them as they stood, aghast, in the doorway. Her hair was dishevelled, her eyes blank and shining. She stumbled and fell onto the bed.

"Where's Dominic?" Sophie strode into the room and pulled the woman into a sitting position. "What is wrong with you? Are you drunk?"

"J'en ai plus rien à foutre ici." She lurched to her feet, pushed Sophie out of her way, and vomited onto the rug.

"Antoinette! What the fuck—"

They turned. Dominic stood in the doorway, his face a mix of fury and distress, his yellow shirt stained, hanging loose, and torn at the shoulder.

"Leave us," he said. "I'll deal with it."

"Goddamnit, Dominic," said Hadir. "She's throwing up and screaming like some crazy *jinn* from the underworld."

"I said I'll deal with it. Leave us alone."

Amina backed into a corner. The wild stare on Dominic's face scared her. He looked menacing.

"What the hell have you taken?" Hadir persisted. "Do we need a doctor?"

Dominic raised both hands and tugged at the back of his hair, a habit Amina had noticed when he was stressed or clearly wishing to be somewhere else. "Goddamn it, Hadir. It's no big deal. A harmless hallucinogen. We went to the American club. She drank too much. Okay? Please, everybody…just go."

Swearing under his breath, Hadir ushered Sophie and Amina from the room.

Up on the roof again, he went straight to the bar, poured himself a cognac and slumped into one of the chairs. "No wonder he wasn't at the dinner. 'Harmless hallucinogen', he tells us. Like those two words fit naturally together. Is that the same woman as last time? The one from Grenoble? I lose track."

"I think her name is Antoinette," said Amina. "She wanted to see more of Morocco."

"What the hell part of Morocco were they seeing tonight?"

"Calm down, Hadir." Sophie stood behind her husband and massaged his shoulders. "Dominic's been working hard to get ready for the trip. We knew he wouldn't be around for a few days."

"What is it with these women of his? They're all basket cases. None of them last more than a month."

Dominic's girlfriends were a constant source of gossip. They were usually French, pouty lips, long legs, high heels. They would curl up on the low couches in the courtyard rooms, their loose, V-necked sweaters falling away from their creamy shoulders as they leaned forward for drinks or reached for a cigarette. They desisted with coy looks and graceful shrugs when Sophie told them there was no smoking except on the roof, and then giggle when Dominic pulled them to their feet and chased them up the stairs. Once, he called for a bellboy to bring wine to the rooftop, but the boy returned, saying there was no sign of them. He could hear low voices in Dominic's room…should he knock on the door in case they wanted the wine in there? "Don't be ridiculous," Sophie had said. "Give it here. Amina and I will drink it."

Amina had not enjoyed the wine.

She looked down now at her plain comfortable sandals, chosen because she was on her feet most of the day, and thought about her wardrobe. Flowery cotton skirts, loose blouses. No high heeled shoes or painted nails. Nothing that any man would find sexy. *Don't be stupid. You're the little sister. He'll never look at you any other way.*

Hadir swigged the last of his cognac. "Well. This one is likely on her way out."

When they turned in for the night, Amina stood for a moment in the corridor outside her door, straining to hear the intense muffled argument in Dominic's room. She could not deny herself the tiny spark of pleasure.

Chapter 3

Amina gathered an armful of files and took them over to Hadir's office. It was the end of the month, and she was working late, bringing the accounting up to date. Hadir wanted hard copies of everything and kept an old steel, three-drawer filing cabinet for this purpose. He was leaning over his desk, one hand on his hip, the other flicking a pen back and forth between his fingers, peering at a large blueprint. Despite the hour, his shirt was buttoned to the neck, his pants had a sharp crease, and his shoes were still shiny. Dominic was stretched out in the chair, one sandalled foot crossed over the other.

She hesitated, not wanting to interrupt, but Hadir beckoned her in. "It's late, Amina," he said. "That could have waited until tomorrow."

"I'd rather do it now. Then it's out of the way." She placed the pile in an empty spot on his desk and began jamming the new paperwork into bulging folders. A year ago, she had completed a bookkeeping course to supplement the hotel management training, anxious to prove her worth.

"Hadir, what's with all this filing?" said Dominic. "Don't you know Amina has scanned, uploaded, downloaded, organized, and cross-referenced everything on the computer? It's all online."

"It's online until it isn't. Network outages, blackouts, cyber theft…"

"I don't mind," said Amina. "Perhaps it's best to be safe."

"It's a waste of your time," Dominic scoffed.

"*You* are a waste of *my* time, brother." Hadir stabbed at the blueprint. "Why can't you get those final estimates? Too busy cleaning up yesterday's disaster, whatever her name was?"

Dominic winced. "She left on the first train."

"So?" Hadir persisted. "Final estimates?"

"I keep telling you, there are a few unknowns. It will get resolved. Stop fussing."

Amina smiled to herself as they continued sparring and jabbing at each other.

The El Hassan brothers were born and grew up in France, with Moroccan blood from their grandfather. They spoke fluent French, Arabic and English. Both had a classic Mediterranean look: medium height, slim build, olive skin tones, dark eyes, dark hair. But that was where any similarity ended. Around the hotel, Hadir was known as "Head in the Sand" and Dominic, several years younger, "Head in the Clouds." They would go along with this. "You'll have to ask Head in the Sand about that," Dominic might say if asked to explain an invoice. Or, "Marketing?" Hadir would put on a terrified look. "That's Head in the Cloud's territory. He's the schemer. But he'll be pestering me when it's time to pay for it."

Amina was often caught between them, with Hadir stressing caution and the need to make sure there was a healthy reserve, while Dominic wanted to *spend* money, claiming they'd never make more unless they spent more.

"Look at the people we got for *Moroccan Cuisine* week," he reminded his brother once.

"The mess in the kitchens! We nearly lost our chef," Hadir shot back.

"And the group from England. They loved it. Their reviews were the best yet. If I hadn't spent the money on social media, we'd never have got their attention."

Hadir had walked off waving his hands and muttering that the English were cheap. But he confessed to Amina once that Dominic was usually right.

Now, Dominic said, "Amina, come see me when you're done with this dinosaur. I've got renovation photos to show you." He roused himself from the chair and folded the blueprint. "It won't take long. I'll be in the gold room."

In the gold room, Amina found Dominic shuffling a deck of cards. He moved the cards to the side and indicated the photos of furniture accents and accessories laid out on the coffee table: tall copper vases, heavy candles on elaborate pedestals, miniature date palms in terracotta pots, colourful ceramic water pitchers, and more.

"Sophie and I are going shopping for some of these tomorrow," he said. "Zahra said we should get your input...says you've got a good eye."

Zahra was their interior design consultant. Amina had helped to move and re-arrange things under her direction but had no idea of leaving any impression at all. She was delighted to be consulted. They discussed each item and Dominic made a list of those they felt best about.

Getting up to leave, she noticed more boxes of cards on the low table by the couch and saw the writing on the side of one. "Are those Tarot cards?"

He gave her a quizzical look. "You're not offended, I hope."

"Some people say they're evil."

"That's nonsense." He patted the seat beside him. "Come on, I'll teach you a little, if you like. But don't tell Hadir. He'll blame our mother's Roma blood."

Amina knew her father would have vehemently disapproved, but was thrilled that Dominic would take her into his confidence.

"There are all kinds of decks." He pulled a few out. "The Rider-Waite, the Deviant Moon, Wildwood, Thoth...many others. They have seventy-eight cards. The difference is the symbolism, the way they are illustrated. Everyone has favourites. These belonged to my mother."

"Thoth. Is that the Egyptian god Thoth?" Amina pointed to a beautiful soft cream and blue leather case with a brass clasp, an image of the god with the head of an ibis on the front.

"It is. Did you learn much about those guys at school in Egypt?"

"A little."

"I know from my mother that Thoth is the god of writing, magic, wisdom...languages too, I think. He's the husband of Ma'at—the one who watched over the universe, insisting on justice and harmony. And that's where my knowledge on that whole subject starts and ends, I'm afraid." He opened the clasp and pulled out some of the cards.

Laying them face down, he explained a few different spreads: the *Horseshoe*, the *Tree of Life*, the *Celtic Cross*. "The cards help you think about different things that are happening, your past and present, the challenges you face, the possible outcomes."

Amina doubted the validity of all this, but the way Dominic's voice dropped into a serious, whispering tone as he lifted each card and explained it, made her want to learn more.

She ventured a sideways look at him. He wore a classic kaftan tunic shirt, white with black embroidery around the neck, white pants rolled up at the ankles. He was particularly striking in the half-light of this curtained room off the lobby. The walls were lined with low, plush sofas overflowing with woven cushions in gold and yellow and deep burnt orange. Small tables were scattered around the edges, some with silver pots and glasses for mint tea and, on every surface, gold, sandalwood-scented candles. The light from the candles played on Dominic's face, softening his sharp features, and lightening his thick dark hair. Amina noticed the kink in his nose that apparently was once broken. She didn't want to ask how. He was nearly thirty and had never married. "A playboy, Amina," Sophie told her. "Of course, he would never harm a hair on *your* head but, nevertheless, be warned." Amina had blushed furiously, hoping that Sophie could not tell how much she secretly admired him.

"The cards can help to ease your mind," Dominic said. "They suggest new paths, different ways of looking at something that worries you."

Only one worry plagued Amina's dreams: *what really happened all those years ago in Cairo?* Fragments of conversations, half-stories and gossip would steal into her mind on the edge of slumber, making her sleep fitfully and wake with new anxiety. This much she knew: her father was sent to prison, wrongly accused of setting a fire that killed the man he worked for. A few months later, he was released for lack of evidence. But, too late; too late to repair the humiliation and heartache…her school friends with their cruel teasing, parents whispering and pulling them away. Her father had been involved with foreigners, something to do with drugs, a cousin told her. She remembered one of her uncles trying to defend him. "He told the police everything. He had nothing to hide. They had to let him go." "Well, they still didn't believe him, did they?" said another. "And why not, I ask myself. Poor Fatima. The shame of it."

Fatima was her mother. When she died, the family blamed her father and refused to have anything more to do with him. Finally, unable to take the hatred of relatives and the hostile looks of neighbours, he took Amina and came back to Fez, the city of his birth.

Amina admired the cards Dominic was explaining: *The Knight of Cups*, a winged young man on a white horse, holding a golden chalice in his right hand; *The Empress*, seated on a throne, blue twisting flames around her; *The Three of Swords; The Seven of Wands; The Chariot*. They were like fairy stories, she thought, surely not to be taken seriously?

Dominic picked up the next card from the spread. "The one in this position will tell us what's happening at this moment, the influences on the current situation."

He flipped it over. *The Tower:* a tall, grey stone tower breaking apart, on fire, people falling from it, a lightning storm in the background, orange and black flashes, a large all-seeing eye above it. Dominic replaced the card carefully and leaned back, his hands on his knees.

"What does it mean?" Amina was alarmed by his silence. He looked like a trapped animal in the candlelight.

"Sorry, I didn't mean to frighten you." He picked up the other cards without turning them and put the whole deck back in its leather case. "I think that's enough for tonight."

She got up, torn between relief and regret. "*The Tower*. It's not a bad omen, is it?"

Dominic held her gaze for a moment, weighing his words. "It's a harmless hobby of mine. I shouldn't have bothered you with it."

As she walked away, he called out to her. "Amina. I'm sorry about last night. Antoinette. I'm sorry you had to see that."

Chapter 4

Dominic watched his brother pacing the kitchen. It was late and the staff had gone home.

"*The Tower.* Are you nuts, Dominic? Why are you messing with that stuff again?" Hadir picked up a wooden spoon and banged it on the counter. "All through our childhood we sat with those wretched cards and listened to Mother warning us about this or that and driving our father out of his wits with her crazy predictions."

"She was always right."

"She took it too far, and you have too."

"Something is going on, Hadir. It's weird. I've been getting this strange tingly feeling. I wanted to try and figure it out."

"So why didn't you turn over the rest of the cards? Who knows what you might have learned? Maybe we're going to win the lottery. How about that for a tingly feeling?"

"You shouldn't have such a cavalier attitude. The cards should be treated with respect." said Dominic, but he couldn't stop the reluctant smile. Trust his brother to think about possible financial gain.

"You are the one with the cavalier attitude." Hadir threw the wooden spoon back in its jar. "One thing I remember from mom is 'don't start unless you want the truth.' What is the matter with you?"

He is right, Dominic thought *The Tower* is a frightening card. It heralds unexpected, disruptive changes, the breaking down of old beliefs and habits. Perhaps he had unwittingly shone a light on something that was not ready to be revealed. That's what his mother would have said.

"I've got a strange feeling it's all connected to Ahmed," he said aloud. "It's been on my mind again. I don't know why. Like something more is expected of us. What had we done to deserve that break, to get back all that money?"

"*Mon Dieu*. Will you never let this go? For all we know the circle is closed. If Ahmed had not returned that money, we'd never have been able to pay off those scumbags, and you would have had more than a broken nose. In fact, we'd likely both be at the bottom of the Mediterranean. And who knows what would have happened to Ahmed and Amina."

"Amina was such an innocent party in the scheme of things."

"And don't you go destroying that innocence. If she ever knew you consulted Tarot cards and pestered the Gods, she'd leave us in dismay."

Dominic turned away, hoping Hadir could not see the guilt on his face. "I am sorry, brother. I can't help the feelings I have."

Hadir took the lid off a jar on the counter, his eyes widening with delight to find it full of soft coconut cookies. He popped one in his mouth. "Next time you get these funny feelings, go up on the roof and talk to the stars. Maybe they'll be in a better mood than the Tarot cards."

Dominic bristled at this sarcastic reference to his other passion. He had soaked up all his mother's love of nature. When he was a boy, she would let him sit on the porch with her late at night to listen to the crash of waves from the ocean, and gaze in wonder at the night sky. She told him that the stars knew the future, the wind whispered secrets, the desert hoarded mystery, and the earth told its stories only to kindred spirits. Hadir, nearly eight years older and already into girls, had written him off as a nature freak.

He was about to defend himself again when the door of the kitchen opened, and Sophie strode in.

"What are you two doing here at this time of night? Arguing, no doubt. And there I was hoping you might be teaching yourselves to cook something more than a rudimentary *tagine*. Do you know what time it is?"

Hadir dusted the flour from his hands. "At least I can cook better than this half-witted brother of mine," He squeezed Dominic's shoulder then cuffed him on the back of the head on his way out. "God protect me from my own family. Nagged and bothered from all sides, I am. And when the two of you are out shopping tomorrow," he called back, "don't forget we've got a budget."

Unable to sleep, Dominic made his way up the narrow stone steps that lead to the roof of the hotel. In cooler weather, guests would enjoy their meals here, or stretch out on one of the canopied daybeds to drink a mint tea and gaze over the rooftops toward the Atlas Mountains.

He made for one of these beds now. The three cats who had claimed the hotel as their home, gathered round him, clearly pleased at the unusual chance to be stroked and fussed with at this hour. Lying flat, arms behind his head, he listened to the sounds of the night: the odd car passing on the highway at the edge of the medina, the hushed laughter of young men on the street below, the cautious growl of a dog.

It had been overcast all day and most of the easily recognized constellations were partly covered by cloud. Straining his head back, he could just make out Pegasus, the white horse, the sire of Poseidon. There was Algenib, the star that defined the wing, he thought, but couldn't be sure. He had forgotten so much. Years ago, he had bought a decent telescope. Where the hell was that now, he wondered.

His mind meandered through the week ahead and the tasks that had to be taken care of before his trip, including promotional plans for the fall. He would get Amina involved—Hadir was useless at any kind of marketing. And he should call Antoinette, if only to make sure she had made it back to France. She had been in a rare temper and wouldn't even let him drive her to the train station. God knows how she got there. He couldn't remember what they had fought about. Why was he attracted to spoiled women with a well-honed sense of entitlement, Sophie had asked him this morning. It was as though he wanted the relationships to fail. *Was that it…was he so scared of commitment that only the most fleeting affairs, the most erratic and volatile women suited him?*

One of the cats climbed onto his chest, demanding attention. He loved the darkness. It was restful and soothing under the stars, especially on such a warm night, with the lingering smell of the disappearing orange blossom carried on the soft breeze. No matter where he travelled, he felt a flush of pure happiness to be home.

No, he was not scared of commitment, he thought. He looked with such admiration at his brother and Sophie, the two smart kids they raised, and the high hopes they had for the family's future. It was a treat to watch the two of them when they sparred: Sophie storming off in a huff, Hadir grabbing her arm and pulling her into a tight hug while she pounded her fists into his shoulders. That's what he wanted—that selfless, unconditional kind of love. No point in consulting the Tarot cards over that. Perhaps, it was not destined for him.

He rubbed the cat under its chin. It purred and stretched out full length.

The Tower. Shit. In his mind, the card signalled traumatic, disruptive change, but his mother would tell him it was much more subtle than that. He longed for her reassurance, her wisdom. They shared the same strong instincts, the same intuition, but he knew only the most basic, clumsy interpretations of the cards. And he was too impatient. "You can't keep knocking on the door of destiny, asking what it has in mind," she said once when she found him using the cards. "Sometimes, events are unfolding that you are not yet aware of. Stay quiet, listen to your heart. Everything will eventually become clear."

The night had fallen totally silent, but the fierce heat of the day still hung oppressively around him. He exhaled a long, deep breath and gently nudged the cat away. The puzzle of his future would remain unsolved; no matter how many attempts he made, there was always a piece missing.

Chapter 5

"You can't be serious. I'm not paying that for two copper urns. I bet if I scratched them with a knife, the paint would come off." Dominic checked the base of one of them. He knew it wasn't painted but the price was way too high.

He and Sophie were nearly finished with the shopping for renovation accessories and had arranged for a mule driver to pick up their purchases and wait for them in Nejarine Square. This store was not one of Zahra's usual suppliers, but the display of decorative copper urns and planters had caught their eye.

The merchant scowled and walked away. "Take your knife and scratch them, if that's how you feel," he said, over his shoulder. "That you should insult me. I, who have been in business here since before you were born. I, who have been consulted about the furnishing of homes for our most esteemed residents, ensuring authenticity, generously offering my time for the benefit of our city."

Dominic rolled his eyes at Sophie. He wasn't up to a protracted bargaining session.

"Let's get out of here. I need a break," said Sophie. "That café across the square has good mint tea. We can take stock of what we've got and what we still need."

Dominic was not fond of mint tea, the favoured beverage across the country, and was always pleased to inform hotel guests that the coffee in Morocco was among the best in the world. "You go," he said. "I want to drop in on Youssef. I'll meet you there in fifteen minutes."

He sought any excuse to meander through the Medina and headed now for the *Aïn-Allou* souk which he loved, particularly for its leather goods: everything from large brown and cream travel bags, satchels and purses, to belts and braces, sandals, and the traditional flat-heeled slippers in every possible colour. The tanneries in Fez were a "must-see" for the tourists, despite their unpleasant smell. Dominic insisted that every piece of leather furniture in the Riad Capella started there, and would often visit the tanneries, marvelling at the work still done by hand, at the men preparing the hides under a blazing sun, and large stone vessels filled with dyes spread over a huge surface, like the multi-coloured pallet of a giant painter.

The merchants in the *Aïn-Allou* souk knew him well and he could barely take two or three steps before being exhorted to come in for tea, to sit with the family and catch up on local gossip, to be asked about his love life and why he hadn't settled down and "made lots of children."

"Ah, he's still a foreigner," said Youssef, a leather and jewelry merchant, and a good friend. "You know these French men. They have a roving eye."

Dominic picked up a couple of watches with wide, grey and burgundy leather straps, and thick gold stitching. He decided to buy them for Alex and Rafik, his two nephews in New York. Sophie would say they were too expensive, and that the boys should not be spoiled. *Too bad. What are favourite uncles for?*

"Do you know that man?" Sophie asked, when he joined her at the café. "He keeps looking at us." She pointed to an elderly, heavy-set man with a long blue *gallabiyya* and a white scarf wound around his head and neck, sitting at a table farther over.

"I think I saw him outside that store, the one with the touchy merchant. Looks like he's headed this way."

"*As-Salaam-Alaikum,*" the man said, approaching their table. "Forgive me, but I believe you are from the Riad Capella? I couldn't help but notice that you have purchased a number of items. I saw you with the mule driver earlier."

Dominic nodded but said nothing.

"Allow me to introduce myself." He pulled a card from his pocket. "I am in the business you see. In Egypt. I am visiting and I have some connections with the store you were in earlier. If you are interested in the merchandise there, I can get you a good price. No problem."

Dominic slid the card into his jacket. "Thank you. But I think we're done for today."

The man nodded and backed away, both hands raised. "Of course, but call me any time."

"How would he know where we're from?" said Sophie as they left to meet the mule driver.

"Come on, Sophie. We're known around here. We've certainly spent enough money."

The driver made sure all the goods were securely strapped to the little cart. "I see you know Da'ud," he said, as they made their way back along the narrow winding laneways, edging around the huge barrels of potatoes, apples, figs, walnuts, and long trestle tables with soaps and detergents, brushes, mops, and other household cleaning products.

"Who is Da'ud?"

"The man you talked to at the café. You mean, you don't know him?"

"He offered to get us a good price at one of the stores. We thought he was just visiting."

"The merchant at that store is his cousin. He lives there with him."

"What?" said Dominic. "So, he doesn't live in Egypt."

"Maybe part-time." The driver could not keep the smile off his face. "Good trick. He is drumming up the business. Sometimes he pretends to argue with his cousin to get a good price for people."

"What a shyster. There are too many good people trying to make an honest living. They all suffer when no one knows who to trust."

"He's trying to help his family. Not such a bad thing," said the driver. "Maybe the prices in there are fair."

"Maybe. But that's not the point," said Sophie. "The point is his dishonesty about the relationship."

Dominic squeezed her arm. He loved his sister-in-law's high sense of honour, her righteous indignation, and the fact that she usually tried hard to believe the best of people.

Chapter 6

Dominic put the encounter at the café out of his mind. Therefore, it was with considerable surprise that, one morning, he found himself face to face with the Egyptian in the courtyard of the hotel. Amina told him he had a visitor, a Mr. Da'ud Karaoui. The name did not ring a bell until he saw the old man, hunched up on one of the stone seats by the fountain, drinking a mint tea. The dainty tea glass looked fragile in his meaty hand.

"Yes, we've met before." Da'ud said. "*As-Salaam-Alaikum.*"

Dominic muttered the traditional response. "Come to sell me your cousin's merchandise, have you?" he added.

Da'ud shrugged. "A man must make a living, *Insha'Allah.*" He waved his arm to encompass the dramatic architecture of the courtyard. "Yours is a good one, I believe."

"What can I do for you?"

"Is there somewhere we can talk, I wonder? Private."

Dominic led the man to his office and closed the door. *Some nerve.*

The old man took his time getting seated. He removed a gold tasseled cushion from the guest chair, saying "May I?" and placed it on the couch by the wall, nodding appreciatively at the ornate furnishings. He ran his fingers over a carved, painted box on the desk, nodding to himself, and eased his large frame slowly into the chair.

"Your business is doing well?" he asked.

"We are proud to have many loyal guests."

"Repeat customers are important." He began to rummage in a well-used leather satchel hanging from his shoulder.

Here it comes, Dominic thought.

"However—" the old man continued, finally retrieving two stapled sheets, and placing them on the desk. "That is not why I came."

Dominic frowned. "Why, then?"

"The young woman." Da'ud nodded his head towards the door.

"What young woman?"

"The one who brought me the tea."

"Amina? What about her?"

"I knew her father."

"A lot of people knew Ahmed. He worked here for several years."

"I knew him in Cairo."

The outside sounds of wheeling food carts, guest chatter in the lobby, and ringing mobiles fell silent for a second.

"You know about that time of course?" A sly smile hovered over Da'ud's mouth.

A rush of unwanted thoughts crowded Dominic's head. *Is there unfinished business in Cairo, is there a relative who had some claim on Amina?* He tried not to show his concern.

"I assume you know what happened to the man Ahmed worked for?" Da'ud continued.

"You mean the astronomer? I've heard a few things."

"A well-respected man. Lectured in many distinguished universities. In America too. He died. Ahmed was accused of setting the fire that killed him. Such a tragedy. I believe Ahmed told you about this."

"How do you know what he did and didn't tell me?"

Da'ud twisted the ornate silver ring on his little finger. "We saw each other from time to time. The past played on his mind. I believe it helped him to talk to someone who knew the people involved."

Dominic frowned. The family always hoped that Ahmed felt comfortable enough to discuss anything with them, but there may have been stories he was too embarrassed to share. And he was superstitious—if you speak of unpleasant things, you give them energy. "You knew those people in Cairo, then?"

"The man, Karl Gustav, was also an Egyptologist. He had a passing interest in Egyptian antiques and consulted me from time to time."

"And what has all this got to do with Amina?"

"You can decide." Da'ud indicated the papers on the desk.

Dominic picked them up. Both sheets had a twelve-section circle. They looked like horoscope charts, dense with symbols and meticulously scripted words. He peered closely. Ancient Egyptian hieroglyphics and the standard astronomical glyphs covered them. Notes in the margins were written in a neat, sloping hand. On the top of the first sheet, a name and birth date in English and Arabic announced: Amina Gamel, 24th July 1999; on the second, a date and a question mark: 27th November 2014?

Something about that second date was familiar to Dominic. *Two days before Hadir's accident.* He remembered the fierce pain in the pit of his stomach when he got that call and learned that his brother was in hospital, seriously injured; and later, sitting at the bedside with Sophie and the ten-year old twins, hearing him whisper that the money was gone.

"I don't get it," Dominic said, putting the two sheets aside. "What's this all about? How come Amina's name is there?"

"An interesting story." Da'ud checked his watch. "If you have not eaten lunch, perhaps you will be my guest. Anywhere close would be fine."

At a small restaurant down an alleyway near the hotel, they took the last free table under a covered archway. The cook was carving slices from a leg of lamb turning on a spit and delivering them to customers with slices of bread drizzled with olive oil.

Da'ud ordered a *mezze* meal for both: small dishes of spicy lamb mince, tahini sauce, fried cauliflower, cucumber salad, hummus, and pita bread. Dominic ate hungrily. The family and staff usually had leftovers in the hotel kitchen, or sometimes Henri took pity on them and made something special.

Ahmed had told Dominic that the astronomer he worked for in Cairo was Swiss by birth but loved Egypt and made it his home. He was apparently a spiritual type, a mystic, interested in the paranormal. Aside from serious writing and lecturing on cosmology, he developed star readings to help people discover their true path. Not the common fortune-telling horoscopes, Ahmed insisted, but rooted in the mythology and wisdom of the Ancient Egyptians. Interesting type, by the sound of it, Dominic thought, bit of a dark horse. Despite all the later trouble, Ahmed never spoke ill of Karl.

"Ahmed got drugs for him, right? Was that a factor in his arrest?"

Da'ud pursed his lips. "Perhaps."

"What kind of drugs? Blue Lotus?"

"*Salvia divinorum*. A plant. Native to Mexico. Ahmed knew someone who knew someone, shall we say. 'Diviner's Sage,' they call it. Perhaps you have heard of this?" Another wry smile. "Made the star gazing even more exciting, I believe."

Dominic made a mental note to investigate it.

Da'ud pushed his plate aside. "Let me tell you about the star charts."

Apparently, after the fire, Da'ud was called in to help go through what remained of Karl's possessions. There was an old leather satchel—he pointed to it hanging on his chair—unnoticed and unharmed. Much later, he discovered the two stapled charts with Amina's name in a zippered pouch inside and brought these papers to give Ahmed on one of his trips to Morocco. But, when it was clear how sick his friend had become, he changed his mind. The poor man would worry about what had prompted Karl, whom he was accused of murdering, to plot his daughter's star chart. It may only cause more grief.

"So why did you keep them?" Dominic asked, scooping the last of the hummus from the glass dish.

"Clearly a lot of work went into them. Properly interpreted, they could be instructive, enlightening for Amina. I believe she has turned twenty, am I right? Perhaps she is thinking of her future now, of marriage?"

"She is secure, happy, and busy. I'm sure marriage has not entered her mind."

"Such a lovely young woman. I am sure there are many candidates."

Dominic glared at him. "Do *you* understand any of what's written on them?"

"In my work, of course, I had an appreciation for the ancient history of my country, but I have no real understanding. On one of them, something is written in the margin about the 'wrath of Sekhmet' which is supposed to be a formidable force, if you believe in these things." Da'ud chewed thoughtfully on a small piece of pita bread and looked along the street at the hustle of the crowd. "There is some suggestion of dire consequences, karma at work." He turned back to Dominic. "I thought about giving them to Amina myself, but then felt it was not my place. You and your brother are her family now. I felt you should have them, and you can give them to her."

Dominic felt a reluctant respect for the man. Maybe he did, after all, have a sense of honour. "Amina was born in Egypt as you know. But I doubt she can read that stuff, and I certainly can't."

"It would be a pity to ignore them. Perhaps I was meant to find them."

This comment took Dominic by surprise. It was the kind of thing he himself would believe. *The Tower* came back into his head, along with a tiny shiver down his spine.

"There are several people in Cairo, Egyptologists, who might be able to help you," Da'ud went on. "Let me know if you'd like me to make enquiries for you. I will be staying with my cousin for a while." He placed his business card on the table "In case you have mislaid the other one I gave you."

Dominic picked up the charts again. "You haven't mentioned this second page. What is it? No name, just a date with a question mark."

"Karl had a child, a son. I believe he was born on that date—some months after his father's death."

"Really? What happened to this child, and the mother?"

Da'ud shrugged. "They lived in Italy for a while. But now? I'm not sure."

Chapter 7

Amina navigated her way through the market stalls with Dominic's imminent trip to North America on her mind. Her vision of the world on the other side of the Atlantic came mostly from movies, and she longed to learn more about life outside Morocco. She had studied English in school and taken refresher courses while at the hotel, but still lacked confidence. How long would Dominic be gone this time, she wondered, trying to head off that inevitable aching, empty feeling.

While paying for dates and apricots, and juggling bags to retrieve her wallet, she felt someone was watching her. She looked over her shoulder, but saw only the hustling crowd, people elbowing past each other. And then, a few stalls over, an elderly man caught her eye. For a second, he seemed surprised, then he raised a hand in greeting and gave her a slight bow. *Isn't that the man who came to the hotel a few days ago to see Dominic, the one who asked for tea in the courtyard?* Acknowledging him with a quick smile and a nod of her head, she moved away.

Coming to the market was such a treat, and she always offered to do so if the kitchen staff were busy. Henri was very particular. Some years ago, he had gone back with her to return a couple of bruised onions from the bottom of a paper bag. The old vendor, squatting on a low stool surrounded by rope baskets of vegetables, was dismissive and rude, but Henri stood his ground. On the way back, he told Amina they paid a fair price for these goods and were entitled to expect the best. After that, the vendors would tease her, calling out to each other in loud voices, "That young lady works with Henri. Don't try to pass off yesterday's bread on her!" She was both embarrassed and proud. Proud that she was earning money and could now hold up her head in the marketplace.

She hurried past the section where she had been sitting with her father five years ago when Hadir was struck by the car and badly injured.

On sleepless nights, the scene played over in a continuous loop in her mind, the details blurring into half-dreams.

Her father was running, clutching the bag of money to his chest, gripping her hand so tightly that it hurt. "Baba, baba, what's happening?" she cried, barely keeping up with him. Through the narrow alleyways that sunlight never reached, through tented souks and spice markets they ran breathlessly, until he pulled her into a tight corner that smelled of garbage and cat pee, and stuffed the bag under his jacket. Backwards and forwards, backwards and forwards, he rocked, saying nothing, nothing at all.

But now there was so much colour, bustle, and happy noise here. It would be easy to spend the whole morning, sit for a while under the twisted, thorny branches of the *argan* tree and watch the world go by.

"Amina!" Her friend Tabani called from across the aisle. "What are you doing here? Why didn't you tell me you were coming?"

"Last minute decision," Amina jostled her way over. "What are *you* doing here? I thought you had all sorts of wedding preparations to worry about."

"I had to get away. My mother is frantic, driving me mad. She wants every detail nailed down. Which sauna to go to, who will be coming to the henna party, how the *amaria* will be decorated. She is constantly texting relatives and getting different advice. She is worried about offending someone. I keep telling her it is *me* who is getting married."

Amina hugged her friend. "You must be excited, though, Tabani. Come on, admit it."

"Of course. But it's a full-time job keeping *Oumi* at bay. I know I shouldn't complain, though. Probably all mothers are like that, don't you think?"

Amina pretended for a moment to be engaged in shifting the weight of the groceries. Were all mothers like that, she wondered? *What might it be like to plan a beautiful, traditional wedding with your mother?*

"I'm so sorry." Tabani touched her arm. "That was not very sensitive of me."

"I barely remember my mother. I'm lucky to have Sophie watching out for me." Amina checked her watch. "Nearly ten. I still have spices to get. Henri will be pacing."

She made her way to the rows of covered tents where the spice sellers gathered. The market was getting busier, and she had to jostle her way through. The strong smell of ginger drew her to a vendor grating ginger root into small, sealed plastic bags.

"A special fresh ginger tea for you this morning, Amina?"

"I never have the time, Kamal. I need two fresh, good-size roots."

"You must come sooner. Good ginger tea makes for a happier day."

She stood for a moment taking in the giant woven baskets and pyramidal piles of saffron, paprika, cumin, turmeric, cinnamon, and listening to the enthusiastic cries of the vendors. Henri told her that in most countries, people buy spices in supermarkets, already sealed in small glass bottles. How could they tell if they were fresh, how could they see the colour and the texture properly, she wondered. She loved the spice market most of all and thought, surely, if those people could see this place and take in all the potent scents, they would prefer to shop here.

Finally, the shopping was done, and she headed home. Walking past the long rows of tented stalls, the old man reappeared. Her father would have told her that gazing at women is extremely rude, and that looking back at him could be taken the wrong way. On the other side of the square, she pulled her scarf across her face and chanced a quick glance over her shoulder. He was still there, gazing unquestionably in her direction.

***

"What kind of a man?" Sophie asked her.

They were in the kitchen, discussing a special occasion dinner for eight that one of the hotel guests had requested. Amina mentioned the man at the market, and Sophie became upset about it.

"Can you describe him?"

"An older man. He wore a *gallabiyya*. He might be Egyptian."

"Egyptian?" Sophie frowned. "Something rings a bell, but I can't think what."

"I've seen him before, here, at the hotel. It seemed strange…I don't think he meant any disrespect."

"You saw him *here*?"

"He wanted to see Dominic. I took him tea in the courtyard, and they went into Dominic's office and closed the door."

"What? Dominic has said nothing to us about a meeting like this."

Amina wished she had never mentioned it. When they got to Dominic in his office, Hadir was also there.

"Ah, yes, I forgot to mention it," Dominic said, after Sophie relayed what Amina had told her. "Sorry. It was that guy who introduced himself to us in Nejarine Square." Dominic waved his hand. "No big deal. He was looking for business."

"Looking for business," Sophie exclaimed. "And you let him in? After that little game with the merchant, not telling us it was his cousin? Are you mad? And now that creepy old man is following Amina around the market?"

"It's all right, everyone, really."

"It is not all right, Amina," said Hadir. "Bumping into you once is one thing. Staring at you as you leave the market suggests he was following you. That is very bad, very worrying behaviour. Dominic? What the hell is this? Why would you entertain a discussion with the man? He's not one of our suppliers and he sounds pretty shifty to me."

"If you'd all let me get a word in——he came because he knew your father, Amina. His name is Da'ud Karaoui. They knew each other in Cairo and continued the friendship here. I guess he wanted to use that connection and get some business out of us. But his behaviour is outrageous. There is no excuse for that, and I will call him on it."

"Please don't. If he was a friend of my father, then that explains everything. I remember my father mentioning the name Da'ud at one point."

"You didn't tell us about this, Dominic." Sophie gave her brother-in-law one of her famous skeptical looks. "Especially as we were both appalled by his deception, coming over to us all obsequious in that café."

"I'm sorry, I'm sorry. I've had a lot on my mind."

"Okay. Enough," said Hadir. "The mystery is solved. Dominic and I will discuss it."

"Come on, Amina," Sophie said. "We have to give the men a chance to feel important."

Amina left, relieved that the man was a friend of her father. He probably missed him too and that's why he was looking at her.

Chapter 8

Dominic watched his brother processing this latest development, staring at the two stapled sheets on his desk, shaking his head and taking a deep, noisy breath of irritation. After Sophie and Amina left, he felt he had no choice but to tell Hadir the truth, the real reason for Da'ud's visit.

"First, you stand there and tell all three of us a bare faced lie, and *now,*" Hadir's voice rose an octave with outraged incredulity, "you tell me you had *lunch* with the guy, and he gave you these damned things. Whatever the hell am I looking at here...*horoscopes?* For God's sake, Dominic." He sat down heavily and threw his hands in the air.

"I didn't tell you because I knew you'd get worked up, just like this, and because I don't want Sophie or Amina to know. Not yet."

"You lied."

"A white lie."

"There is no such thing in Sophie's lexicon, as you know. And what about Amina? Doesn't she have the right to know about these?"

"What if they have some kind of bad news, some dire prediction?"

"Oh please. It's all mumbo jumbo. Surely?"

"I wanted to think about it. I was *going* to tell you, of course. How could I know the old guy would be skulking around the market?" Dominic perched on the edge of the visitor's chair with a nauseous feeling as though he'd had too much to drink.

"What exactly did he tell you about these?" Hadir picked up the sheets..."over your nice friendly lunch?"

Dominic recounted what he could remember of the Ancient Egyptian interpretations that Da'ud had offered. "I don't have any understanding of that stuff. That first chart is about Amina's life. And it was done by the guy her father was wrongly accused of killing. Amina might try some amateur way of reading it and find something sinister in there."

"Can't you look it up online?"

"Not this. I've tried. You can get a hundred astrologers with one click but I doubt they are into hieroglyphics too. I'm not sure anybody does this kind of thing. Da'ud said an Egyptologist might be able to help."

Hadir turned to the second sheet. "And this one underneath is the guy's son? What has he to do with it all? With Amina?"

"Who knows? Maybe the astronomer did these for people he worked with, their kids, his own kid."

Hadir tossed the paper aside. He took a sip from his glass of tea and put it down with a grimace. "Stone cold." He went to find a bellboy to bring another.

Dominic looked around his brother's office. It was less ornate and more practical than his own but there was one stunning piece of *kellij*, the traditional Moroccan mosaic art on the wall behind his desk. It had classic geometric florals with colours ranging from the dark matte browns to yellow, cyclamen pink and vivid blues—so intricate with hundreds, thousands, of pieces of tile. The same artist had designed the beautiful arched wall behind the fountain in the lobby. Dominic had always been surprised at Hadir's willingness to pay the price for these things with "no functional value." But the artist was local and well-known, and Hadir claimed it was important to support local people and culture.

"I'll admit this much," Hadir said, coming back. "It's all weird." He looked as though he was about to say something and then had second thoughts. Dominic wondered if he was thinking about the Tarot cards, *The Tower,* just as he was. "I don't feel good about keeping this from Amina, but you're right. Who knows what upsetting bits of nonsense they might contain?"

The bellboy brought a new pot of hot mint tea and insisted on pouring it, lifting the pot high above the glass and pouring a long thin stream of the beverage to fill it perfectly, without spilling a drop.

"Well done," Hadir said. The young boy beamed and offered to pour one for Dominic who shook his head.

"Brahim, you know my brother prefers coffee. He's an alien." Hadir waved his hands and the boy scampered away.

"What should we do?" Dominic felt quite unable to make a decision on his own.

"Sophie is no doubt expecting us to rough up the old guy in a back alley." Hadir inhaled deeply. "I will visit him. Alone. A friendly chat, 'man to man'. Now that you know him so well, you are compromised. And you can't control your temper."

"I will try hard to improve, sir," said Dominic.

Hadir threw an eraser at him, shaking his head. "You can come with me and wait in a café. In case I need you. Or in case he murders me."

***

Dominic sat at a restaurant patio table not far from Nejarine Square. He had brought paperwork from the hotel and tried to apply himself, but it was mostly accounting issues that required his signature, and he had little interest in reading them in detail. He tried to argue with Hadir that surely one signature was good enough—Hadir's. But his brother had insisted that anything over a certain amount should have both.

He ordered another coffee. This was a new, upscale restaurant compared to its nearby competitors and it attracted a lot of tourists. Potted palms were placed among tables circling a miniature fountain at the centre. Two feral cats helped themselves to the bubbling water, constantly looking back over their shoulders. Each table had a bright red and yellow tablecloth and a small Moroccan lamp shaped like a twisted pyramid, with a tea light candle underneath. Nice touch, Dominic thought. He knew the owners, an older man and woman who did this to keep themselves occupied, they claimed. He hoped they did well.

"*As-Salaam-Alaikum,* Dominic." And there they were, coming out with his coffee and a plate of almond *ghriba* cookies with lemon cream. "May we join you?"

He was only too happy to put the paperwork aside. They chatted about the tourist business, the customers they had, and Dominic's impending trip to North America.

"You are a restless soul, Dominic. No chance you will be settling down any time soon?"

"Time enough for that, Yasmeen," Dominic said, taking a second cookie. "Why does everyone want to get me married off?"

"Because you are letting yourself go to waste. And you love children. Look how good you are with your nephews. They adore you. Here you are, an eligible bachelor with at least three women I know finding ways to cross your path accidentally on purpose."

Dominic said he knew nothing of any interested women and was much happier left alone.

"Yes, much better left alone," said a voice behind him. Hadir leaned over his shoulder and took one of the cookies. "Here I am doing the hard work and my brother is whiling away the morning at your lovely restaurant without a care in the world. No papers signed, I see."

The hosts insisted Hadir join them for coffee and would not accept payment. With some difficulty, the brothers extricated themselves after another half hour and took their leave.

"Well?" said Dominic when they were out of earshot.

"He will not be bothering Amina again." Hadir imitated the gestures of the old man. "'Begging most gracious pardon. My eyesight is failing, and it is possible I am staring and not realizing. Such a lovely young woman, such a comfort to know that your family is taking care of her. Her father was a good man. Forgive me if I have caused distress.' On and on he went."

"What a creepo," said Dominic.

"He pressed me about the charts. Had we given them to Amina? Were we planning to get help to interpret them? I told him we hadn't brought it up yet, that she had a lot on her plate with your impending trip. He was anxious to curry favour, to make up for the 'misunderstanding.'

He gave me the card of some Egyptologist. Spent forever fishing around for it. He's not sure if the guy could help or if he has time, but suggested we call him. He's in Ouarzazate."

"What's an Egyptologist doing in the middle of the desert in Morocco? Making movies?"

"Yes, actually. He's a consultant on some film projects."

Dominic shook his head. "Let's wait. We don't know enough about the guy who did these charts. Might have been a Machiavellian type. And I still don't get why that other page, the child's, was stapled to Amina's. If they happened to be together, that's one thing, but stapled? Seems odd."

"I asked him that. He just shrugged. 'Why would you worry?' he said. 'The child is not important.'"

PART II — THE LEATHER BRACELET

Chapter 9

"The child is strange," Robert insisted in another frantic phone call from England.

Nigel choked on his morning coffee. "What?" He coughed to gain time. "I mean, what kind of strangeness are we talking about? Not *The Omen* or *Rosemary's Baby*, surely?" He rolled his eyes at his partner, Philippe, who hovered nearby. This was the third or fourth call from Rachel's brother in the past few months. Nigel was tired of the drama. He went out onto the balcony of his high-rise condo in Toronto, needing air. Several sailboats plied the choppy waters of Lake Ontario in the brisk morning breeze.

"They are now telling us that he is gifted and will need constant stimulation, that he might become more emotional than other children." Nigel detected a note of panic in Robert's rising voice. "He mumbles to himself in two or three languages for heaven's sake. I can't put my wife through this anymore. She has enough on her mind. It's…I'm sorry. It's a bad time."

"Gifted? Who is saying this?" Nigel had met Rachel's son, Lukas, only a few times when he and his mother lived in Italy. There was indeed a certain 'knowingness' about the child, as though he were weighing you up. Obviously, the father's influence.

"Some child therapist the woman at the kindergarten suggested. I mean he can read like a six, seven-year-old and he's extremely observant, doesn't miss a trick. But…he's withdrawn, over-sensitive…and who knows what else is coming. And with our own three children. All too much."

"He might just be smart, Robert. His parents were very intelligent. And he will surely adjust, in time. I know I'm the wrong person to be expressing an opinion on children." But if anyone were mad enough to have three children, he thought, what difference should a fourth make? *How to phrase that, exactly?*

"Forgive me, Nigel, but I'd be grateful if you'd step forward here. In many ways you were Rachel's best friend, a father figure to her, *and* the Executor of her will. But it was me who had to bring the boy to England, sort out the Italians, the house, Uncle Vanni, that whole convoluted business with the death certificate."

"I *had* to defer to you on those matters," Nigel said, getting increasingly hot under the collar. "*You* were her brother, for heaven's sake. And half Italian yourself, *Roberto*."

"Oh, cut it out. *Dove sono il bagni.* That's about it." Robert went on about the child not wanting to play with the things "normal" four- or five-year-olds would be drawn to. And as for his own teenage children, the novelty of inheriting a young cousin had worn off. "Don't get me wrong, we love him dearly. We simply don't know what's best for him anymore."

Nigel turned his gaze reluctantly from the lake and went back inside.

"With the summer holidays coming up, we thought a change of scene would be good for him," Robert said. "Melinda and I were hoping you'd drop by when you come to the UK next month. He might appreciate a friendly face from the past. That way we can discuss a few ideas in person. What do you say?"

It took Nigel a full minute or two to realize that one of the ideas the man was proposing was that they, Nigel and Philippe, invite the child to Canada for the summer holidays. As soon as this sunk in, he protested madly, making excuses about their age, the fact that their antiques store still required work, other plans etc., etc., but Robert kept saying "Of course, of course, just running it up the flagpole, you know, discuss it when you arrive, very flexible…"

***

As Nigel drove along the A40 towards Cheltenham, he marveled that he had allowed himself to get this far. He could have stayed longer in Guildford with his friends, spent a day or two in Oxford visiting his old university haunts, and ventured into those pretty Cotswold villages where there was always an antique auction or two to get excited about. But no, here he was, driving past Oxford and bound for the home of Rachel's brother in Cheltenham. To top it all, traffic was slow and drivers increasingly bad tempered.

Philippe had professed great excitement at the idea, googling away to find *"Ten super fun things to do with young kids this summer,"* things Nigel could barely bring himself to imagine.

Finally, pulling into the driveway of the prim, pseudo-Tudor house, he cast a wary glance across the manicured front garden, its perfectly round boxwood shrubs, lupins, and columbines, and clusters of hydrangeas pruned to within an inch of their lives. A stone cupid, hands behind its back and eyes cast heavenward, provided a touch of whimsy. *No grinning gnome, thank heavens.* Was that a curtain moving at the leaded bay window, or could he slam the car into reverse, risk backing into one of the ornate urns, and then phone? *So terribly sorry. Unavoidably detained.*

Alas, here was the good wife Melinda on the doorstep.

"Nigel! So good to see you. How was the journey? You must be tired. Come in, come in." She stopped at the foot of the stairs. "Robert. Nigel's here. Hurry down." She ushered Nigel into the living room. "Up there, getting some papers together. You know Robert. Bit of a fusspot."

Papers, Nigel thought, a slight flutter in his stomach. Melinda urged him into an overstuffed, winged armchair with a matching footstool.

"Sherry, perhaps?" she asked, hovering by the drinks cabinet.

"No, no. A cup of tea would be just the thing." Who on earth drinks sherry, he wondered? *Surely, it's only for the Queen's speech at Christmas with a nice mince pie?*

Melinda went to put the kettle on. Nigel thought she had lost weight since he last saw her. She looked drawn, frail. The clock on the mantlepiece struck the half hour. *Dear God, please get me out of here before the sun goes down.* He looked around the room: Astoria Grand armchairs with beige and gold striped upholstery, an oak buffet sporting Wedgewood crockery, a British Colonial rosewood coffee table on fat, spiral-fluted legs. Not even a nod to the modern age, he thought, and no art to speak of. On the far wall was a print of that Constable classic, *The Hay Wain*, that must surely be in every third or fourth living room along the entire length of this country. *Where did they hang Rachel's paintings?*

"The man himself!" Robert entered the room with a flourish and shook hands vigorously. For a fleeting second, Nigel caught a resemblance to Rachel. Dark hair and olive skin tone that defied the English climate. But in another instant, it was gone, and here was this tall, skinny man with thick-rimmed glasses, looking so British with his Shetland wool V-necked cardigan, his hair just over the collar,

Over lunch in the austere dining room, flanked by floor-to-ceiling bookshelves, Nigel tried to follow the plaintive chatter of his hosts. Through the window, he saw purple clouds looming over the trees in the distance, adding to his general sense of gloom.

"They'll be home shortly," Robert said. "Fiona, our eldest, stops by the pre-school to walk home with Lukas every day."

"Of course, she'd rather be with her own friends," said Melinda.

Nigel detected a note of distress in Melinda's voice. Robert kept taking her hand and squeezing it. They told Nigel a long tale of woe, how Lukas never wanted to go on play dates with other kids his age, never wanted to watch children's television, always had his nose in his iPad or in one of those star books his mother gave him. "Sometimes we'll go into his room at night and find him sitting on the windowsill trying to look at the stars. He gets all upset if it's cloudy or raining…which of course, it usually is."

Nigel raised his glass of *Greco di Tufo* and took a sip. Rather nice. Robert knew his wines. The Italian bloodline still worked at some level. Nigel replaced his glass carefully on the coaster. "We must not forget that he saw his mother drown just a few months ago."

A few uncomfortable seconds ticked by. Melinda busied herself stacking the plates.

"I know. PTSD. That's what Uncle Vanni is saying. But what can we do? We've tried everything."

"Talking about Uncle Vanni—surely, he'd be delighted to see his great nephew again. No?" Nigel realized too late that this last word came out like a desperate croak.

"Vanni's too old. Not long for this world, I fear. Look, we know it's a tall order. Of course, we'll cover all expenses, anything you need. We thought you could tell him more about his mother. In the later years, you knew her better than any of us did."

Nigel wondered if anyone had truly known this woman who had become one of his closest friends. Her life had taken a dramatic turn all those years ago—and at *his* instigation. God, how he had often regretted facilitating that meeting with the man who would turn her life inside out, the man she loved beyond reason. She never got over his death; it was only the boy who had kept her going these last few years. He remembered his last visit to her home in Italy. There was a photograph that stayed in his mind. It was taken in the desert near Cairo with the pyramids on the horizon. Karl had his arm around her waist. Strands of long fair hair floated across his face. Rachel was leaning into him. Both had a wistful, half-smiling look as they gazed into the distance, as though they knew the answer to everything was out there, beyond the grasp of others.

His reverie was broken by Robert laying out some paperwork. The conversation now took a decidedly pragmatic turn: timing, airlines, the young relative who would accompany Lukas on the flight, passport details, the need for a letter—proffered with a flourish—giving Nigel temporary guardianship of the child in Canada. *Guardianship.* Nigel felt untethered from reality.

"Ah," said Melinda, peering through the dining room window to the driveway, "here they come."

Chapter 10

Lukas stood in the doorway of the dining room, next to Fiona, the eldest of his cousins, who bore a look of strained tolerance. He was dressed in knee-length grey shorts and a white shirt. Slim and tall for his age, he had the blonde hair and sculpted features of his father. And the same clear grey eyes, like some mythical Norse creature…a little unnerving, Nigel had to admit.

For nearly an hour, Lukas sat on one of the dining room chairs, his hands resting in his lap, his legs swinging constantly back and forth. His uncle outlined the plans and his aunt tried to stay jolly and positive. Poor kid, Nigel thought, he's probably dreading it the same way I am.

"Philippe has already found some interesting things for us to do," he said, desperate to make conversation. "Would you like to see Niagara Falls?"

The boy's eyes lit up for the first time. "Really?"

Nigel was relieved by the boy's show of interest.

"I've just remembered something," Robert said. "There's a bag of things Rachel wanted you to have. To be honest, I'd forgotten about it. It's in the storage room off the garage. Let me check."

"I'll come with you." Nigel was anxious to release Lukas from the scrutiny.

It was a generous garage, Robert's Range Rover taking up less than half of it. Nigel's gaze was drawn to an opaque sheet of plastic covering something tall and wide, leaning against the opposite wall. The bottom part was torn away, and the corner of a painting showed through: earthy tones, a few fallen leaves. He stopped in mid stride, one hand to his heart. "Please tell me that is not what I think it is."

Robert followed Nigel's gaze. "Aah, that. But what is one supposed to do with it? It's far too large."

It can't be. Nigel pulled up the plastic and took a moment to collect himself. There was a man standing at cliff's edge, a sun gathering strength behind far hills, a sky of smudged pinky-grey, and dark greens of cypress trees bleeding through dawn's light. *Aphelion.* He dropped the sheet of plastic and turned to face Robert, the blood rising to his face. "Goddamnit Robert. This is a very important painting. I assumed you had left it with Uncle Vanni. I can't believe it's sitting in a garage in this frightfully damp British climate. It will be ruined."

Robert foraged around in a storage room off the garage. "Cut the dramatics, Nigel. How can a bloody painting be *important?* The damned thing is enormous. I couldn't saddle Uncle Vanni with it and where the hell would *we* put it?" Nigel nearly suggested the depressing oak buffet and hutch could be sacrificed but bit his tongue. "And she had so many. Some are in Lukas's room, but he's not interested."

"He might be one day."

Robert pulled out a small step ladder and climbed up to rummage on higher shelves. "It's not just the paintings. The books…astronomy, astrology, all that mumbo jumbo she was into in Egypt. Strict instructions not to get rid of any of it. I mean, there are limits."

"This painting meant the world to your sister. She bought it anonymously from that gallery in Rome, as I'm sure you know. If you won't hang it, it should be in a climate-controlled vault."

"Here it is." Robert handed him a canvas bag. "I've no idea what's in it." He came down off the ladder.

"Look Robert, I'm serious. You do know who painted this, don't you?"

"Of course, I do. Steven someone. My sister's fling in Italy. Not to our taste, I'm afraid. Sorry, I know he's a friend."

Nigel recalled the last time he had seen the painting, at Rachel's home in Calabria, where all the rooms were wide and tall and smelled of the sea. Lying back on one of her large wicker chairs, feet on the coffee table, a glass of wine in hand, his eyes would be drawn along the tumbling rows of bookshelves, across the fireplace and over to a low trestle table on the far wall, coming to rest on the painting that soared above it. It always made his heart flutter. No wonder she loved it so much.

Her brother is a complete moron, he thought, a bloody philistine. "It's not yours to question, Robert. When Lukas is older, he can choose to keep it or donate it to a gallery, or even sell it, although his mother would not have wanted that. But it cannot stay like this."

For the first time in this strange encounter, Nigel felt he had the advantage. Robert needed to keep him on side. "If you can stomach the cost, I will make arrangements to have it shipped to Canada…along with any others you don't care for."

Robert reluctantly agreed. Melinda materialized again, pressing another cup of tea on him, but he finally persuaded them it was time to leave, blaming the traffic and his flight the next morning.

Robert came out to the driveway to see him off. "Look Nigel… I don't want you to leave with the wrong impression. Melinda, you see… she has the brunt of it all. I've got my work to distract me. She has to deal with the day-to-day. And…" He turned his head away for a moment. "She's not well, you see."

Nigel looked at him with alarm. His lower lip was trembling. But Robert shook his head and made a dismissive motion with his hands. "Won't go into that now. Needs a break, that's all." He suggested an alternate route to Heathrow and urged Nigel on.

***

Nigel shifted in his business class seat on Air Canada's flight back home, cradling the last half inch of a dry martini in one hand and picking at the tiny bowl of cashews with the other. *What on earth have I done? Must be getting soft in my old age. And Melinda not well…what did that mean? Bit of a shocker at the last minute.*

He extended an arm to catch the attention of the rather fast-paced flight attendant and ask for another drink and a replenishment of the cashews. She delivered these with a practiced smile and an assurance that the meal would be served in fifteen minutes. Thank God, Nigel thought. The martinis were going down too easily.

With some difficulty, he unbuckled his seatbelt and managed to extract the canvas bag Robert had given him from his overstuffed carry-on case. Inside was an envelope with his name on it. Rachel's writing. He had not expected this and took another swig of martini.

My dear Nigel,

These are a few things that were saved from the fire. Lukas is too young to appreciate them, but he already loves the night sky and all the stories of the stars. I put them aside for you because I don't trust Robert to realize their value or hold on to them.

*At the bottom there is a decorative box with hieroglyphics on it. It contains charts and photos and sky maps, and also a notebook. It's a miracle it was unharmed. Karl must have started putting all this together as soon as he knew I was pregnant. I had no idea, and you can only imagine the tears I shed looking through it. We knew we were having a boy, but had not chosen a name. Pasted on top of the box is a celestial map for the day Lukas was born. It was supposed to be two days earlier, but Karl was confident it would be the 27*th *and of course it was. He was never wrong. In the notebook, he described some of the good and not so good events of our lives, and the course of our love and fate…things that Lukas is far too young to grasp. I think he meant to keep it going for years, like a diary, believing they would share the same passion for the stars and the mythology and wisdom of the ancient Egyptians, and that, one day, they would discuss these things together. I leave it to you to decide when Lukas should have it. Please keep it safe. I know you still shake your head at me. But I love you and trust you, as you know so well.*

Rachel

A wave of sadness passed through Nigel. He thought his tears for Rachel had all been spent, but perhaps he would never fully "move on" or whatever that saying was. Every time he had seen her in the years after Lukas was born, it was as though she were literally fading away, becoming more ethereal and elusive. Her thick hair began to thin, her voice weakened, her eyes were locked on the middle distance. Near the end, she could barely get one full breath. No wonder she drowned.

Yet now she was gone, a pale impression of her personality lingered perpetually on the edge of his consciousness.

The canvas bag was a treasure trove: a miniature antique brass astrolabe with moving plates and all the astronomical markings, a medallion of the Egyptian Dendera zodiac, a carved silver flask, an *ankh* talisman on a chain, and other pieces of jewelry. At the bottom was the box with the hieroglyphics on it. It was filled with diagrams, star charts, tables, maps of the heavens, photographs of constellations, verses, poems, and many notes. He took out the notebook that Rachel had mentioned and scanned the lined pages, densely written, in several languages, in Karl's fine, sloping hand.

Nigel gazed through the aircraft window. For many years he had wrestled with the mystery of this strange relationship, always fearing it would come to no good. And here he was, thinking the whole drama had ended, being thrown right back into the middle of it. He wiped an errant tear with the cuff of his sleeve.

Chapter 11

In the lounge of a swanky hotel in midtown Toronto, Steven waited for his daughter to join him for a drink. He checked his watch. He was having dinner with Nigel and Philippe tonight, and Nigel had just texted: *Don't be late. Big news.* Trust Nigel to drop a juicy morsel and hold back the detail, he thought. Another ping. Toby, his art agent. *Need you tomorrow. 10 a.m.?* Toby would be fretting about the upcoming show in Toronto and the big one in Stockholm in the Fall.

Steven had flown in from his home on the west coast the previous day and was already feeling "commitment stress," as his latest ex called it. The few women who had shared his life in recent years claimed he was disinterested and self-absorbed. They didn't understand that he was simply content. He made money from something he loved to do and didn't have a "happiness meter" to be continually nudged upwards, degree by anxious degree. He lived where he felt well, on the coast on the edge of Canada, the huge, generous country sweeping out to the east, the big ocean to the west; he took great joy from watching the sun creep over the land towards him and sail blithely out to sea at the end of each day. He had few friends, people to play squash with, people to visit.

Shifting his weight in the plush leather armchair, he felt something digging into his thigh. He checked, saw nothing, and sank back again. But it was still there. He got up and ran his hand along the side of the seat cushion. Wedged at the back was a kind of strap with something metal on it. He pried it loose with difficulty: a band of soft black leather with a red metal symbol and a buckle that was broken. It looked like a man's bracelet. He took it to the lobby.

"Fantastic," cried the man at reception, seizing it joyfully. "One of our guests has been searching frantically for this. He lost it last night."

"Glad I could help." Steven smiled and turned to leave.

"Please, would you give me your number. I'm sure he would like to speak with you."

"No, no. I'm just glad he's got it back."

"But he will be so relieved—and so upset if he can't thank you."

Steven relented and left his name and number.

When he returned to the lounge, Catherine was there. He had been looking forward to seeing his daughter. They had been getting along very well lately, but he still braced himself for the attack-defense maneuvering that characterized many of their conversations. He often wondered if she still resented him for the breakup with her mother.

"Quite the ritzy place you chose, Dad," she said. "Doesn't fit with the west coast tree hugger image."

"Good to see you too," he said, leaning over to give her a hug. "It's on the subway. Convenient for *you*, I thought."

She pulled one booted leg underneath her. Her jeans and grey hoodie were clearly well-used but looked good on her. Nigel claimed Catherine was one of those women who could throw a scarf around her neck, put on any kind of earrings, and look fabulous. She *is* attractive, he thought with fatherly pride: clear skin, shaggy, neck-length auburn hair, bright eyes—like her mother—and with that same endearing but deceiving look of innocence.

"I'll have a white wine," she told the waiter. "And since my dad's paying, some of those cheese dippy things too."

Steven got off on the wrong foot right away. "How is your mother?"

"Oh Dad. You don't give a shit."

"You know what, Catherine, I *do* give a shit and I'm not sure that giving a shit is something else I should be criticized for."

She gave an exasperated shrug and raised both hands. "Mom's the same as always. Nervous, complaining, freaked out about everything."

"And dare I ask about your Aunt Amy?" Amy was his brother Colin's widow who had remarried long ago. He had the right to ask, he told himself. He felt like an exile on the west coast; no one ever reached out with news. After all these years, he hoped the blame and remorse were done with.

Catherine hesitated. There had been a family celebration for Amy and Nick's tenth anniversary at their place in Nova Scotia, she finally told him.

A bunch of contradictory thoughts danced in Steven's head. Amy and Nick deserved to be happy. But it should have been Amy and Colin. And if Colin had been there, he, himself, would have been there. He tried to stifle the unreasonable hurt that arose, not because this big happy party had happened, but because no one had bothered to tell him.

"What did you expect, Dad?" Catherine said. "A fucking invitation?"

"Hey, I might have sent flowers."

To change the subject, he asked about her teaching plans. For years, she had loved to paint, and he hoped she might follow in his footsteps. However, fearing to be "condemned to walk perpetually in the shadow of my famous father," she had opted to teach and had just graduated with a Batchelor of Education. She was applying to teach art history at a local secondary school in the fall and claimed to be excited about this. But he wasn't convinced. She was impatient and easily bored, not the best qualities for a teacher.

"I've been thinking. I might take a year off," she said, as though reading his mind.

"To do what?"

"I don't know…travel, work abroad, climb Kilimanjaro …anything. Once I start teaching, that's it, I'll be stuck for the long haul."

"And money?" He knew she was sensitive about this and clamped his teeth together in anticipation of a sour response.

"I don't need any more of yours, if that's what you're thinking. I'm resourceful. I'll get by. So…big show coming up, eh?" She raised her glass to him. "I might even go. Geez, Dad, you must be raking it in these days. When are you going to buy a bigger condo here? That place you've got is a shoebox. How the hell can you stay in it for weeks on end?"

"Because it's an art studio with a bedroom. And that's all I need when I've got a ton of work to do. And do you have any idea what a shoebox in this damned city costs?"

"Don't pull the starving artist with me. You've gained a few pounds since I last saw you. And that 'cabin' out west would buy four times the square footage you've got here. Hey, you're having dinner with the boys tonight, right? Maybe there's something in their building. Three million plus. Pocket change, Dad."

"I'm not sure if I should be offended or not. I never know with you."

"That's the way I like it." She grinned and raised her glass, clinking it with his.

I like it too, he thought.

He asked whether she was seeing anyone…another tricky subject. He suspected she was freewheeling with the men in her life, but knew that even the slightest hint of a raised eyebrow would result in the "apple not falling far from the tree" lecture.

"There's a guy from college, Gavin. Mom doesn't like him. Says he's got no ambition. She's a fine one to talk."

Steven felt a guilty pinch of pleasure that she confided this off-hand, negative comment about her mother. For a fleeting moment, it made him feel closer to her.

Too soon, they had to drink up and get going. When they parted, she blew him a kiss, and he realized how much he missed his daughter. Maybe he'd have to get over this west coast idleness and come here more often.

Chapter 12

Nigel and Philippe were already at the door. Philippe had his hands to his heart, then opened them wide for an embrace. Steven submitted to the hugs and fussing, offered his jacket for hanging up and accepted the proffered glass of wine. He made his way into the large living room, with its eclectic mixture of contemporary furniture and antiques, and admired the stunning, almost aerial view of the lake, sparkling in the early evening sun.

The "boys" stood silently behind him. He turned to the side and nearly dropped the glass of wine. *Aphelion* hung on the far wall over a low, white console table. A million unconnected thoughts flew through his mind. "Oh my God, guys. Jesus. What the fuck!" He put the glass of wine on the coffee table and fell back onto a sofa opposite the painting. It took a minute for him to get a full breath.

The man in the painting was stretching his arms way up to the sky. The rising sun spilled pink-gold light down distant hill tops, bringing faint definition to the olive groves and terraced vineyards. The man leaned far over the edge of the precipice; his feet rooted into the earth; he would not fall.

Memories flooded back: Tuscany, his beautiful home with its terracotta tiles and creamy paint peeling off stucco walls, the studio with northern light, early morning walks to the ridge. And the woman he once loved. This painting had been a turning point for him, an homage to his passage through guilt, depression and self-doubt. Five years ago, it was the anchor for his exhibition at a gallery in Rome and all this time, he believed it had been sold anonymously.

"For Christ's sake, Nigel. Don't tell me it was you—"

"It was Rachel. She made a deal ahead of time with the gallery owners—made us promise not to tell you. It got put in storage until. . .until the baby was born and she moved to Italy. It hung beautifully in her home there. Of course, her son will inherit it one day."

Steven took a deep breath. "How the hell did it get here?"

"Long story. Come, let's sit on the balcony. I'll explain everything. The hors d'oeuvres are waiting, more wine is chilling, and it's a lovely summer's evening. So much to catch up on."

Over the next hour, Steven listened, with mounting disbelief, to Nigel's tale of his trip to meet Robert in England, the impending visit of Rachel's son, and the plans they had put in place.

"Holy shit, guys," he said when they stepped back inside for dinner. "That's a lot to take in. Not exactly the summer you were expecting. Sure you're up to it?"

"*Mais bien sûr*," said Philippe. "It will be an education for all of us, a big adventure."

"Philippe will be in charge of the adventure part. Lord only knows what use I'll be."

Steven stared once more at his painting, already finding the odd flaw, a few places he'd like to get at again. "I gotta tell you. . .I'm not sure how I feel about this. I liked it better thinking it was just 'out there' somewhere."

"But it must bring back lovely memories, *non?*" Philippe said, urging him to the table.

"Sometimes I still struggle with all that stuff."

"All that stuff is over with."

Not quite, Steven thought. A few months ago, when Nigel called to tell him Rachel had died, drowned in the Mediterranean on the beach by her home, he found himself curiously devoid of sensation, as though the love and the anger had finally drained away. *But is that it? Or am I still trying to shut off this damaged heart, scared to let the sadness in again?* He kept telling himself it was done with, but sometimes, out of nowhere, a memory would rear up and wreck his mood. *And now the child. Coming here. Nigel must be out of his mind.*

"When is he coming, exactly?"

"Early July," Nigel said. "He's starting school in September. Want to meet him?"

"I'm not good with children."

"How long are you going to be here?"

"A while. I have a lot to do. I might fly back and forth a few times."

They fell into a companionable silence, each thinking about the past, Steven surmised. He noticed both the boys had aged. Silly to keep calling them "boys," but the affectionate term had stuck. Nigel must be sixty-five and looked quite distinguished with his grey hair combed back, red-framed glasses, and an unfailing sense of style: tonight, cream pants and a mauve shirt with the collar turned up. Even Philippe had let himself go grey, devoid of the purple streaks that used to be his "thing." Steven wondered, with a flash of vanity, if they thought the same about him. He would turn fifty this year. But he worked out, still played squash, had never gained serious weight, despite what Catherine said. He glanced down at his faded blue jeans, reluctantly acknowledging that fashion was not his strong suit.

"Any news on your social scene?" Nigel asked.

"Apparently I'm too much hard work."

"Well, you are a bit heavy-going sometimes, my friend."

Should I mention Natalie? She was not at all like the "culture vultures" who had gravitated to him these last few years, women who constantly strived to reassure him of their artsy sophistication as though this were a mandatory credential for dating a painter. Natalie was natural and uncomplicated. She worked in a bank and had helped him with an investment issue. He had felt an odd sense of relief when his name meant nothing to her on meeting, and she knew little about art. She was interested in *him*, the man, not the artist and her comments about his work were unfiltered and refreshing. But it had only been a few months. Way too early to start feeling good.

"Yes?" Nigel persisted. "Do I detect a glossing of the eyes, a smothered smile?"

"I'll tell you something when it's worth telling," Steven said, catching the delighted exchange of looks between the boys and the not-so-discreet "thumbs up" from Philippe.

He enquired about their antiques store, a passion that had brought them a great deal of pleasure—and money—over the years.

"We can't let go of it," Nigel said. "Our Manager, Derek, is still with us, God bless him. We just do what he says. You must drop by. He's a big fan of yours and would love to see you."

"And what are you going to do about this?" Steven jerked his thumb over his shoulder to the painting. "It could be twenty years before the kid gets a place of his own, and he might curse his mother for bestowing it upon him. Why don't you sell it? Put the money in trust for him."

"Rachel would not have wanted that."

"Damn it, Nigel." He put down his knife and fork and sat back, surprising himself with his sharp sting of annoyance. "None of us should be worrying about what Rachel would or would not have wanted. She lied to us for a long time. She can't be directing from the grave."

There was a moment of shocked silence before Philippe tapped his arm. "You have not forgiven her, *mon ami?*"

Steven frowned and began to eat again. "Forget I said that."

They talked about his exhibition in Stockholm in the late fall, and more about the upcoming Toronto show they planned to attend, as they had with all his exhibitions over the years.

He started to help them clear up, but they tut-tutted and pushed him into the living room. Stretched out full length on the couch, he watched his two good friends working together with such relaxed efficiency. They had all shared a lot of joy and grief over the years. Steven searched for a way to describe how he felt in their company and decided on the simple but loaded word: *safe*. That was it. He could say anything, admit anything.

They might tease or admonish or cajole, but they would never judge. Their home had always been a safe haven.

His phone vibrated. Probably Toby again, he thought, ignoring it. After a minute or two, he checked voicemail and listened with growing interest.

"Hey, guess what," he called over to the kitchen. "I've got a lunch invitation from a complete stranger."

"Goodness me. Do tell."

"I found a guy's leather bracelet in the hotel lounge this afternoon. Just got a voicemail. He's in town on business, apparently. *So* grateful. Insists on buying me lunch at some new restaurant. And now…" he struggled to his feet. "I've eaten too much, and I should be going. I've got an early meeting with Toby tomorrow."

He hugged Philippe goodbye.

Nigel walked him to his car. "This man you're having lunch with," Nigel said. "Not some elaborate scam, I hope. There's a lot of that happening these days."

Steven shrugged. "Sounded like a good guy. French, maybe. I'll call him in the morning. Dominic someone."

Chapter 13

As Steven approached the restaurant, he could see it might be a part of the 1920's neo-gothic boutique hotel that stood next to it, undergoing what looked like a major renovation. His first thought, as the Maître D' ushered him inside, was what a truly unusual place this was, what a feast for the senses: a classic Moorish horseshoe archway at the entrance, intricate wrought iron railings separating the different seating areas, tables inlaid with mosaic and mother of pearl, low-hanging multi-coloured glass lamps, walls painted terracotta and bright blue, carpets, cushions, and candles—everywhere, an indulgence of colour. He picked up the smell of cinnamon and lemon and could hear soft music: a low, rhythmic drumbeat and a female voice singing in what sounded like Arabic. Yet, despite the typical décor, there was nothing cliché about the place. It was warm and welcoming, contemporary.

And this must be the man he was meeting, coming towards him. Yikes, Steven thought, he fits right in with the décor. Slim, attractive, maybe thirty; full dark hair hanging below the collar; a white linen shirt that showed off olive skin, and an open vest that was a patchwork of different shades and shapes of brown and burgundy leather, cross-stitched in red and gold. It would have looked ridiculous on most men, but this guy pulled it off.

"You must be Steven Farrow," the man said. They shook hands. "I am Dominic El Hassan. Please sit down. What will you have to drink?" He signaled to someone standing nearby.

Immediately, a waiter appeared with water and olives, nuts, and dates, another one to offer the menu and a glass of wine, and yet another to ask if he would like his jacket to be hung.

"You've obviously got some pull here," Steven said.

"I hope so. My family owns this restaurant and the hotel, which of course is not open yet. What do you think?" Dominic swept his arm around. "Please tell me your first impressions. I'm anxious to hear. I have learned you are a well-known artist. I Googled you. I hope you don't mind. I am so impressed with your work and honoured that you accepted my invitation."

"Thank you. Well, what can I say? This place is incredible. I wish you the very best with it."

They clinked glasses. Steven noticed his host was wearing the bracelet. He must have mended the buckle.

"You are wondering about this, why it is important to me." Dominic extended his arm and pointed to the red metal symbol. "This is the Roma chakra symbol. I wear it when I travel. Foolish, some would say, but I am superstitious. It was my mother's. I was dismayed when I lost it."

They fell into easy conversation. Dominic apologized for his English—which Steven thought was impeccable—and told him about his family and his home at the hotel in Fez. The hotel here would be opening at the end of the summer, he said. It was being renovated to reflect the main features of the Riad Capella.

"Why did you pick Toronto?" Steven asked.

"We have a good Moroccan friend who is in the business. He's married to a Canadian woman, and they live here. When this property came on the market, he told us we should snap it up. It's the perfect boutique style, and the location is excellent. He's going to run it for us."

"I look forward to seeing it. Do you plan to expand into other cities?"

"Ah, that's a big question. On the one hand, we dream of building a franchise, getting bought out by an international chain and retiring on the French Riviera. On the other hand, we know we'd be bored on the Riviera. And we never want to be away from Morocco too long. You must come and visit. It is a beautiful country. I am proud of it. You would be an honoured guest."

They talked about travel. Dominic had been to many parts of the Middle East and Europe and had spent a short time in the United States several years ago. "A woman," he explained, looking embarrassed. "And a mistake."

"I was just in New York," he added. "My twin nephews are there for a year—part of their international school curriculum. My brother and his wife wanted me to check up on them. *Mon Dieu,* they already sound like Americans and even have that 'New York' attitude." He grimaced. "You can be sure that will not go over well when they get home."

Steven told Dominic about the time he spent in Italy but admitted that, as a rule, he preferred to stay put. "I'm a homebody, I'm afraid. Not a very adventurous person."

"My brother, Hadir, sometimes wishes I was more of a…what did you call it? Homebody? I have our mother's restless gypsy blood."

He asked Steven about his art, where he got his inspiration, his own family. Steven mentioned the upcoming show in Toronto and the later one in Stockholm that he was nervous about. It would feature stark landscapes: sweeping arctic spaces, winter dreams, endless dances of cold and ice. One critic here had labelled them "bloodless."

"Critics be damned," Dominic said. "We are at their mercy too, but have learned you can never please everyone. How is the meal?"

Although usually a plain eater, Steven enjoyed what he learned was a traditional Moroccan *tagine,* with lamb and apricots, and a bunch of spices he had never heard of.

At the end of the meal, a young man appeared with a small teapot and two tiny glass cups in silver holders.

"Don't feel you have to do the mint tea thing," Dominic said. "My countrymen are obsessed with it. Would you like a coffee?"

Steven declined anything further. The restaurant was bustling, and this man was probably anxious to get back to work.

Weeks later, looking back on that lunch, he tried to remember if he had felt any sense of premonition. He had spent an unexpected and pleasant couple of hours with a nice guy in a great new restaurant. When they parted, he gave Dominic his card and invited him to attend his Toronto show opening if he was not busy that evening. He never expected to see him again.

Chapter 14

In the middle of the night, Nigel got up for the bathroom and checked on Lukas. The boy had been with them for two days and was settling in, but Nigel couldn't stop himself from fretting. What on earth must it be like to have children of one's own, he wondered, having to worry about them twenty-four hours a day. He concluded that most parents must be teetering on the brink of emotional collapse. Easing the door of the guest bedroom open, he couldn't make out the shape of the boy on the bed and risked switching on the main light. The covers were pulled back. The bed was empty. *Must be in the bathroom.*

"Sorry, Lukas," he called toward the bathroom door. "Just making sure you are okay."

No answer. He checked the kitchen, the den, the hallway. The main door was double-locked, and the boy's jacket hung in the closet. He stood in the middle of the living room and took deep breaths.

"What's the matter?" Philippe's voice from the bedroom. "Why are the lights on?"

"I can't find Lukas."

"What are you saying?" Philippe stumbled into the kitchen. "He's not in his room?"

"Go and check. I might be having a bad dream."

Philippe went frantically from room to room. "No. Not here. Not here. *Quelle horreur.*"

Nigel leaned on the countertop, trying to slow his increasingly rapid heartbeat. "All right, let's stay calm. Think for a minute and—"

The balcony door opened with a couple of slow, laboured wheezes, and they both let out a strangled yelp.

"Lukas, *mon petit.*" Philippe rushed over and flung his arms around the boy. "What are you doing out there?"

"Looking at the stars."

Nigel, one hand to his heart, sat down heavily on the kitchen stool. "What a scare you gave us. I was about to call the police."

Lukas stared at his feet. "Sorry. I'll go back to my room."

"Certainly not. If you can't sleep, there's no point in going back to bed. What time is it? Good Lord, three-thirty. I do believe I need something chocolatey."

Philippe splashed cold water on his face at the sink. "Good thinking," he whispered. "Lukas, come and help me fix something to eat."

Lukas hesitated, as though not ready to believe this. "I love the nighttime."

"In this weather we should probably have ice cream."

Nigel turned on the balcony light and eased into one of the chairs. "Goodness me, still so hot out here," he said to himself, putting his feet up on the coffee table and trying to remember if he had ever been up at this hour. The big city skyline off to the left was eerily quiet, with few lights still on in the tall towers. There was a faint hum of a generator in the near distance and, behind him, the happy chatter of Philippe and Lukas. *Perhaps this will all work out after all.*

He had been plagued with second thoughts when picking Lukas up from the airport. First, there was the interminable wait with the huddled masses, then the bubbling excitement and long list of instructions from the young woman who had accompanied Lukas, some relative of Melinda's who would be staying with friends here. The poor child was tired, his blond hair tousled, his blazer all crumpled. *Fancy making a small kid wear a blazer on such a long flight.* And there was far too much luggage. Robert and Melinda obviously had no idea what was appropriate for a Toronto summer. An officious young man in a uniform with a badge hanging round his neck asked for his ID and the letter authorizing him to assume guardianship. In a tiny, windowless room, an equally pushy woman from Customs checked things off on her tablet and kept shooting him wary looks, no doubt thinking he was a cyber pedophile.

Philippe had gone to a lot of trouble to make Lukas feel welcome, putting up "age appropriate" posters in the guest room and getting some tattooed creature from an electronics store to load a video game player with games involving dragons, bandicoots, and zombies that didn't look at all appropriate to Nigel.

They had worried about what exactly the boy had been told about the two of them, how much he understood, how much he might have resisted. But, to their surprise, he had settled in right away. He had never been in a "skyscraper" and was enthralled by the view from the balcony and wide-eyed with the prospect of going to the top of the CN Tower. On the first day, he spent a lot of time in his room, putting his clothes away (neatly, Nigel observed), setting up his iPad and iPhone on little stands, getting all the cords and plugs and adapters sorted out and placing a few well-thumbed books on his bedside table. Robert said he could read exceptionally well for his age, one of the reasons for the "gifted" conjecture. Nigel glanced at the books: *Animals in the Sky, Our Planet and its Neighbours, My First Book of the Stars.* Obviously in the blood, he thought. He remembered one night drinking a glass of wine on the terrace of Rachel's lovely home in Italy, overlooking the sea. It was dark but still warm. She brought the boy out in his pyjamas, barely a toddler at the time, and read to him from a book like this. He had sat quietly on her lap with his thumb in his mouth, looking up at the stars.

When he and Philippe gave him the items in the canvas bag that Rachel had left, he was spellbound. He turned over each one in his hands and carefully lined them all up on a shelf in his room. They had held back the box with the sky charts and the notebook, thinking it was far too complex but when they saw his delight with all these other things, they showed him this too. It was as though they had given him a puppy.

"You mean my own dad did all these?" He was sitting at the island in the kitchen, sorting through the box wide-eyed.

"Your mom kept it for you. She thought you might understand it more when you're older."

"I know already that's Sagittarius on top of the box. It's a fire sign. It's my own. He has a bow and arrow. See?" He turned the lid for Nigel.

"I think I see," Nigel said, not at all sure what he was looking at. "Your mother taught you, I imagine."

"And she said my dad was a well-known expert."

Now, on one of the balcony chairs, Nigel saw the box, open, with the notebook and some of the charts and maps beside it. A small flashlight lay to one side. *Don't tell me he's been out here in the dark trying to read that?*

Philippe and Lukas finally emerged with a couple of trays of cold juices, slices of chocolate cake, and bowls of ice cream.

"Look at us all in our pajamas on the balcony," Philippe said. "What on earth will the neighbours think? Let's see if anyone else is up."

They leaned over the rail, Lukas's head just clearing the top, and scanned the circular driveway below, the corner parkette and the boardwalk along the shoreline, parts of it visible directly under the iron lamps. The Gardiner Expressway passed behind the tall buildings farther east. Other than the odd car hurrying by, there was no one about. Before them the lake stretched away and melted into the blackness of the sky.

"How big is this lake?" Lukas asked.

"Never mind the lake," said Philippe. "We'd better eat this ice cream before it melts."

Nigel sat back, smiling to himself as he listened to the two of them chatting about the kind of food they liked, Philippe making fun of how people ate in England, especially "that strange Marmite you put on toast, and those hot, rubbery things called 'pikelets.'" He described the outings they had planned: the zoo, the Science Centre, the Museum of Illusions, Niagara Falls, and more.

"I see you've been looking inside that box and the notebook your dad kept," Nigel said. "Found anything interesting?"

"He drew this." Lukas sorted out a page from the box. "It shows where all the planets were on the day I was born."

"Isn't that Italian?" Nigel asked, looking at the writing underneath.

"My dad spoke lots of languages. Even Arabic. I want to speak in Arabic like my dad." Lukas stared up to the sky. "You can't see all the stars tonight because of the moon."

Nigel followed his gaze. There was a perfect half moon directly south.

"I'd like to have a telescope," Lukas went on. "My mom said I could one day, but Uncle Robert says I'm not old enough yet."

Good old Uncle Robert, Nigel thought. What a killjoy.

"Lukas, one last slice of cake for all of us," Philippe said, passing the plate.

"Uncle Robert says you shouldn't eat between meals." Lukas took a big mouthful.

"No doubt we will all wake at noon with dreadful stomach aches. But, in for a penny," Nigel said, taking his own slice. *Uncle Robert be damned.*

Chapter 15

On the opening night of his art show in Toronto, Steven had the strong feeling that he had fallen down a rabbit hole.

First, the gallery was packed. He had not expected anywhere near this number of people. The gallerist was already on the phone, looking furtive, pleading with the caterers for more "nibbles platters," as he called them. The work did look good, Steven thought. These paintings were from his new surreal, abstract phase and many had already been sold. He stood with the buyers on the raised platform, getting their names, writing a personal message on the back, posing for the obligatory photographs before they were hung back on the walls with their red "sold" dots. He had never been good at self-promotion and was always grateful when these niceties were over.

And then, a tap on his shoulder, and there stood his daughter, looking stunning in a sleeveless red shift, long silver earrings, and red high heels. He could not remember the last time she showed up at one of his exhibitions, and certainly, she had never looked like this.

"Catherine! My God, you came." He gave her a big hug which she submitted to without her usual pullback. "I'm honoured."

"Hey, I was at a loose end and thought, what the hell." She swept her arm around the gallery. "Pretty cool stuff."

A compliment. "You like it? Really? You're not just saying that?"

"I never 'just say' anything, Dad. You know that. I like these better than landscapes. Enough already with those. These look like you're enjoying yourself. I see you've made a ton of sales already. Anything left for the show in Stockholm?"

"They want the northern series there."

Catherine rolled her eyes and grimaced. "Not all that shivering Arctic stuff? Greys and blues, and bleached white suns barely making it over the horizon?"

"Never expect praise from your own family, I've learned."

She punched him on the arm. "I'm kidding. Well, half kidding. Whoa, incoming. The boys are here. Fighting their way over. Looks like they've got some young kid with them."

Steven groaned inwardly. Of course, it was inevitable that Nigel and Philippe would find a way for him to meet Lukas, if only out of some warped sense of mischief. Now he'd have to explain it all to his daughter.

"Hello Steven. And Catherine…how wonderful to see you again," Nigel exclaimed, standing back to appraise her. "Don't you look just *ravishing*. Let me introduce you both to Lukas. He's over here from England. Spending the summer with us."

Steven could see nothing in the boy that reminded him of Rachel. He was clearly his father's child. A memory of the only time he had met Karl leapt uninvited in his head. The exhibition in Rome. What a fucking jerk the guy was. All superior and dismissive, making him feel like a total loser. The boy had the same sculpted facial structure, the same clear grey eyes.

"Hello Lukas," he managed. "I knew your mom. She helped me a lot."

"I know. You lived with my mom in Italy. She told me you were famous."

Steven felt a sharp jab in the ribs from his daughter and caught her stifled laugh. "That's a bit of a stretch, but nice."

"I have some of your paintings at my uncle's house in England."

Steven thought that strange: "my uncle's house," not "my home."

"One day, you'll have a place of your own," Nigel said. "They will look splendid there, I'm sure."

"Do you like looking at paintings? Or did Nigel and Philippe make you come here?" Catherine asked him.

Lukas stumbled for a response. "I don't know much."

"Well, it's your lucky day. I'm into art and I'm going to be a teacher. Come with me. You tell me what you think about these paintings, and I'll tell you what I think, and we won't tell my dad. Deal? And…I spy food on a table by the wall."

"I'm coming too," Philippe said. "No way I'm missing out on an art lesson and something to eat." He hooked his arm through Catherine's.

Steven and Nigel watched Catherine steer her charges away.

"Shit, Nigel. Does he ever look like his father? Gives me the shivers. To think I met his mother at that gallery up the road. And she wrote that rotten review. I can't believe you brought him here. He'll be bored to tears."

"We'd never miss an opening of yours and we can hardly leave him home alone."

"Is he settling in?"

"Much better than I expected. Such a serious little boy and easily bored. He's interested in things you wouldn't expect of a child that age and asks a million questions. But he's also happy to curl up for hours with that iPad. God knows what he's looking for. We're off to Niagara Falls soon and I shall be pressed onto that wretched boat, draped in plastic, with a serious risk of drowning." He glanced over Steven's shoulder. "I spy that mealy-mouthed critic from *The Art of Life* or whatever it's called. Off you go. Circulate."

Steven gave himself up once again to the embrace of the crowd. He exchanged a few words with the critic who looked happy, although good reviews were never assured until printed in black and white. More and more people streamed in, exclaiming, high-fiving him. Sustaining enthusiastic conversation became challenging.

He needed another drink. Catherine was at the bar area, alone. "Where's your entourage?" he asked her.

"Busy eating." She clinked glasses with him. "So, Dad. The cute kid…not my stepbrother I hope?"

"Come on, Catherine. I can't believe you said that."

"Well… entirely possible. He's Rachel's son, right? The one who dumped you for some dude in the desert."

"What the hell do you know about all that? Nothing."

"Don't look so shocked. The more hush-hush you make it, the more people are determined to find out. Karl, right? The father?"

"Why does it matter?"

"It doesn't matter, Dad. It's just *interesting*." Catherine sipped on her generous glass of Chardonnay and surveyed the room. "Your big red and yellow one is attracting a lot of attention…including a rather gorgeous creature, staring quite intently. Do you know him? Don't make it obvious you're looking."

Steven turned. "Shit. I don't believe it. I'll be damned." More and more he felt he was down that rabbit hole. "Come on over. I'll introduce you."

The man looked up as they approached and broke into a wide smile. "Steven. Good to see you again. This is truly wonderful. Amazing work."

"I'm so flattered that you came. Dominic, this is my daughter, Catherine."

Steven noted the way Dominic's eyes slid over his daughter. It felt strange and uncomfortable to watch a younger man give his daughter the eye.

"So how do you two know each other?" Catherine asked.

Dominic told the story and showed her the leather bracelet. "You'll think I'm crazy, but losing it was upsetting. Having it returned is like a course correction. Fate is back in control. All will be well."

"Have you had a chance to look around?" Steven said. "I'd be happy to—"

"Don't worry, Dad. I'll show off your work to Dominic. I'm the official tour guide. Why don't we all meet up a bit later? Go have a drink?"

Steven was once again left watching his daughter take control. His new Moroccan friend put a hand on her shoulder to steer her clear of a clutch of people.

After a while, the crowd began to thin. The gallerist and his agent, Toby, over in the corner, were both a study in contained enthusiasm, no doubt already calculating the night's earnings. After bidding farewell to the stragglers, he found Nigel in the back room, fishing about in a jar of cookies.

"Where is everyone? Did Catherine leave?"

"Waiting for us at Fitzgerald's. Come, come, let's get a move on. How exciting all this is." Nigel ushered him out onto the street.

"Did you meet the French Moroccan yet?" Steven asked.

"Absolutely. Philippe was practically drooling. I had to intervene. We should hurry. He might be making a fool of himself."

"No worries there, Nigel. Catherine's got her claws into him, I fear. Or vice versa."

"What fun. A juicy romance in the offing. He is quite something."

In the bar, a waiter directed them to a round table in its own booth. Dominic had one arm draped over the back of it, resting casually but unmistakably behind Catherine's shoulders, Steven noted. Lukas and Philippe sat opposite and all four were laughing. Something was not quite right, and Steven felt another rabbit hole moment. They were speaking French.

"Can you believe this?" Philippe said. "Lukas already speaks Italian and he's even learning French. *Génial!*"

"I grew up in Italy," Lukas said. "My mom was half Italian."

"You're amazing," said Catherine. "I swear your French is already better than mine." She summoned the waiter and ordered another bottle of wine. "Anyone want anything different?"

Steven shook his head. *Who is this self-assured young woman?* He knew she had enjoyed French in high school but had no idea she could hold a conversation in it. He looked at his daughter with new admiration. *Is she showing off for Dominic or does this* savoir faire *come naturally to her?*

"How long are you in town, Dominic?" Nigel asked.

"A couple of months at least. Until the hotel is open and running smoothly."

"It used to be the Kensington Arms, right? I wondered what they were going to do with that place. It closed with barely a squeak. It's more like an inn. Will you keep it that way?"

"That is why we bought it. It has a lovely courtyard that we have redesigned with a Moroccan feel. It will be called The Darija. That's the Arabic dialect of Morocco."

"Wonderful. I bet it's a lot of work, though."

"Yes, but I love it. I'm thinking of bringing over someone from Fez. She's amazing. Part of the family. Knows how we like things done. It would be a good experience for her. I must convince my brother, though. He worries too much."

Steven leaned back and took in this strange end to a strange day: Rachel's son at the same table as his daughter. *How the hell did this happen?* Philippe unashamedly ogling Dominic; Dominic unashamedly ogling Catherine. The Moroccan had dressed less exotically today, with jeans and a dark blue linen jacket that looked expensive. Catherine nudged herself closer to him. *So much for Gavin, or whatever his name is.* He wondered if Dominic was a genuinely decent guy or simply a charmer. Hard to tell, and not something he was prepared to worry about.

Lukas had gone quiet and was clearly overwhelmed.

"Lukas," said Dominic, as though thinking the same thing. "Philippe tells me you know a lot about the stars. How did you learn this?"

"My mother taught me."

"Really? I know a little, too, and it was my mother who taught me. What is your birthday? Do you know your star sign?"

"Twenty-seventh of November. I'm a Sagittarius."

"Ah, the centaur. Travelers, risk takers, forging their own path. And what about the rest of you?" Dominic looked round at the others.

"Taurus," said Nigel. "But definitely *not* into all that hocus-pocus."

"*Tu sais, Dominic, il est un cas typique!*" Philippe said. "*Vraiment têtu.*"

Nigel put on his pained, affronted expression. "Please. I'm getting *un petit peu* fed up with the French. I'm *not* stubborn. I am just always right."

There was a lot of teasing and laughter around the table. Steven made the stop sign with his hands and shook his head, refusing to get into it, but Catherine leapt in—"Dad's a Leo. Ambitious, demanding, intolerant. Right, Dad?"—and he was forced to defend himself.

Yet another bottle of wine was brought to the table and the conversation became more animated and ridiculous. Eventually Nigel, alarmed at the hour and concerned about Lukas needing sleep, declared they should be on their way. He called for the bill, and everyone rummaged around for credit cards. But Nigel insisted it was his treat and claimed that Taureans were surely the most generous of the signs.

"I hope we'll see you again, Dominic," said Philippe. "Maybe you'd like to visit Niagara Falls with us. You haven't been there yet, have you?"

"I have been meaning to but, please, I would not want to intrude."

"Oh, you wouldn't be," said Nigel. "You can sit with me and drink wine while we watch Philippe and Lukas go on that awful boat. Maid of the Pissed, I call it."

"Excuse me, Dominic," said Lukas, causing all heads to turn his way. "Is it easy to get to the desert from where you live?"

"It certainly is. My favourite way is through the Atlas Mountains to Merzouga. About a day's drive. Merzouga's a small desert town. It has the most amazing sand dunes. Why do you ask?"

"I went in the desert once, with my mom. It was…" He looked down for a moment. "My dad said it's the best place to see the stars."

"Where does your father live? Perhaps he will take you one day."

There was an uncomfortable silence before Nigel jumped in. "Both Lukas's parents have sadly passed—"

"My dad died before I was even born," Lukas said. "He was murdered."

Jesus Christ. Steven felt a cold hand on the back of his neck. *How the hell does the kid know this? Surely, his mother never told him?* Dominic looked appalled and tried to apologize.

Philippe pulled the boy into a hug. "Ah Lukas. It's all a bit uncertain. It was most likely an accident."

There was a lot of shuffling about and several simultaneous changes of subject, and then they were all outside, saying goodbye, going their separate ways.

Catherine gave her father a peck on the cheek. "Quite a night, eh, Dad?" she whispered. "What do you know about this…what Lukas said? Something else you're hush-hushing?"

"I know very little, Catherine. And it's none of our business."

"I think I might muscle in on that Niagara Falls trip, see what I can squeeze out of Nigel."

"Something tells me that wouldn't be the reason you'd go. Where is he, by the way, our Moroccan friend? I didn't see him leave."

"He waved goodbye. Seemed to be in a bit of a hurry all of a sudden."

Chapter 16

"Dominic, it's five thirty in the morning. Is everything all right?"

"This is important, Hadir. You've got to get up, go down and get those charts. I'll explain. They're in *your* office. You kept them. Please go and get them. Don't wake Sophie."

"What? You've woken me up for this? What do you want with those damn things at this hour?"

"Stop talking and just get them. Please."

Dominic heard his brother saying something to Sophie who had obviously woken. He heard Hadir swearing to himself and then, eventually, making it into the office and rummaging around in desk drawers.

"Second drawer, right hand side. That's where you put them, I think."

"Yes, yes, I've got them. Now what?"

"The child. What was his birth date?" Dominic closed his eyes, bracing for the response.

"You mean the second sheet? 27th November 2014. With a question mark after it."

"Oh fuck." Dominic sank onto the bed in a cold sweat. "I don't believe it. It can't be." His hand holding the phone was shaking. "Give me a minute." He took the terrycloth robe from the bathroom and draped it around his shoulders. "I'm shaking, Hadir. This is too strange."

"Settle down, brother." Hadir's voice had a sharp pitch of concern now. "Tell me what's wrong."

"I've met him. That kid. His name is Lukas. It must be him. Same birthday. He's going to be five this year. So, born in 2014."

Hadir was incredulous and began to protest but Dominic cut him off and explained the whole series of events: Steven finding his bracelet, their lunch, going to the gallery, meeting his daughter and the friends who were looking after Lukas.

"But you don't know that the father was in Cairo. The boy didn't say that, did he? Hundreds of children would have been born on that date."

"Not with a father who loved the desert and the stars, who was murdered."

"No details? Like *how* his father was murdered?"

"He never got a chance. They cut the conversation dead."

"So how are these people connected to him? How come he is in Canada, staying with those two men? Are they related?"

"His mother was a friend of theirs. And the painter, when I had lunch with him, he said he had lived in Tuscany for a while. I have a feeling he's connected to it too, but I can't figure out how. The mother, she's dead, I know that."

"Do we know her name, the mother?"

"No, *but* Da'ud said the mother and kid lived in Italy, and Lukas said his mother was half Italian. He was born in Italy and speaks the language. Come on. It has to be him."

"*Putain de merde*. Why didn't you ask a few more questions?"

"You've got to be kidding. When he let that out at the end—'my father was murdered'—what could I say? It was too awkward. Everyone tried to talk about something else, and then we left. But I will see them again. I mean I should, no?"

"Let me think a minute, brother. I'm barely awake."

Dominic imagined his brother sitting in the chair at the desk, digesting this news, weighing his thoughts, trying to come up with logical conclusions. He imagined Sophie padding down the stairs in search of her husband, worried about what could be going on. A wave of tenderness washed through him. He missed them.

"How are you going to see them again, these people?" Hadir said.

"They are taking the boy to Niagara Falls. They asked if I'd like to join them. All I want to do is find out more. Don't you trust me?"

"No. You'll be dragging out the Tarot cards next."

Dominic felt a bolt of fear, remembering the unfinished Tarot reading. *The Tower: disruption to everyday life, upheaval, disaster. And losing the bracelet, the chakra wheel…something is broken, something has to be put right.* He felt nauseous and pulled the robe more tightly around him. "Hadir, what could this mean? Maybe I've drunk too much."

Hadir was silent for a moment or two. "Let's try to stay cool and think things through. These people…you like them by the sound of it. They are kind, generous. What's to worry about? I'm not going to tell Sophie about this. When you are home, we will discuss it with her and decide whether we should tell Amina. We can describe it as an amazing coincidence, a way of showing us how lives intersect and, in the grand scheme of things, everything works out fine."

But when Dominic eventually said goodbye to his brother, he felt neither of them really believed that.

Chapter 17

Dominic leaned over the concrete balustrade and into the enormous avalanche of water with its loud roar that took the breath out of him. A light breeze blew whirling flashes of wet spray into his face and hair.

"Wow," was all he managed, thinking about the barren sands of his own country and what a fickle mistress Mother Nature was.

"Look at the American side," Catherine said. "We Canadians love to gloat that *our* Horseshoe Falls are so much grander."

"This is amazing, magnificent. Thank you all so much for including me today."

Lukas ran back and forth in great excitement, taking shots with his iPhone.

"There are lots more vantage points farther along. Philippe and I will stay here. Send photos to your uncle, Lukas. And don't wander off."

"From what I know," Catherine whispered to Dominic as Lukas ran ahead, "The uncle was only too happy to get the kid off his hands. I doubt he's too worried."

"This uncle," Dominic said. "Exactly what is the relationship?"

"His mother's brother, Robert. They took him after Rachel died. Hey—" she called out to Lukas. "No climbing until I can hang on to you."

Rachel, Dominic thought. *Had Ahmed ever mentioned that name?* It didn't ring a bell. He watched Catherine grip Lukas's belt with both hands so he could balance steadily on the stone barrier and lean over for a good shot.

Dominic had looked forward to this day with a strange mixture of foreboding and excitement, anxious to learn the truth of Lukas's background, but not wanting to appear nosy or arouse suspicion. If, indeed, this boy was the son of that man in Cairo that Ahmed worked for, and these good people had assumed that Ahmed had intentionally set the fire that killed him…well, he could put them right. But then, he thought, none of them may know any of the details or anything about Ahmed, and revealing the connection would be upsetting and unnecessary. He resolved to assume only mild interest, hoping everything would come clear naturally.

In the car on the way here, however, he had fought with different feelings. Catherine sat in the back between him and Lukas—she had insisted Lukas get a window. He wondered, with a twist of excitement if she had manoeuvred that on purpose. She wore a sleeveless T-shirt and a light summer skirt with a slit up the side that exposed a beautiful, tanned leg he longed to touch. He had to keep swallowing hard and looking out of the window, glad for the jacket across his lap. Once, Nigel winked at him in the rear-view mirror. *Shit, am I that obvious?*

"Do people go over in barrels like the pictures on my iPad?" Lukas asked climbing down. "Do they die?"

"Probably," said Catherine. "They're all idiots. No sympathy from me."

They ambled back to Nigel and Philippe.

"Look at this," Nigel beckoned them over to the rail. A rainbow hovered in the fine mist over the top of the Falls. "Let me take the shot of the three of you. Quick, before it goes."

He positioned them against the railing. Dominic stood in the middle, sliding his eyes sideways to Catherine and hoping his dark glasses concealed his intent. He was certain she wasn't wearing a bra. He draped his arms around both her and Lukas, acutely conscious of the sharp tingle along the full length of his spine.

Nigel snapped away. "Lovely, lovely. A Hallmark greeting card."

"Enough," said Philippe. "Lukas and I will miss our boat ride."

"Right. Off you go, then. We'll be watching you from on high." Nigel pointed up to the Skylon Tower. "Make sure you're both thoroughly dried off before you venture near our table."

Over lunch, Dominic had to battle once more to stay focussed, feeling Catherine's knee right up against his own in a way that was surely not accidental. He didn't trust himself to look directly at her. As the restaurant slowly turned, he was grateful for the excuse to keep gazing at the different views of the Falls, the boat being tossed around in the thundering water at the base and, in the near distance, the vineyards that Nigel claimed were producing some excellent wine these days. He wondered how he was going to steer the conversation, but there was no need. As soon as they ordered, Catherine launched right in.

"Hey Nigel. Bet you guys never thought you'd be babysitting at this point in your lives."

"You are right there, my dear. He is a funny mixture. Sometimes his mind is scattered in all directions, sometimes it's totally focussed on something. But he is no trouble. Philippe, I swear, is enjoying every minute."

"How is it that you know Lukas?" Dominic asked. "I think you said his mother—"

"Rachel, yes. She was a good friend of ours. She was an art critic."

"She had a thing with my dad when he lived in Italy," said Catherine. "He and my mom were divorced years before. She helped dad's career along. An enigmatic woman from everything I've heard. Right, Nigel?"

Dominic caught the brief look the two exchanged but couldn't read it.

"Steven was just becoming noticed when they met," said Nigel. "As I'm sure you could tell at his Toronto show, he is now well known, very successful. We had hoped they would stay together. But it was not to be."

"Well, who can blame her? I mean I love my dad, but there's way too much baggage there. *And* the other man—Mr. Mysterious, the astronomer. No contest. Talking of which—what a friggin shock that was the other night at Fitzgerald's. Lukas saying his dad was murdered. What's the story there, Nigel? I can't get a damn thing out of my father.

He does his exasperated sighing routine if I ever bring up that tale of woe."

"I'm not surprised. Poor man. But, Catherine, it was all uncertain. I know so little."

"I don't believe you. You know everything. Hey, maybe you're covering up for my dad. Maybe he killed his rival in a fit of jealous rage. That's why he won't talk." She burst into a peal of laughter.

Nigel gave her a coy look but said nothing.

"Come on," she persisted. "It sure stopped the conversation. Poor Dominic must have been embarrassed."

"I was so sorry I had asked the question," Dominic said. "Did you know his father, Nigel?"

"I was responsible for Rachel's introduction to him. With our antiques business, I used to travel through the Middle East quite a lot. I knew someone in Cairo who introduced us. It was only a chance meeting. I never had any dealings with the man."

Cairo. Dominic clasped his hands in his lap. *It has to be him.* "Was he Egyptian?"

"No, no. Swiss. Karl Gustav. An astronomer and Egyptologist if you please. The boy has inherited not only his angular blond looks and his love of the stars but all that Teutonic precision. Rachel worked with Karl on a project there. Such a strange affair."

Dominic felt he'd been kicked in the stomach. *Lukas is the astronomer's child. Karl Gustav. That's him. How could all this have possibly happened?* His body trembled.

"But he died in a fire, right? He wasn't *murdered?*" Catherine said.

"How did you even know that?" Nigel asked her. "You amaze me. Surely, Steven has never told you?"

"I *am* connected to the art world, you know. My father probably spilled his heart out to some art groupie on a drunken night. And people talk."

"Women talk," Nigel said, wagging his finger at her. "Yes, Karl died in a fire, but some believe the fire was set deliberately. What is most mysterious is that *Lukas* knows this, or at least has picked up the idea of murder. Rachel didn't want him to know any of it."

Dominic felt like someone was holding him under water. He was desperate to take a breath but couldn't open his mouth. *Could this really be a coincidence?* It was unbelievable.

"This Rachel," Catherine said, "was a woman with a secret—"

"I hardly think it's necessary to go into that in front of our guest," said Nigel, frowning now.

Catherine turned to face Dominic, ignoring Nigel. "She spent more than two years with my Dad, off and on, helping him get over himself, kick-starting his career. Like, why? What drove her to do that? I mean, she was in love with this other guy, right? Big mystery. Nigel knows all the details, but he and my dad have this conspiracy of silence. I don't get it. Why can't people tell the truth?"

Why can't people tell the truth? He felt for a moment that the world had paused, waiting for his next words, and tried convincing himself this *was* a coincidence, nothing more. Perhaps he should say, "Lukas's father, Karl Gustav…"

Catherine put a hand on his shoulder. "Sorry, you must wonder what kind of people we are. Where is the damned waiter?" She got the attention of the nearest server and gave him a big questioning shrug of her shoulders.

Dominic's moment was gone.

Their food followed quickly, and the conversation turned to easier subjects: good and bad restaurants in the city, Nigel and Philippe's antiques store, Catherine's misgivings about starting work in September and getting "trapped in the system" as she called it.

"Ah, here come the sailors, home from the sea," said Nigel.

Philippe and Lukas were making their way across the restaurant, Lukas flushed with excitement. "Brilliant, totally brilliant," he kept saying.

Philippe tore off two pieces of the pizza Nigel had thought to order for them and handed one to Lukas. "There he was, standing on the deck with two feet apart like a born sailor, staring right up into the *déluge*." Philippe said, "*Mon Dieu,* I was too busy hanging on the rail."

"Weren't you a bit scared?" Nigel asked Lukas.

The boy shook his head vehemently. "It was fun. You don't have to be scared."

The light began to change. Dark blue clouds had drifted over, and the lowering sun pierced through with bright yellow shafts. Dominic went to the window and joined other diners, exclaiming, taking photographs. He turned and took a shot of his new friends raising their glasses of wine, Philippe acting the fool with rabbit ear fingers behind Nigel's head.

He texted his brother: *Lukas is the boy on the chart. His father is Karl Gustav. His mother is Rachel. They lived and worked together in Cairo. It is definitely him. I will call you tomorrow.*

Why was he here, he kept asking himself…what strange circumstances had contrived to bring him to this restaurant above this famous waterfall, so far from home, with people who were total strangers until a couple of weeks ago, people who had no idea of his disturbing connection to them?

He looked up to see Lukas smiling at him. The little boy's eyes were clear and grey and questioning, as though wondering the same thing: *What are you doing here, Dominic?*

Chapter 18

On their return journey, Catherine claimed the front seat. Lukas asked Dominic nonstop questions about Morocco. "Is it different from Egypt?," "Does it have the same desert?," "Does it have any pyramids?" The boy's curiosity was astonishing. Dominic felt unaccountably drawn to the child, almost as though he had known him before in some other life—something he would never admit to Hadir for fear of ridicule.

"My dad knew everything about stars," Lukas said. "And he wrote in the notebook that it's real, what the stars say."

"The notebook?"

"It's a kind of diary. My mom had it and it's mine now. Nigel and Philippe gave it me."

"And you can read it?"

"A lot of words I can't read. Some are in Arabic." He drew in his breath suddenly and twisted in his seat. "*You* could read it." His eyes widened with excitement. "I mean, could you read it for me? The Arabic? Could you tell me what it means?"

"I'd be happy to take a look at it. Your dad was a very clever man from what I've heard. I hope I can understand it."

Nigel put on some classical music, and they fell silent for a while. Dominic gazed at the back of Catherine's head, that brown and gold shaggy hair that looked like she had just run her hands through it, and her lovely profile when she looked through the window.

As they neared Toronto, the traffic on the highway that hugged the shore of Lake Ontario began to snarl, and progress was slow. No matter how many times Dominic travelled in North America, he still marvelled at the endless highways, the skyscrapers pushing higher and higher as though competing for sunlight, the sprawling shopping malls, and the unseen infrastructure that made everything work. He thought about the crowded alleyways of the medina in Fez, the chaotic open markets, and the skinny, barefoot street kids who, for a price, would find whatever it was you could possibly need: cigarettes, batteries, SIM cards, light bulbs, scissors, umbrellas, toothpaste, and deliver it to you in under five minutes. *In its own way, that too is infrastructure…and it works.*

Lukas had fallen asleep against him. He moved his arm around the boy's shoulder and squeezed him closer.

When they finally drew near to Nigel and Philippe's condo on the lake, Catherine insisted that she and Dominic take a cab into town from there. Nigel tried to protest but she convinced him it was crazy to battle another half hour of traffic both ways just to drop them off.

On their way through the downtown neighbourhoods, Catherine chatted to the cab driver, ignoring Dominic. He was acutely aware of the heavy ache in his groin and glad he did not have to make conversation. Was he imagining everything? Was she just a flirt, playing him along? If he asked her to dinner, would she shake that lovely head, telling him she was flattered but no thanks, or she had a boyfriend, or she was too busy.

But when they got out of the taxi, they stood for only a few seconds in front of his hotel. There was no question as to what would happen next. They barely made it to the elevator before crushing into each other, hands groping furiously. His belt undone, his shirt pulled from the waist, he fumbled for his room key card and tried several times, in mounting frustration, to get the green light on the door to engage. Once inside, they tore off each other's clothes.

Dominic's memory of the next few hours was nothing but a mad, magical blend of sensations: the warmth of every inch of her body on his lips and under his hands, those silky legs and velvet thighs, the sweat on her temples, the surprising strength of her calves locked around him as she pulled him deeper, her breath on his face when he collapsed beside her. They made love intensely, continually until darkness fell outside.

Some hours into the night, he woke and found the bed empty beside him. There was a soft noise of traffic outside, and a strange but familiar smell drifting across the room. He struggled to sit up. Catherine was perched on the arm of the couch, right up against the window that was open a fraction. She had a big towel wrapped around her and was smoking a joint.

God, she is gorgeous.

"Want some?" she said, her arm extended towards him.

He got up, slid one hand around her shoulders and pulled the towel away with the other. "I want *you*."

"You've had me five or six times already. I lost count." She blew smoke in his face.

"Not nearly enough." He took a deep drag from the joint, pinched it into the ashtray and pulled her back to bed.

At six thirty, his alarm went off.

"Merde," he grumbled, pulling the covers over his head. "I've got a meeting at eight and I'm starving. Let's get breakfast."

Catherine was already out of bed and retrieving her clothes from different places on the floor. "I've got to get going."

"What's so urgent?"

"Places to go, people to see. I have a life."

"Can I be in it?"

"Doubt it. You're G.U. Geographically Unacceptable."

"Not so. It's a small world. And I'm here now." He grabbed her T-shirt from the floor and stuffed it under the covers.

"Give me that or I'll walk out topless and cause a scene."

"You have to come and get it."

She took a step toward the bed. "Don't even think ab—"

He pulled her down on top of him. "I want to know exactly how unacceptable I am."

***

Of course, he was late for the meeting, and quickly became engulfed in the endless stream of decisions to make, questions to answer, delays, setbacks, mishaps and all the other paraphernalia connected with the opening of a new hotel.

Finally, he found a quiet moment to call Hadir.

"I'm still trying to get my head around this," his brother said. "The coincidence is too weird. Leave things alone. If anything was intended, it will become clear. Otherwise, it wouldn't have been intended, would it?"

Over the next few days, Dominic could barely think straight and realized that trying to manage a grand opening with unfamiliar contractors, in an unfamiliar city was foolish. Their friend Joel was an excellent manager and had been in the business for years, but there were too many critical decisions to make, and all had a domino effect on each other. It was not fair to leave it all to Joel.

And of course, there was Catherine. He had managed to get one of the rooms in the hotel finished for his own use so that he could move in and be permanently on site. That helped, but they saw each other almost every day and got little sleep. She was different from any woman he'd been involved with. Confident, challenging, and, although she appeared to be enjoying the relationship as much as he was, never possessive or needy. If anything, he found himself in an unusual position—he was the one asking when they could see each other again, whether they could have dinner, what she was planning for the weekend.

"Have you told your father?" he asked her one night.

"Told him what? That we have a lot of great sex together?"

He wondered, not for the first time, if that was the only reason for her interest. "You haven't said anything?"

"It's none of his business."

"But we will all be together on Saturday. At the baseball game. And then back at Nigel and Philippe's."

"Well, it will be a nice surprise for him."

This woman certainly knew her own mind, he thought.

Although he was tempted, he resolved not to tell Catherine and the others about the strange connection to Lukas. If Amina did come over, it would be unfair to her and if she herself knew, she would want to defend her father to them all, even to Lukas. He wished he knew exactly what the boy had heard or thought he knew. In the end, he believed it could all get emotional and complicated. *Silence is the best course.*

One night when Catherine had another commitment, he worked late at The Darija, going through the administrative work that had slid off track. He had a hard time remembering what was online and what was hard copy, and spent a lot of unnecessary time looking for things that were right under his nose. Either he would have to adopt his brother's ways and get binders and labels and a decent filing cabinet or have everything digitized. In frustration, he pushed it aside and went for a walk along Bloor Street, the main cross artery of the city. The city had grown on him in the last few weeks. It was alive, diverse, and bustling, and it felt successful, even though it lacked the grandeur of Chicago and the hyperactivity of New York.

He sat on a bench near the Royal Ontario Museum, trying to get a grip on his wandering thoughts. *What to do about Catherine?* Stop it, he tried to tell himself…the affair will end when you go back to Morocco. He felt a pinch of fear with this thought, an emptiness. *Maybe Steven finding my bracelet is another part of fate's devious plan?* Catherine made him think about the future, something Hadir always nagged him about. His brother thought of the future as a long road that you take step by step, plan by plan, decision by decision. Dominic thought of it as a funfair, filled with exciting rides and games to try purely for the challenge, the joy. "You are a thrill seeker, brother," Hadir said, "looking for the constant high."

Is that what this affair is all about? Is Catherine another thrill? But no, there was something else going on, a deeper need she must be filling. He thought about her face in the dimmed lights of the patio restaurant where they last had dinner, the mischief in her eyes as she held his gaze over the rim of her wine glass and slid her bare foot up to his groin under the tablecloth. But the feeling that pulsed through him was not only sexual tension. It was something that pressed against his chest and made his breath come fast and shallow. It didn't feel like love. *But what else could it be?*

Chapter 19

After a particularly stressful day, Dominic plucked up the courage to broach the subject of Amina with Hadir. The remaining furniture and décor were coming soon, and she would be invaluable. She would know exactly how to organize and place everything and could help him with the endless paperwork.

Sitting at his makeshift desk in the office at the hotel, Dominic pulled out the financial papers and punched in his brother's number, wondering what kind of a lecture he'd get about his relationship with Catherine, which he had not yet revealed.

They talked for a while about finances, and he was pleased to be able to reassure Hadir that there was no undue debt, that payments were being made on time, and the bank was "on board."

"You might be promoted to Head in the Sand one day," Hadir said.

"Thanks, but no thanks. There are a few staffing issues. Do you want to put Sophie on?"

"Just fill me in. No need to bother her."

This was odd. Staffing was not Hadir's forté and he was usually happy to put his wife on the line for this part of the call. Dominic quickly summarized the latest hires, some of the employment regulation issues, and the fact that Ethan, the deputy manager, was up to speed but couldn't start full-time until September. He could tell his brother wasn't listening too carefully.

"I'm seeing those people on Saturday, Hadir. A baseball game, and dinner at Nigel and Philippe's afterwards. Lukas will be there."

"*Baseball?* You hate it."

"Two things. I've grown fond of Lukas. He's a sweet kid, so intense, so curious. And I think he likes me. He wants me to translate some of the

Arabic in the notebook his father started. He's bringing it to the game. And, well, I may as well come totally clean. There's a woman."

A big sigh from Hadir. "Of course, there's always a woman. You've been there at least a month."

"Thing is, though, she's the painter's daughter."

Hadir swore, and Dominic winced. Well, he expected this.

"These are new friends, Dominic. They might be good contacts for us down the road. You'll ruin all that when you eventually dump the poor girl."

"More likely, she'll dump me."

"What? I might even pay to see that."

"Look, I need to ask you something. So many things have to happen in the next few weeks. Joel is terrific, but we need someone to take care of the smaller things, get the paperwork organized, worry about the furniture and accessories. The interior design guy is great but hard to work with and expensive. And, as I said, Ethan won't be fully on board until September."

"Ethan?"

"The deputy manager, Hadir. God, are you even paying attention?" Be business-like, Dominic told himself. "I was thinking about Amina. For a few weeks—"

"Absolutely no way. Too much. It would stress her out."

Despite knowing his brother would put up a fight, Dominic was struck by how vehement he was. "Let me finish. Just to get us past the opening. Think about what a great experience it would be for her, what it would do for her confidence. She'll learn new things."

"No, Dominic. What are you thinking? Of introducing her to your new friends? *This is Amina – the daughter of the man who murdered Lukas's father.*"

"Goddammit, why did you say that? Ahmed did NOT murder him."

"But the boy might think he did. We don't know what he knows."

"How could he know who Amina is? And *she* doesn't know who *he* is. I would never put her in a difficult position."

"But she would certainly be meeting these new friends, right? What if it all came out? That woman would no doubt be climbing out of your bed every morning and bound to meet Amina."

"*That woman*'s name is Catherine. She knows nothing about this. I haven't told any of them."

"Good to know. Look, Amina coming to Toronto is not an option. She would need a visa. It could take weeks."

"Don't give me that, Hadir. With *your* connections. A week at most. And Hadir…have you told Sophie yet, about the charts, about Lukas? You can't keep her in the dark. Let me at least talk to her about Amina. She's got a better perspective on these things than you."

This time there was a much longer silence at the other end. Dominic grew alarmed. "Hadir? What? What's going on?"

"I guess I can't keep it from you. Sophie and Amina are on their way to Ouarzazate. They are driving there. They're seeing the Egyptology guy. The one Da'ud recommended."

It took Dominic a second or two to take this in. Ouarzazate was a long journey across the desert. *What the hell has happened?*

"It's my fault," Hadir said. "Those damned star charts. You woke me up at some God-awful hour of the morning and I was confused. I left them on my desk. Amina found them."

PART III — THE SYNASTRY

Chapter 20

Through the window of the car, Amina stared at the High Atlas Mountains in the distance. The straight road before them shimmered and disappeared in the fierce heat of the afternoon sun, and the rocky hills switched between burnt orange, deep red and dark grey as they fell in and out of its relentless glare. Scattered among the foothills were outcrops of cedar, cork, walnut, and palm, and tiny fields and pastures that the Berbers had cultivated for centuries.

"What was I thinking, bringing us out in this blistering sun?" Sophie said. "We should have left earlier. No wonder there is no traffic." She pressed her foot harder on the gas pedal.

Not wanting to do the whole journey in one day, Sophie had arranged to stay at a modern hotel in Beni Mellal the previous night, one popular with tourists. It felt strange to Amina to be waited on, to be asked if everything was in order, and whether she would like something to eat. She noticed how effortlessly Sophie handled herself: tipping the bellboy with money already in her hand, asking him to take the luggage to their room after directing them to a shady spot by the pool, and to have two glasses of chilled white wine brought out.

Sophie and Hadir had engaged in a fierce argument before they left, and Amina was mortified to be the cause of it. It began so innocently. She had taken some invoices to Hadir's office and was writing him a note, when she noticed her name on a strange looking sheet of paper on the desk: a big circle with many sections, filled with signs, symbols, and handwritten notes. She thought she must be mistaken and looked more closely. But there it was, Amina Gamel, and her birth date, 24th July 1999, in the top right corner in both English and Arabic. She picked it up. Stapled beneath was a similar page with a date and a question mark, no name. Could they be horoscopes, she wondered, having seen something similar in a magazine once. But not with these strange symbols. Some of them looked like hieroglyphics. In the margin on the sheet with her name were several notes:

Sekhmet, from the Ancient Egyptian word 'shm' – power, might. Mistress of Dread. Sekhmet left Egypt angered by deception. The hot winds of the desert are her breath. Lower down was an arrow pointing to a symbol and the words: *Ascendant: Cancer 13°50'35 – sensitive, passionate when wronged.*

Amina felt something squeezing the air from her lungs. The charts fell to the floor.

Up in her room, she sat on the bed and rocked back and forth, a thousand frightening questions ricocheting through her mind. *What is this? Who did it? What is it doing in Hadir's office? Does Dominic have something to do with it?* She thought back to the night with the Tarot cards, and how Dominic had stopped so abruptly. *Please, please don't let this be something to do with the past, about Baba…*

Memories of her childhood flooded her brain: the sadness and humiliation in her father's eyes; the money falling from the sky; the two of them hiding in the dark alleyway, terrified they would be found by others who would fight them for their treasure. She shivered and pulled the sheets over her. The tears flowed heavily, and she struggled for breath.

There was a sharp rap at her door. "Amina, it's Sophie."

"I'm sorry, Sophie. I'm not feeling well. I'll be down in a minute."

"Please. Open the door."

She struggled off the bed and eased the door open.

"Let me in. We have to talk." Sophie scooped Amina into her arms. "I know what happened. One of the bellboys saw you go into Hadir's office, then run up the stairs like the devil was behind you. I went in there. I saw those papers."

They sat beside each other on the bed and Sophie told her what she, herself, had just found out: that the Egyptian, Da'ud, had given these charts to Dominic, that they were almost certainly done by the man

Amina's father used to work for. She tried to reassure her that there was nothing harmful about them. The second sheet was probably for his own child, a son. This is what he did all the time—read people's stars.

"Hadir and Dominic did plan to give them to you at some point, Amina. But it went out of their minds, what with how busy things are getting and Dominic over in Canada. And to be honest, they worried it might upset you. That's what held them back."

"But that man…why give the charts to Dominic? He knew my father; he knew I worked here. Why not give them to me? I'm not a child."

Sophie pulled her close again. "You are right, Amina. But you know how overprotective our men are. They have honourable intentions but lack emotional intelligence. First, Dominic didn't tell Hadir. Only when that old man followed you around the market, did he finally let on about the charts. And then, the two of them kept it from me. Hadir and I just had a brief *discussion*. I believe he is on the roof with the shisha pipe, licking his wounds."

Amina smiled through her tears and felt sorry for Hadir. She was relieved, but Sophie's next question took her by surprise.

"So. What do you want to do about this?"

"You mean…I'm not sure what you mean?"

"They are in the safe now. But they are yours. You can rip them up, burn them. You can summon Da'ud to see what else he knows. You can do whatever you please."

Amina went to the window. The lowering sun had cast the busy alleyway into shadow. A stray dog foraged for scraps.

She thought about one of the phrases: *Mistress of Dread*. "I wish I could understand them…those symbols and words. Perhaps there is someone I can talk to. But not if it costs a lot of money."

"I thought you might say that." Sophie got up. "Let's go and tell Hadir that decision. He is supposed to have been doing some research for us." She took Amina's arm and guided her out of her room and onto the roof.

Hadir was on his phone. He dropped his voice and got up when he saw them coming and walked back and forth along the edge of the terrace. Eventually, pocketing the phone, he motioned for them to join him on the deck chairs under the big striped canopy, moving two cats out of the way to make room. Sophie told him what Amina wanted to do.

"I'm sorry you are upset, Amina, and I understand your curiosity." He shook his head slowly. "Finding Egyptians is one thing…finding Egyptologists is quite another."

"Did you call that woman, that friend of Henri?" Sophie asked him.

"Yes, I did. And I also called our young friend at the tourist bureau. His mother is Egyptian. They used to live in Alexandria."

"And?"

"What are you hoping for, Sophie? How many star gazing Ancient Egypt gurus do you expect them to have in their contacts?"

"Then we should go and see the man Da'ud recommended. In Ouarzazate."

That's when the argument started. Hadir was incredulous.

"You have to be kidding. I cannot leave the hotel with Dominic away, and there is no way I will allow the two of you to drive across the desert to see a man we know nothing about. It is out of the question."

"Since when are you 'allowing' or 'disallowing' anything I decide to do? Amina wants to understand what is on these charts, and so would I. It could be a lot of mumbo jumbo, or it could be interesting. Regardless, it is her right to do with them as she pleases."

"But the man in Ouarzazate. He could—"

"He can read all that hieroglyphic business. Do you have a better idea?"

"Sophie, *mon amour*, Ouarzazate is a nine, ten-hour drive. You don't know the region, you would be two women travelling alone."

"You mean, without a man? Heaven forbid! How would we know which direction to go, how to talk to strangers, how to handle an emergency? For God's sake, Hadir. This country is our home. And

Ouarzazate is a fascinating town. Africa's Hollywood. If nothing else, it will be a nice break for Amina and me."

And on it went: Hadir questioning why a meeting was necessary, why not email or Facetime; Sophie saying it could be a long discussion, complicated; Hadir insisting it was probably nonsense and could surely not be complicated.

"What *is* the matter, Hadir?" Sophie said, clearly exasperated. "Is there still something you're not telling us?"

"Enough. Can't a man even *worry* in peace?"

Sophie prevailed, of course. She always did, Amina thought, smiling to herself.

Up ahead, the road made a sharp swing to the right. Rounding the bend, Sophie abruptly slammed on the brakes and swore. Amina had to put her hands on the dashboard to brace herself.

"*Merde*. Sorry, sorry," said Sophie.

Off to the side, in a clearing under a walnut tree, was a police car. Two policemen were leaning against it, smoking. One of them waved his arm indicating Sophie should pull over.

Once more in awe, Amina watched as Sophie walked over and greeted both men. She stayed there several minutes and, before long, all three were chatting and laughing. Eventually, one of the men put both his hands over one of Sophie's and gave her a slight bow.

Amina cracked the window open a fraction to overhear the conversation, but a whoosh of oppressive hot air blasted in. She quickly closed it. Another phrase on the chart came to her mind. *The hot winds of the desert are her breath*. Despite the heat, she felt a pinch of cold on the back of her neck and began to worry about what they would learn the following day.

"Did they charge you with anything?" she asked when Sophie got back in.

"They gave me a lecture about speeding. It is important to be friendly to the authorities. Most of them are good people."

In another hour, they drew close to Ouarzazate and could see the famous Kasbah Taourirt, straddling the far hillside. No wonder so many movies are made here, Amina thought. The sandy brown buildings climbing over each other on the hillside, the green canopies of palm trees, the crescent moon in the darkening sky, all looked magical. Her friend, Tabani, had told her *Game of Thrones* was filmed here. Tabani managed to download some of the episodes on her tablet, but it wasn't of good quality, and neither of them understood it.

They drove through town and up a steep hill to an imposing hotel that was more like a castle: massive stone pillars on either side of the entrance, tall, iron-studded wooden doors open to the lobby, high-backed chairs with heavily carved wooden arms and legs, huge statues of lions and elephants and other African wildlife scattered around.

"Makes our own Riad look humble, don't you think?" said Sophie.

"But it must be so expensive. I didn't want you to spend this money, Sophie. Last night too. I feel badly that you're doing this."

"Don't be silly. This is a treat for me, too. And it's always good to look at what attracts tourists these days."

After a light meal, they shared a pot of mint tea on the terrace and admired the view. The muezzin's soulful *Salat al-'isha* reverberated over roof tops. What had Dominic thought about these two charts she was carrying halfway across the country, Amina wondered? *Does he share the same feeling as Hadir…that it is all nonsense?* She doubted this. Dominic believed in strange things. She wanted to ask Sophie how the three of them felt, what they had discussed, but sensed there was something Sophie was holding back, something that troubled her. If *only Dominic were here.* Maybe he would have talked to her more freely. He had been gone such a long time. Day-to-day life went on as usual, but nothing felt the same.

"Come, we should have an early night." Sophie stretched her arms above her head. "I need to call my dear husband and reassure him we have not been sold into slavery. And we have an important meeting tomorrow."

Chapter 21

Masoud Burhan greeted them at his home. He was young, possibly early thirties, if that, and not at all the kind of person Amina expected. She had imagined an older man, a "sage," with a wizened face and hooded eyes, wearing the traditional Egyptian *gallabiyya*. Masoud wore western dress: blue jeans, sandals, a pale cream shirt with sleeves rolled up at the wrists. His face was rough with sharp cheekbones, skin deeply tanned and weather beaten. He had black, wiry hair, a short beard, and dark eyes under heavy brows.

"Please, come this way." As he led them into his home, Amina noticed he was limping.

The room was furnished with low, decorative benches around the walls, and well-stuffed cushions. A large, circular copper table stood in the centre, with a silver tea pot and small orange, green and blue tea glasses. Masoud sat across from them. He told them this was the traditional *koshary shai* tea, common in the north of Egypt, and asked if this would be acceptable or would they prefer a different kind. Having been assured this was fine, he went through the relatively long ritual of adding fresh mint leaves, steeping and pouring. By the side of the tea were plates of figs and dates and many kinds of nuts. He encouraged them to help themselves.

He divided his time between here and his home in Cairo, he said, in answer to Sophie's questions. This house was owned by the production company. He was a consultant for films being shot in the area and was required for his expertise on the Ancient Egyptians. He knew Da'ud because they had once worked together on a film project, in which Da'ud sourced the furniture and artefacts for the sets. Despite his somewhat fierce appearance, Masoud had a gentle manner and spoke quietly, with the Cairene dialect that reminded Amina of her childhood. He nodded his head slowly while Sophie asked her questions, and showed no discomfort with her direct manner and overt scepticism.

"You told me the reason for your visit," he said. "I am interested to see the charts you speak of. But first…" his dark eyes settled on Amina, "I want to know whether this is curiosity or whether there is another reason?"

Amina retrieved the charts from her bag and took a moment to gather her courage. "My father worked for the man who created these. I don't understand why this man wrote *my* birth chart unless he was trying to understand something himself. And if so, what?" *What exactly happened all those years ago in Cairo? Who were these people her father worked for? And if that man's death was not an accident, then who was responsible for it?* All her knowledge was rooted in rumour and innuendo. And now, she had a strong feeling that Sophie and the brothers had learned something more. Despite her love and gratitude, she harboured a seed of resentment. "I don't know what to believe about things like this," she added. "Perhaps it will influence decisions I make for the future."

Masoud inclined his head, letting her last statement hang in the air. "You need to understand something before we start." He took the charts from her. "Neither these, nor anything I tell you will unveil the future. I have an astronomical *and* astrological understanding of the universe and the movements of the planets—this is essential for a full appreciation of the lives of the Ancient Egyptians. But I do not believe in the principles of astrology, and I am not a fortune teller."

"We are not suggesting—" Sophie began, but Masoud raised his hand to stop her.

"I care only that you are not misled or that what I say may cause you to take action with no foundation in reason."

"What exactly *can* you tell us?" Sophie asked.

"I will tell you what is *on* these charts, what the hieroglyphics represent, their relationship to each other and their possible significance against the backdrop of the star maps behind them." He turned to

Amina. "The Ancient Egyptians understood things about the mysteries of the universe that even the best Egyptologists will scarcely fathom in their lifetimes. But they did not know *you*, Amina, and they should not influence your life."

Amina could not hold his gaze.

He refreshed their tea and picked up the charts.

"I'm sure you know that the man who did this was an expert in his field," he said eventually.

"How do *you* know this?" Sophie asked.

"After I got your call, I spoke briefly to Da'ud to thank him for his referral. Karl Gustav used to lecture at the university in Cairo. Anyone who studied astronomy or Egyptology at that time would have known him. He was extremely well-regarded. I understand he died tragically."

"But maybe he wasn't a good man."

"I would be sorry to hear that." Masoud looked closely at the charts again. "I need time to study these. I had not expected them to be so densely constructed. How long will you be in Ouarzazate?"

"How long do you need us to be?" Sophie asked.

"Another day. If I may make a suggestion. . .I will study them tonight and tomorrow morning. In the afternoon, I am needed on a film set for an hour or two. Perhaps you would like to meet me there and I could show you some of what goes on behind the scenes. Would you enjoy that? And then you must be my guests at dinner, and we will discuss what I have found."

Sophie said her husband could manage another day without them. Amina was delighted at the idea of seeing a film set and imagined telling Tabani about it. Her friend would be envious.

Masoud struggled to stand up from the low seat and reached for an elegant cane with a silver horse-head handle, that lay off to the side.

"Are you okay?" Sophie asked, stepping towards him.

"Thank you. I must get used to it."

"Did you have an accident?"

"A bad fall from a horse. My father has a horse farm in Abu Sir. Near Giza. I fear the damage is permanent."

He gave them directions to the film studios. "I look forward to seeing you tomorrow."

Chapter 22

In a cavernous building on the film production lot, Amina stood in awe, taking in a scene she could never have imagined. Floor-to-ceiling columns with Ancient Egyptian frescos around them stood on one side. On the other, a wide flight of stone steps with a red carpet led to a large ornamental throne at the top. Scaffolding secured a huge camera fixed to the end of a crane. There were people everywhere: operating the camera, hooking up lights, sitting on benches, stools, and foldout chairs, or squatting on the floor. In one corner, men in Bedouin *thoabs* with the traditional *keffiyah* head scarfs talked to women in Ancient Egyptian sheath dresses. In another, men dressed as soldiers, swords hanging from their sides, shared a shisha pipe. Others huddled over computer screens or shouted into walkie-talkies. Nearby, a man held the reins of several horses in one hand and thumbed through his mobile phone with the other.

Masoud explained that three productions were happening simultaneously on different lots and many of those involved would congregate here in the break as there was a cafeteria, and it was cooler.

He took them in a modified golf cart for a short tour of the outside locales. All around them were sweeping valleys of orange sand, streams flanked by groves of palm trees, buildings that looked like palaces, castles and fortresses, some of them guarded by enormous statues. Masoud pointed to a camera crew on one of the far hills filming a long line of men on camels. He showed them places that had been used in *Lawrence of Arabia*, *Gladiator* and *Black Hawk Down*. Amina took photos but Masoud insisted she stand and pose before the different sights; *he* would take the pictures. He made a production of this, encouraging her to turn this way and that, while he limped about, taking his sunglasses on and off, snapping her from different angles. She beckoned for Sophie to join her, but Sophie demurred. She was preoccupied today, Amina thought, wondering if it was to do with the telephone call to Hadir last night. Or perhaps she missed the twins who had been gone for several months. Amina couldn't imagine being separated from one's children for so long, but the boys were staying with a relative in New York and, from all accounts, were thoroughly enjoying themselves. She glanced over to the golf cart and was relieved to see Sophie smiling, gesturing discreetly with her thumb toward their host with a "knowing" look.

"Well, well, *ma chérie*," Sophie said with a sly smile as the two of them drove back to their hotel. "I do believe our young hieroglyphics man has fallen for you. All that not-so-casual and inappropriate touching of your arm, all the gallantry."

Amina smiled. "I don't think so, Sophie. And anyway, I'm not interested."

"The man who bewitches you one day will be a lucky man indeed."

"Maybe there isn't such a man."

"Well, there are plenty standing in wait."

Amina thought about her intense but brief relationship with an intern at the clinic where her father was treated. She had so quickly lost interest in him.

Sophie began to list the young hopefuls on the hotel staff, evaluating each and their chances. Amina played along with her teasing but could think only of the one man she longed for. Sophie would never name *him*.

***

They sat on the terrace of Masoud's home that looked over the top of a grove of palm trees. A welcome breeze from the mountains blew the leafy fronds back and forth. Masoud had poured wine and suggested they discuss the charts before dinner—a simple chicken couscous with raisins and pine nuts.

"So, where to begin," he said, putting the first chart in front of Amina and anchoring it with decorative stones from a bowl. "Let's start with the classic planetary positions. What interested Mr. Gustav is the significant influence of Leo. Your sun, ascendant and Mercury are in the Leo constellation. His interest almost certainly stems from the mythology of Leo in Ancient Egypt and its connection to the Goddess Sekhmet." He pointed to different sections of the sheet. "I have referenced the hieroglyphics and, in separate notes, have given you detailed descriptions of what they stand for. Sekhmet was a warrior goddess. She represents vengeance. Wrongdoing invokes her fury. She breathes fire and unleashes her lust for punishment. Not someone you should cross."

Clearly enjoying his descriptions, Masoud went on at some length about this goddess, the possible daughter of the sun god Ra. Amina was grateful he had typed it out for her. She tried to recall what she'd learned about Ancient Egypt in school. Most of it had gone totally over her head.

"And here is the hieroglyphic for the Goddess Ma'at. The ostrich feather on her headband represents truth. She symbolizes karma, the balance and harmony in the universe. Upsetting this balance has dire consequences and that's often when Sekhmet steps in with her rage and fury. Amina—" he touched her hand. "Nothing here should cause you concern."

"But what has all this got to do with me?"

"You are an Egyptian, Amina. You might be a modern echo of the powerful Sekhmet. Who knows what kind of temper may lie behind that lovely face?"

Amina blushed and sharply withdrew her hand.

"I did not mean to offend you," Masoud said. "Here," he pointed to the paper again, "right next to Sekhmet, is her consort Ptah. Ptah was a fascinating creator-god, an artisan, a highly imaginative individual. And this, here, is the symbol for Shai, the Ancient Egyptian concept of fate and the path you are destined to follow…"

Amina began to wonder whether all this had been a waste of time.

"I can see it is a lot to take in." Masoud handed the sheets to her. "You should wait a few days and read them with a fresh perspective. I'm sure you will have further questions and I hope you will call me. But—" he reached behind him and picked up more typed sheets. "There is the matter of the second chart."

"We think it's the man's son," Amina said. "I don't care as much about that one."

"I will summarize quickly. Of all the hieroglyphics on this chart, the most significant, the one that was clearly on the mind of the father as he created this, is Nefertem. In Egyptian mythology, Nefertem represented the first sunlight and the blue lotus flower, and was *eventually* thought to be the son of Ptah and Sekhmet. I have included screen shots of mosaics and paintings of Nefertem. Most often, he is depicted as a beautiful, ethereal young man with Egyptian blue water lilies around his head."

Amina felt a slight stiffness from Sophie at her side. "All very interesting," Sophie said. "But nothing to do with Amina."

Masoud raised a cautionary hand and placed the two charts side-by-side. "Amina, you and this child were born fifteen years apart and you have never met. But here is what is most interesting. This second analysis, with his date of birth at the top, is *not* a nativity, or horoscope, in the classic sense of the word, not like this first one that was done for you. It is a *synastry*. A synastry is the overlay of *two* charts. It maps out the relationship between two people, how their lives intersect, their compatibility. The two people in this analysis, an analysis that indicates an inextricable connection, are the child…and you, Amina."

On the drive back to their hotel, Sophie was silent. When they arrived, she suggested a nightcap on the terrace. There, she went through the details of her conversation with Hadir on the phone the night before. First, she told her that Dominic wanted her to go to Canada. Amina was beside herself, barely able to process this scary, exciting possibility. And then Sophie told her about Lukas.

Chapter 23

Steven took a long hard stare at his latest painting, cursing the cramped confines of his condo and the need to retreat to the hallway to get a good perspective of the work. He had returned yesterday, having flown back to Vancouver for four days—an extravagance, considering the distance and the cost of the flight. But he convinced himself he needed a little time off.

Now, he missed the beautiful high-ceilinged studio of his home out west, and he already missed Natalie. She had listened attentively to all his descriptions of the events of the past couple of weeks: meeting Dominic, Catherine's affair with him, Lukas—and that whole "down the rabbit hole" feeling at his show. Of course, a couple of bottles of wine later, this led to him spilling his heart out about Rachel. They sat on his deck in the two red Adirondack chairs, staring across the Georgia Straight toward the Gulf Islands. The sun had gone down, and it was chilly. They pulled the big alpaca wool blanket over them. The horn of one of the BC Ferries sounded in the distance. He loved hearing that. It meant he was home.

Over the years, he had confided in few people about Rachel, not wanting to stir old memories or resurrect the anger and hurt. Natalie asked him no questions, just squeezed his fingers. "Rachel was unique…and good for you," she said. "That's what you should remember." She had a way of oversimplifying even the most complex issues, but it was comforting after the angst he allowed himself to wallow in.

He approached the painting again and fussed with the white brightness of one of its focal points. Exploring abstract expression felt good; it suited his pensive moods, and the success of his Toronto show made him feel good about the decision to stick with it for a while. There was still one more painting to complete for Stockholm, and Toby was hyperventilating. His agent had dropped in that morning. *Pathways,*

Steven called it. Sweeps and swooshes of greys and whites and sea blue. There was no anchor but many points of light that demanded attention. The eye was drawn to a meeting point in the centre, but it couldn't rest there because the colours diffused and blended. The painting had a sense of mystery, but also excitement, possibility. Toby agreed and was all for wrapping it up and getting it put aside, so Steven could start on the next. But he insisted on one more day to be sure.

He checked his watch. An hour before the game. He was a big baseball fan, but had fretted about taking more time off. He stood as far back as the space would allow, closed his eyes, opened them again and let the painting wash over him. *Right. It's done. And it's great.*

***

Nigel had secured a private box for the Blue Jays game at the Rogers Centre, courtesy of one of his good customers. Behind the dedicated, comfortable tiered seats that overlooked the stadium, were couches, a coffee table, a wet bar, a huge TV with live coverage, and gourmet food on order.

"This is not what you'd call an *authentic* baseball experience," Steven said, pouring another beer. "You'll give our international friends a totally false impression."

"My dear chap," said Nigel. "If you thought for one moment that I would sit for three hours on a hard seat, pay twenty-five dollars for a beer and a rubbery hot dog, and then get up and sing part way through, you are mistaken. This is as authentic as it's going to get, and I believe both Lukas and Dominic are thoroughly enjoying themselves…albeit for different reasons."

Steven looked over at the seats. Lukas paid rapt attention to the game while Catherine explained it. Dominic had one arm around her shoulder and was twisting and fondling her hair. *Shit. Where is this going?* Catherine had described it as "a thing" when she called to tell him. "What kind of a thing," he asked naively. "Lots of fun," was all he could get out of her. Well, he'd seen that coming. Apparently, her mother was horrified she was dating someone "one quarter Arab." Typical, he thought. Lilian probably hadn't met anyone outside of her own neighbourhood in twenty years.

"Looking at the lovebirds?" Nigel dug an elbow in his ribs. "What a handsome pair they make. I do believe Philippe's heart is broken."

Philippe placed a large bowl of tempura shrimp and dipping sauce on the bar in front of them. "*Au contraire.* My heart beats soundly. My life is complete," He grabbed a shrimp and popped it into Nigel's mouth. "My admiration was but a fleeting dream."

"It won't last," said Steven, still looking at his daughter. "They never do. And this one will actually be leaving the country."

"Don't be such a sourpuss." Nigel wagged his finger. "He'll be here for several more weeks and is even bringing over someone from their place in Fez. Tomorrow, I believe." He spread his arms wide and looked up at the ceiling. "Ah the first blush of love, 'tis a rare and wonderful thing. Let them have fun while the mood is upon them."

A loud roar went up from the crowd. "Whoa." Lukas jumped up. "Two runners now. First and third." He looked at Catherine for confirmation.

"That's right. What do you think our guy on first might do?"

"Steal second?" Lukas shouted.

"How do you know these things?" Dominic asked him. "We've only been here half an hour. And what is 'home'? Is that where they are all sitting?"

Catherine explained home base, the dugout, and the bullpen. All three munched on charbroiled hamburgers and gourmet fries.

"That kid," Steven said to Nigel and Philippe. "What's he all about?"

"Robert was told he is gifted. Who knows? Maybe just extremely smart."

"He wants to be loved," Philippe whispered. "*Pauvre petit…*his father killed, his mother…" he trailed off, probably thinking that the subject of Rachel was still off limits.

"What do they mean 'curveball'?" said Lukas, his eyes on the TV screen.

"Can't help you with that one," said Catherine. "Ask my dad."

Lukas hesitated, as though not sure whether to interrupt the adult conversation at the bar. "Can you tell me, Steven?"

Steven was surprised at the wave of delight he felt. "Come over here and I'll demonstrate." He looked around. "Of all the bells and whistles we've got here in this Opera Box or whatever it is, there's no friggin' baseball." He crumpled a couple of paper napkins from the bar into an approximate baseball size and explained the different ways of clutching and throwing the ball. As the boy earnestly tried to copy him, he was struck once again with the absurdity of the situation. Here was *Rachel's son*, asking him questions in a baseball stadium in Toronto, five years after he had last seen her, five years after that beautiful, terrible day on the terrace of his home in Tuscany when the mailman brought her letter.

Lukas gave an elaborate shrug when it was clear that the pitches were beyond his grasp and returned to his seat. For a second, Steven saw Rachel. It was the exasperated look she would sometimes give him, usually followed by that Italian-style "I give up" wave of her hands. But there were few Mediterranean genes in the boy. The shock of blond hair, grown longer, and those grey eyes. Those were the father's. *What was it that guy had, what kind of magic did he wield?*

"What did you learn, Lukas?" Dominic slid his arm around the boy.

"I learned fast ball and breaking ball and—" he thought for a moment—"slider. But I can't really do them."

The boy unsettled Steven. He tried to analyze his feelings. Was it only the memory of that one day he'd met Lukas's father, the sense of unfinished business from the past? He looked at Lukas focussing intently on the game, his feet kicking underneath the seat. No question he was a sweet, endearing kid, he thought, a bit precocious. But unwittingly, he was rubbing salt into an old wound.

Dominic looked back. "Steven, I repeat my invitation to Morocco. I will take you to the Mohammed V stadium in Casablanca to see our national team and get you hooked on the beautiful game of football."

"Why don't you go? To Morocco, I mean," Nigel said. "It might inspire a whole new style in your work, like Tuscany did. Such a vibrant place, so colourful, so alive. Why not?"

Steven was about to question why his work needed yet another new style, but caught himself. Nigel would accuse him of defensiveness, which was right, of course. The "why not?" hung in his head. He had always felt he should travel more. Avid travelers would look at him strangely as though the only thing stopping anyone was money, and that wasn't a problem. At first it was his ex. Lillian never wanted to go anywhere except Florida in the winter. She had no dreams of Paris or Rome. When Catherine was born, travel was off the table for a while anyway. *And then?* Two years in Tuscany. That had been a pretty damned brave move, he told himself, took a lot of guts.

"I have a feeling your lovely daughter might get there before you," said Philippe.

Steven looked back at the seats. He swore Dominic's hand was halfway up her thigh. *Jesus. Get a room.*

Chapter 24

"What kind of car is this?" Lukas asked.

The game was over. Nigel suggested Steven drive the boy to their condo for the pizza dinner they had planned, and he and Philippe would take the "lovebirds." The Blue Jays had squeaked out a win at the bottom of the ninth and the whole city was clearly in a good mood with people spilling out all over the sidewalks, smiling, high-fiving.

"It's a Mercedes C43. I might sell it. I don't like driving here."

"My Uncle Robert has a Range Rover. For all the damned kids."

"What?"

"You know, my cousins and me."

"Yes, but 'damned kids?'"

"I heard him say that on the phone."

Steven was about to make a turn but realized it was one way in the opposite direction. "Every time I get used to this city, they change it. Your cousins are a lot older than you, right?"

"They don't like me."

"Do they say that, or is that just what you think?"

"I kind of know it."

"I bet you were sad to leave Italy."

"It was always nice and sunny, but it's not where I belong."

Steven had never thought of "belonging" anywhere, but he knew Rachel believed strongly in this and had even predicted he would live on the west coast one day.

"Where d'you think you'd like to be one day, when you grow up?"

Lukas stared down into his lap. "I don't know."

Leave that alone, Steven thought.

"What's a Humane Society?" Lukas suddenly asked. "It was on a poster back there."

"It's where they take care of stray cats and dogs, or pets that terrible people have abandoned. I think you call it something different in England."

Lukas fell quiet. From the corner of his eye, Steven saw him crumpling a tissue into a ball and rubbing it back and forth in the palms of his hands. Thankfully, they soon arrived at Nigel and Philippe's building.

***

Steven surveyed the elaborately set dining table. "I thought you said pizza." He snuck an olive from the antipasto dish.

"Pizza *pesto Genovese* and Pizza *alla diavola*," said Philippe, distributing the napkins. "And a simple salad with mango and avocado. We can't let our distinguished international visitor think we are all fast-food junkies."

"Lukas," said Nigel. "Get your nose out of that book and come help me pass round the appetizers." He turned to Steven and dropped his voice. "I told you about that notebook and those charts that his father did. They're never out of his sight. God knows what he's learning."

"Wow," said a voice behind them. "This is unbelievable."

They spun around to see Dominic staring at *Aphelion* on the wall before him, his hands on his hips, his head tilted back. From Steven's angle, his body hid a good part of the painting, and he became its central figure. Steven was reminded of that day in the gallery in Rome when Lukas's father stood in a similar position and stared at this same painting with such cold eyes.

"This is yours, Steven?" said Dominic. "It's magnificent, a masterpiece. Have you ever exhibited it?"

"Thank you. Yes, in Rome, five years ago. I learned recently that Lukas's mother had bought it. Bit of a long story as to how it ended up here."

"My uncle said it was too big. He put it in the garage," said Lukas.

"Can you *imagine?*" said Nigel, a hand at his throat. "Don't get me started on that. We are keeping it safe until it finds a permanent home."

Steven was delighted that Dominic liked the painting. Learning that Rachel bought it had been a disappointment. He preferred to think of it being appreciated by a chance visitor to the gallery, someone who would have been drawn to the textures and colours, the big dip and sweep of the valley below the precipice where the man was leaning forward to greet the rising sun. That visitor might have caught their breath and said "Wow" like Dominic did.

"It's the best thing you've ever done, Dad," said Catherine. "It tells a story, not like all these grey-blue hallucinations you're doing these days."

"Yes, yes, you've made that clear," said Steven.

"What is the story it tells?" Dominic asked.

Steven rolled his tongue across his teeth. He did not like having to explain his work. He saw the challenge in his daughter's eyes, the expectant raised eyebrows of Nigel and Philippe. No way he was going to regurgitate all that pain and drama. "It was a turning point for me, that's all. Rachel pushed me a lot. Helped me to deal with my insecurities. She saw this painting as a kind of liberation. It meant something to her too. That's why she bought it, I guess."

"The title, *Aphelion?* What does that mean?"

"When the sun is far away," Lukas said, causing everyone to look at him. Obviously embarrassed, he put the plate of appetizers down, dived onto the couch and buried his face in the notebook again. "That's what my mom said."

"It's when the earth is farthest from the sun on its ellipse, it's orbit," said Steven. "So, Lukas is right."

"Hey, Lukas," said Dominic. "If you want to sell it to me when you're older, give me a call." He went over and sat on the couch beside him. "Let me see that book of yours. See what the Arabic in there is saying."

Steven sat opposite, next to Catherine. They talked for a while about her planned teaching career. She was unusually candid, finally admitting to nerves and to feeling stressed about classroom management and the "entitled" attitude of many of today's younger students. She was still thinking of taking a year off. He cautioned her about forfeiting a secure position, but she shrugged off his concerns and assured him she had money saved.

The meal was delicious, the wine flowed, the conversation grew animated. As usual with any event involving Nigel and Philippe, there was teasing and laughter and that deep comfort that only old friends could bring. Steven nursed his glass of wine and looked around the table. He felt rooted in the moment, as though they were all meant to be here, to be together—even these two strangers whom he had met only a few weeks ago. He studied Dominic with a painter's eye: easy to see the "one quarter Arab" in him: dark eyes, sharp planes of the cheekbones, pronounced and elevated eyebrows, a slight kink in the otherwise straight nose, a pronounced chin and enviably thick dark hair. He was tanned and relaxed, his shirt sleeves rolled back, one hand holding his wine glass. Steven noted the Rolex watch, the leather jacket over the back of his chair. He caught the eye of Lukas at the other end of the table, raised his glass to him, and winked. Lukas lifted his cola with a big grin. *Too much wine.* He reached for a glass of water.

They had nearly finished the meal when the call came. At first, they weren't sure whose phone it was. Everyone searched their pockets. Then Nigel saw it was his, over on the kitchen counter, vibrating, its face glowing. He rose unsteadily and gave an irritated tsk-tsk when he picked it up.

"Just having dinner," he said into it. "Must be late there. What was that?" He gestured to his friends to carry on eating and went down the corridor to the bedroom.

Steven realized that several minutes had gone by since he had heard the muffled sounds of talking from down the corridor. "Hey, Philippe. Nigel's been a while. He hasn't passed out from all this wine, I hope."

Philippe jumped up. "*Mon Dieu.* He probably fell asleep on the bed after the call."

Steven followed Philippe.

Nigel was sitting on the bed, his face ashen. "Close the door."

"My God, what's wrong?" Philippe rushed over.

Nigel raised his hands to stop him. "It's okay. Bit of a shock. That was Rachel's brother. Wanted to get into a long discussion. I told him we had company and I'll call him tomorrow. But here's the gist of it. His wife, Melinda, she's seriously ill. Doctors saying no more than six months. Needs full time care. They'll have to get somebody in to help." He took a few shallow breaths and started coughing.

"I'll get you some water," said Steven.

Nigel shook his head through the coughs. "No. Don't get the others alarmed. Robert's a basket case. The kids will stay with his sister-in-law. Maybe for the whole school year…however long it takes…I mean for Melinda." He raised his troubled face to them. "This sister-in-law has agreed to take Lukas *temporarily,* but only until 'other arrangements' can be made."

"*Mais quelle horreur.*" Philippe flopped down on the bed beside Nigel. "What does that mean? The poor boy has been through enough."

"He was babbling. It's well past midnight over there and I think he's losing it. Obviously, say nothing to Lukas. We'll figure it out tomorrow."

As the three of them walked back into the dining room, Nigel protesting everything was fine, "bit of a dizzy turn," Steven had the sensation that the quiet world he had lived in a few weeks ago had abruptly stalled and thrown him into an alternative universe. And that universe kept spinning, faster and faster. He put his hand against the wall to steady himself. *What has any of this got to do with me?* He looked over to his painting. Dominic and Lukas sat directly underneath it, deep in discussion over Lukas's notebook.

Dammit, Rachel. Will this never be over?

He realized he was quite drunk and would have to ask Catherine to drive him home.

Chapter 25

Nigel sat on the balcony the following night, nursing a generous martini, and reflected on the traumatic day. It had taken him some time to connect with Robert. The man was clearly still in shock and sounded desperate.

"I'm sorry I ruined your dinner party, but my wife is dying. She's in hospital and wants to come home. We'll have to get a palliative care nurse. I have a full-time job. My own children are old enough to be left alone. Lukas is not. I can't put that burden on my sister-in-law."

"I'm so sorry to hear all this, Robert," Nigel said, bracing himself.

There was a deep inhale at the other end. "Longer term, the only solution may be prep school, flexible boarding."

"What?" Nigel had virtually shrieked. "He is far, far too young."

"I'm talking later, year or two. In the meantime, in the next few months, what can I do? I can't look after him. We'd need a nanny, someone to take him back and forth to school, get his meals. But there will already be a full-time nurse in the house for Melinda. It's just…too much, Nigel, too much."

"But Lukas is starting school this September, right?"

"I can't see how it will work. He would be living in a sad and upsetting environment. Look, there is an alternative for the short term. If you are up to it. I was hoping you might offer to keep him longer, until next term, until Melinda—damnit, Nigel you know what I mean. If I have to beg you, I'll gladly beg."

Nigel held the phone away from himself for a moment and took a deep breath.

"But there will have to be some kind of schooling *before* the new year, surely?"

"One term is hardly a big deal. He's a bright kid as I'm sure you've learned. They've promised to send an outline, suggested lessons. He will catch up in no time."

"Are you asking us to keep him right through Christmas? And what about the young girl, Melinda's niece I believe, who brought him over? She surely can't wait that long? Are you expecting one of us to accompany him home?"

"Nigel, I'm desperate. I'll do and pay for whatever it takes."

"That's another four months, Robert. We are very fond of him but that's one hell of an imposition. And never mind our feelings…what about his?" He realized, with an unpleasant jolt, that Robert might have been planning this from the start. He thought back to his visit there with new clarity. *Did they already know Melinda was unlikely to pull through?* He remembered the huge suitcase they packed for Lukas.

"All I can say, Nigel, is that the longer he can stay with you, the less time he will have to spend with my sister-in-law, with my own children *and* hers. When the worst has happened, we will all take stock and think about what is best for his future here."

Nigel took another generous swig of his martini. *Boarding school. That's what he means.* He thought about Catherine's angry question the night before, after Lukas had gone to bed and they sat in the living room, aghast at the turn of events. "God the British are SO fucked up. Sorry, Nigel, but it's true. They sound like the dysfunctional family that kept Harry Potter in a cupboard under the stairs." But he could understand Robert's predicament.

There was a pleasant breeze up on this thirtieth floor, which was a mercy because the sticky humid days showed no signs of abating. Sometimes, he was uneasy about being this high—too high for a fire truck ladder. Leaning on the railing, he scanned the darkening world below: lots of twinkling lights of sailboats on the lake, lots of people still strolling the boardwalk or sitting on blankets on the sandy beach. And always the low steady hum of traffic in the background, and the odd imperious blast of a horn to remind everyone this was a big, impatient city.

Was he being uncharitable to Robert? Maybe the wretched man was emotionally paralyzed and totally unable to cope. Philippe had been far more sanguine about the whole thing. Four months was not a problem, he claimed. Look how the *pauvre petit* had opened up their lives. They were retired, they had no pressing concerns or commitments, they could get a tutor in to help Lukas prepare.

As they told Lukas the news, Nigel watched the conflicting emotions scatter across the boy's face: the anxiety that his future was once more in limbo, the relief that he would not have to live with Aunt Evelyn whom he had met and clearly disliked, and then the incredulity that he would be able to stay here, for "a whole four more months—really, honestly?"

Philippe hugged him, chattering away in English and French, telling him all the new things they could do, wagging his finger about the need to get some school work done too.

Later, Lukas went quiet, refusing to eat lunch and lying curled up on the bed all afternoon with his iPad. When they checked on him, he had obviously been crying. "I know they don't want me," he said. "Fiona told me one day I have to go to boarding school because I get on people's nerves."

Eventually, they managed to persuade him nothing was decided, and wherever he went in the future, it would be a place to make new friends, find new interests. He kept asking if it was *really* true that he could stay until Christmas, as though unwilling to believe this. Philippe had the brilliant idea of getting on the airline site and changing the return flight to January 4th next year. He made Lukas do it and print the confirmation. That did the trick. By the end of the day, he had perked up again.

And where was Philippe now, Nigel wondered, peering into the living room. He had popped into Lukas's room to make sure he was not lying awake fretting. But that was quite a while ago. They had probably ended up playing some dreadful video game together, closing the door to make sure Nigel didn't hear.

He finished his drink, picked up his magazine, and was about to step inside when Philippe came across the room, finger to his lips, waving his arm for him to go back and sit down again.

"What's the matter? It's late. We should be turning in."

Philippe sank onto a balcony chair, stretched out full length, and stared up at the stars.

"Philippe? What?"

"I've done something terrible. I can't believe what I did."

Nigel stared at him. "What, for God's sake?"

"The notebook. The one his father made. It was in his backpack. At the side of his bed. He was asleep. *Mon Dieu, pardonnez-moi.* I took it out and read some of it."

"Is that all? I thought you'd cooked up some dastardly plot together."

Philippe covered his face with his hands. "There is so much in there, Nigel. His mother…the miscarriage, all those things that went wrong. Even something about the night he was *conceived.* Can you imagine? *Incroyable!*"

"Slow down a bit. How on earth can you tell this from that book? It's all maps and astronomical diagrams. And in several languages, from what I can remember."

"I put the Italian and German in Google translate," said Philippe, his face still covered with his hands.

Nigel pulled one hand away and made Philippe look at him. "Are you telling me you sat there typing foreign languages? At the boy's bedside?"

"I took photos. I went to the study." He put his head back in his hands. "*Je ne suis qu'un scélérat.*"

"Stop being such a drama queen. Let me see."

Philippe gave Nigel his phone. "I didn't do every page. I got scared."

Nigel swiped through the photographed pages and paused on the screenshots of the translations. He read out loud.

— sucked into a field of bad energy that took her strength.

"Dear God. Why on earth write all this for a child?"

"It wasn't *for* Lukas. It's a sort of diary, notes he made to himself."

"But the box had the boy's birthdate on the front, his Zodiac sign."

"Obviously the boy was on his mind when he did all those charts and wrote these notes, but he would not have shared it with him until he was much older, when he could understand it all. Rachel said that in her letter to you. She would never have imagined we'd give it to him *now*." He took the phone back from Nigel and thumbed through it. "Listen to this: *that he will go where fate leads him and not fall prey to the expectations of others*."

Nigel crossed his arms and leaned back. "The boy is far too young to understand all this. It's cryptic, so complicated. And the German? The Arabic?"

"He's got a gift for languages. And Dominic translated some of the Arabic for him—although he would surely have skipped anything upsetting. We should ask him. Look at this." He flicked to another photo. "This bunch of stars. And what it says underneath."

Nigel read: "*I feel the anger of Sekhmet out in the desert. Saturn moving to the eighth. So strong, put in motion long ago.* Philippe, this is serious nonsense. What does 'moving to the eighth' mean? Google translate must be struggling here."

"Eighth house maybe. You know. In astrology."

"No, I don't know. It's a lot of poppycock."

"Remember this was only weeks before the man died."

"Rachel always said he was a mystic. But for heaven's sake. Too much."

"Some people have this skill. ESP or something. There's a lot more. There are more bits about Steven. I saw his name a few times."

"Karl blamed Steven for Rachel's illness, as you know. 'Sucked the air out of her,' or something like that, Steven told me. Truly beyond the pale. We'll have to let it be. Lukas loves it because it's something from a father he never knew. I'm sure he can't read, much less understand, the bulk of it." He stood and urged Philippe out of the chair. "Anything else from your sleuthing that we should worry about?"

"There were other names. *Ahmed.* Wasn't he the one accused of setting the fire? And your Cairo man, *Da'ud.* I think I saw his name. And *Faroul* or *Fadoul.* I can't remember."

"Well. It's all in the past. What possible significance can these people have now?"

Chapter 26

"Dominic, I had to tell them about Lukas. They were already upset about being kept in the dark over those damned charts." Hadir sounded frustrated and tired.

Dominic got up and closed his office door at the hotel in Toronto. "I still wish you hadn't."

"How could I tell them you want Amina to go to Canada, but keep the truth about the boy a secret—the very boy whose chart they had taken to some Egyptologist on the other side of the country? Come on. Imagine Amina finding out about it by accident?"

Dominic had to admit his brother was right. But now he would need to beg Amina to keep it from Lukas and the others.

"I wouldn't have been surprised if the boy's presence in Toronto had put her off from going," Hadir went on. "In fact, I'll be honest, that's what I hoped. How long will he be there?"

Dominic told him what he had heard from Catherine this morning, that Lukas would be in Canada through Christmas and that his future in England was a big question mark. "So how is Sophie now?" he asked. "How is she feeling about all this?"

"I'll spare you the sound and fury and the threats of divorce over the 'continual lying by omission.' She is of course incredulous about the sheer coincidence but—big surprise—she is pleased Amina is joining you. She reminds me that our two teenage boys have been in the United States for months, getting up to who knows what mischief, and yet I am worrying about a mature, highly capable young woman going to Canada."

Dominic had not expected Sophie's support.

"But..." Hadir added, "Amina has not been herself since her return from Ouarzazate. The two of you should get the place up and running as fast as possible, and then get the hell home. Maybe all this weirdness will go away then."

"Dominic," Sophie had taken the phone from her husband. "I believe Amina is 'not quite herself' as Hadir so delicately puts it, because the young Egyptologist was obviously smitten. He even made a visit to Fez on some pretext and called to ask if he may take Amina to lunch."

"You said no, of course." Dominic bristled with annoyance at the nerve of this man.

"You are just like your brother. She has turned twenty and can make her own decisions. One day, she may want to marry. What are the two of you going to do then? Lock her up in a tower? Masoud is a good man, intelligent, and rather attractive. They had lunch here at the hotel. Hadir paced around the lobby until I sent him off on an errand."

Masoud. Who the hell do you think you are, Masoud? Sophie calling the man by his first name gave the situation a kind of gravitas that Dominic found disconcerting. He couldn't articulate why…a protective instinct, that's all.

When he eventually spoke to Amina, she was clearly delighted with coming to Canada and asked him several questions about the hotel, the city, and what kinds of things he would like her to prepare. He apologised for having kept her in the dark over the charts and asked her if she was happy with their interpretation by the Egyptologist. But she was reticent, unwilling to go into any details.

***

The listings on the Arrivals board at the airport rotated and shifted once more. *Yes*, Amina's plane had landed. Dominic secured a good vantage point and watched the big doors whooshing open and closed, disgorging passengers. He found himself on edge, wondering if this was a good idea after all. Wave after wave of arrivals flooded through and finally, there she was, faltering on the walkway, clutching her luggage, not knowing which way to go.

"Amina, over here." He pushed his way through the crowd to her side and gave her a big hug, catching the scent of the jasmine perfume she loved. It reminded him of home. He squeezed her more tightly. "How was it? Did you get any sleep? How are you feeling?" He grabbed her suitcase and shoulder bag and ushered her through the crowds. "A car is waiting to take us back."

On the way into the city, Amina kept shaking her head in wonder. "The buildings…so tall, so close together. And all the cars. It's like in the movies."

She looks sad, Dominic thought, those brown eyes are downcast. He hoped it was just the fatigue of a long journey. She kept fidgeting with the last button on her jacket. With a jolt of surprise, he noted the nail polish on her manicured fingernails.

"You mustn't worry about anything, Amina. The Darija is a wonderful hotel. You'll be proud. It lacks only your magical touch. We've put aside a special room for you. And your office is set up. You'll be running the place in no time."

"How will I find my way around this city? I can't believe how big it is."

"Joel will help you with anything you need. All the staff are anxious to meet you. You'll love it, I'm sure." He bit his lip. There was a great deal of administrative work to be done, and he hoped it wouldn't be too much for her. Catherine was such a distraction; he had not been very conscientious.

Amina fell silent for a while. Finally, she turned from the window and looked directly at him. "Are we going to talk about Lukas?"

He had not expected to be confronted so soon. "Can you believe it? I still can't. What a small world. He's a sweet boy, sometimes a bit too serious. I'm sure you'll meet him at some point. But, Amina, only you and I know of the connection. There is no need for anyone else to know. I think Sophie told you what I found out. Lukas has had a tough life; both his parents are dead and—"

"So are mine."

The defiance in her voice caught him by surprise. "Yes, of course. I'm sorry. But…there are serious concerns about his future life in England. It would be cruel for us to bring up something that happened several years ago and that neither of you had any role in." He realized he was speaking too fast, sounding desperate.

"He might think my father killed his father. I wish I could tell him it isn't true."

Her hands were balled into fists. He uncurled her fingers and was shocked to feel her trembling. "Lukas may not know anything about who was accused. Your father's name may have no meaning to him. What would be the point?"

"But he *might* know. And if not, he will learn one day. He should know the truth."

There was suspicion in her eyes, a challenge. He was reminded again of Catherine's indignation during that lunch in Niagara Falls. *"Why can't people tell the truth?"*

"I know what that Tarot card meant. The Tower," Amina said.

Shit. "Every card has subtle meanings. And you need to understand the context, the bigger picture. I was wrong to treat them so clumsily."

She shook her head. "It means something from the past is coming back, something that might cause havoc."

"You can't trust what you read on the internet. It depends on the source. There are many different interpretations."

"I didn't learn it on the internet."

"Where then?"

"Masoud told me. The man Da'ud reco—"

"I know who he is. I thought he was an Egyptologist, not a Tarot card reader."

"He has studied all kinds of different things."

"Really? What a clever guy he must be." Dominic fought to keep the anger out of his voice. "How about you get a good night's sleep, and we'll talk about this over breakfast tomorrow? Just the two of us. Deal?"

Amina gave him a wistful smile, and his anger melted. There she was again, the lovely, gentle Amina who had been an integral part of his life these last five years, always anxious to please him, always taking his side…not the woman with the nail polish who had doubted his word, who had been hustled by that fucking Egyptian in Ouarzazate. Dominic had always had good feelings about Egyptians but there were now two he could cheerfully throttle.

Chapter 27

Amina had been so tired that she barely took in the details of her room. Waking the next morning, not quite believing the 5.10 a.m. on the digital clock, she thought this must surely be the largest bed anyone ever slept in. *Canada. I'm really here.* She got up with a burst of energy and tried to draw back the drapes. They wouldn't budge, and it took her a while to realize there was a switch on the wall to make them part. Her room looked over a wide road with huge glass windowed shops in both directions, a few cars speeding by but making no sound. What would her father say, she wondered?

Flicking through clothes, hung up hurriedly the previous night, her fingers stopped at the blue silk pants paired with a white blouse that was tied in a knot at the side—a gift from Sophie for the opening night. She held these against her body and twirled around, appraising herself in the long wardrobe mirror and running her hands down the soft folds. She put it back. Today, the slim grey skirt and a scoop neck pink top, cropped at the waist, would be just right.

She waited for Dominic at a table against the wall in the café adjacent to the main restaurant. There were many reminders of home: the central courtyard, benches with inlaid tiles, two small velvet-draped sitting rooms with low couches, silver teapots and glasses for mint tea on the coffee tables, even a shisha pipe on a hexagonal wooden table with low leather chairs on either side. But otherwise, she thought, this hotel was for a different world, everything working with the swipe of a card, the wave of a hand, the gentle push of a button.

A young waiter introduced himself and poured her more coffee. Dominic was late. Amina wondered, with a splinter of resentment, if he was still in bed. Sophie had told her about Catherine. "One in every port," she said, with her usual roll of the eyes and scornful shrug.

Her phone pinged: a message from Masoud, telling her he missed her already. At their first lunch in the Riad Capella, he had told her she was constantly on his mind. If she would agree to see him again, he would drive to Fez as often as he possibly could. At one point, he inclined his head toward the reception area, "I see your gatekeeper is out there. He does not approve." He meant Hadir. "He has no right to approve anyone I choose to be friends with," Amina said, imitating the irritation Sophie had voiced to her husband, irritation that she shared. It was Hadir's air of assumption that rankled. The family had been wonderful, but they did not own her. When they parted, Masoud pulled her into an alcove, out of sight of anyone, and kissed her lightly on the cheek. "You are beautiful, Amina. I want to be so much more than your friend." That same evening, lying naked in bed, watched by the waxing gibbous moon at the window, she ran her hands over her body and enjoyed the surge of heat that coursed through her at the memory of him.

Finally, here was Dominic, hurrying across the restaurant towards her.

"Sorry. Got held up." He sat down, breathless. "Well, you certainly look like you slept well. You look wonderful."

Amina brushed an imaginary speck from her skirt, embarrassed by the intensity of his gaze, and tried to quell the shudder of excitement at the sight of him so close once again. He walked with easy grace, always assuming centre stage. Already, the waiter and the receptionist looked expectantly in his direction, ready to do his bidding.

"I did sleep well. It's a lovely room. Thank you."

He told her about his visit to New York to see Alex and Rafik, how they were speaking English with an American accent and getting a little cocky. She filled him in on life back in Fez, the visits from travel operators, the weekly tantrums of chef Henri, and the day-to-day life that Dominic missed. As they talked, Amina realized how intimately she knew the Riad Capella. None of Dominic's questions posed a problem for her. He listened carefully, nodding at the marketing decisions made in his absence, and she could sense his growing respect. At one point, he moved as though to squeeze her hand, but stopped, questioning the appropriateness.

"Right," he said, in a business-like tone. "Time for you to meet Joel and start weaving your magic."

He took her along the corridor to the administrative offices. *"La voila."* Joel leapt from behind his desk and scooped Amina into a big hug. "At last, the beautiful face behind the beautiful voice."

"Whoa," said Dominic. "Politically incorrect, Joel. Bordering on harassment. Let the poor woman go, or she'll be on the next flight home."

"Amina will forgive me," said Joe. "She is a fellow Moroccan."

"Half Moroccan." Amina laughed.

"Good enough for me. We're all half of something these days. Dominic, what are you still doing here? Get lost. Amina and I have a hotel to run."

Joel would put anyone at ease, Amina thought. Tall, straight-shouldered, with greying hair, and a wide smile, he laughed easily and was constantly taking his red and turquoise-framed glasses on and off, waving them around as he explained things to her.

"May I?" he asked, hooking her arm onto his.

He walked her around the entire hotel, introducing her to the receptionist, the chef, the kitchen staff, the bell boys. In one of the suites, they stumbled upon the interior designer who launched into a tirade about the upcoming grand opening and how "absolutely nothing" would be ready. *"Très difficile,"* Joel whispered as they walked on. "Ignore him." He skipped between Arabic, French and English, sometimes starting a sentence in one language and finishing it in another. He called her the "Chief Operating Officer," and warned the staff that they had better get organized or face her wrath.

***

Over the next couple of weeks, Amina was engulfed in the happy chaos of life at the Riad Darija. She revamped Dominic's haphazard filing system, finalized the plans for the remaining furniture and accessories, and even made a cautious friend of the interior designer. Dominic came to her office every afternoon to go over the increasingly long list of things to be done as they neared the official opening. She looked forward to these meetings, to hearing once more the sound of his voice, watching his long-fingered, restless hands as they shuffled papers, flicked through binders and brochures or tugged at his hair when he was anxious. Sometimes, she felt his eyes lingering on her, but when she looked up, he would give her that simple "so happy you are here" kind of smile; nothing more.

Chapter 28

Amina put the thought of both Catherine and Lukas out of her mind and grew increasingly self-assured with the work. Sophie called her daily, and she took pleasure in the unusual role of *giving* rather than needing reassurance. The staff would often come looking for her help, just like in Fez.

Dominic told her he was proud of her, and relieved that things were working out as he had hoped. In the little spare time they had, he took her to a few different parts of the city: the CN Tower where he cajoled her to walk on the glass floor, and she was petrified but thrilled when he held on to her; the beach where they strolled along the boardwalk and watched the kite surfers, the museum with its enormous dinosaurs. It still felt like a long, strange dream.

She had not yet met Catherine, and wondered if Dominic was purposefully keeping them apart. And she was still anxious to meet the young boy, Lukas.

One day, after she was settled in, they had lunch together and went through the catering options for the opening night party.

"I want it to be a memorable event," Dominic said, leafing through possible menus. "Something people will talk about. Don't tell Hadir how much we're spending."

"We should have different Moroccan food," Amina said. "Something to make us stand apart. I like these best." She set aside two of the menus the chef had suggested.

"As long as it's easy to eat. No knives and forks, nothing too sticky." He relaxed back in the chair and looked around. "I can't believe it's coming together. We'll make it a big, happy party. Excuse me—" he took the phone from his pocket. "Yes, yes. She's here. We're in the restaurant.

Come and join us." He put the phone back. "That was Catherine. She's anxious to meet you."

So here she is. Amina had the impression from Joel and some of the others that Catherine was here every night, but Amina went to bed early and had seen no sign of her.

"And this Saturday," Dominic said. "You will meet my other new friends. I've invited them here for lunch. Unfortunately, Catherine's father can't come. He has flown back to Vancouver for a few days. But he'll be here for the opening."

She folded her table napkin and placed it on the table. "Will Lukas be at this lunch?"

Dominic twisted his fork back and forth. "You will like him, Amina. He's only a kid. . .sweet and charming. . .playful sometimes. And he must be lonely. I think we should leave your fathers out of our lives for a while. Let's not focus on the past."

Over Dominic's shoulder, Amina saw a tall, slim woman approaching. This must be Catherine, this self-confident Canadian woman with her high heels and tight jeans, her short, shiny auburn hair.

Dominic stood up to kiss her. He pulled over a chair from another table.

"I can't stop long. Busy afternoon. Amina. . ." Catherine leaned over and gave Amina a big airy hug ". . .I'm so happy to meet you. Dominic has told me so much about you."

She picked up a strawberry from Dominic's plate and popped it into her mouth. Her nails were long and beautifully manicured. No varnish. She made a move for another strawberry, but Dominic caught her hand and pretended to slap it.

"Hey, order your own."

They chatted for a while, small talk, about Amina's journey, her life in Fez, what she thought of the hotel and the staff here.

"Olivia, one of the receptionists—bit of a ditz if you ask me," Catherine said. "I've told Dominic to watch out for her. Shows up late.

Loses things. And I guess you've met the sous-chef, Jason. Ooh la la, he is something else, eh?" She made a fanning motion with her hand in front of her face. "Imagine, not just a good-looking man, but one who can cook!"

Amina wondered how she could talk about the staff in such a familiar tone. The women Dominic brought to Fez were singularly uninterested in anything but him, or themselves. *Well, Catherine, you don't have to worry about Olivia or any of the others. I'll do the worrying.* Appearing interested and engaged was taking effort because she was battling the swell of anger and the persistent concern that she had been brought here not only to be useful, but because her presence would give Dominic more free time with Catherine.

"Well," Catherine said, looking from one to the other. "I see I've interrupted an important meeting. And I'm already late for an appointment. I'm off. Have a great day, Amina."

Dominic went with her to the lobby, and Amina caught their intimate goodbye kiss.

Back at the table, he was clearly distracted and started checking his phone. "Sorry," he kept saying, whenever texting or answering a call, still trying to sustain their conversation.

"No problem, go ahead." She pretended to read something on her own phone.

Masoud texted her every day, anxious to learn how things were going, and they had talked briefly on the phone the previous day. He had told her this was a good opportunity to develop her independence, not let her gentle nature be taken advantage of, and reminded her of the Ancient Egyptian references on her star chart. *Mistress of dread. Passionate when wronged.* He was joking with her, of course. That was *not* her personality. But at a deeper level, a kernel of resolve took root, a keener sense of her own worth and capabilities.

She looked pointedly at her watch. "I have a lot to do this afternoon. I think I should go."

"Now? Well, yes. Yes, of course."

Rising from the table, she was pleased to note the consternation on Dominic's face, the momentary clumsiness as he spilled some coffee while pouring.

***

Amina stood on the threshold of the restaurant. There he was, the young boy who had plagued her dreams since that day in Ouarzazate when Sophie told her the whole story about him. He was sitting quietly between two older gentlemen, the ones he was staying with, she assumed. Catherine and Dominic sat opposite, hands clasped under the table. They were all laughing about something. Lukas tapped on his iPad. He had fine features: high cheekbones, wide, thin lips, and a shock of blond hair that fell over his ears and into his eyes. He looked up, as though suddenly aware that someone was watching him, and his face broke into a big smile. "Is that Amina?" He pointed towards her. One of the men pulled his arm down and said it was rude to point. "Sorry, sorry," he said. "But is it?"

Dominic brought her over to the table. Chairs scraped and everyone stood for the introduction. Nigel shook her hand, but the other man, Philippe, scooped her into a big hug and greeted her in French.

The boy was excited, anxious to know her. "Amina Gamel." He pronounced it slowly, as though wanting to make sure he got it right. And then "How do you spell that?" He had a notebook and asked her to write it in English and in Arabic, all the while staring at her with clear grey eyes. Dominic had told her about this notebook. She saw that it was filled with maps and diagrams. Lukas turned to a blank page near the back, and that's where she wrote the two versions of her name.

Throughout the lunch, Catherine did most of the talking, telling Nigel and Philippe all about the hotel, telling Amina how smart Lukas was, that he spoke fluent Italian, that he wanted to learn Arabic and that Dominic was helping him translate some of the notes in the book.

Nigel and Philippe were both kind, asking her what she thought of Toronto, praising her English, telling her they had heard such wonderful things about her, and asking her to visit them one day at their antiques store. All the time, the boy kept looking over at her, smiling, and turning away quickly when their eyes met.

Dominic was right, he was very sweet. She tried hard to like him.

Chapter 29

Under the high, domed ceiling of the courtyard in the Darija hotel, Steven turned full circle and took in the décor. Narrow woven *boujad* rugs hung on every wall, each with the traditional square and diamond shape patterns in red, yellow, orange, earthy greens and browns, set off perfectly by the warm yellow stucco walls. Here and there were flashes of vivid turquoise and purple: a leather pouffe, an occasional table with inset tiles, the tasselled runners on the long, intricately carved wooden bar against the far wall. Several mirrors tapered in the classic Moorish shape with heavy silver and gold frames reflected into each other so that, from certain angles, the people chatting and drinking, laughing and clasping hands, multiplied into infinity, and the glint and shimmer of the crystals on the amber chandeliers transformed everything into a dizzy, constantly changing kaleidoscope of light and colour.

Scanning the crowd, looking for a familiar face, he felt suddenly uncomfortable in the frenzied conviviality and wished he had stuck to his guns, stayed home, and watched Netflix.

But Catherine had been strangely insistent. "You've got to come, Dad. It's a big deal. A new hotel in the city, something totally different from all those concrete palaces."

"It's a big deal for *you* for obvious reasons. You don't need me there."

"Well, we do actually. At least, drop by for a while. You can make an excuse to leave early. You're good at that. And, wear something decent."

"Don't tell me it's suit and tie?"

"There's a wide range between scruffy jeans and suit and tie."

He pulled at the neck of the black sweater and hitched up the waist of one of his few pairs of "decent" dress pants. Where the hell was Catherine, after all the fuss she had made? He watched a young woman with flowing blue silk pants and a white blouse tied in a knot at her waist.

Long dark hair, swept back from her face, shone under the cast iron torch lamp on the wall above. She was explaining something in a brochure to two men, one of whom was trying not to look down the deep V of her blouse. Steven rarely did portrait painting, but hers would be one worth trying, he thought, if he could ever do justice to the smooth planes and high cheekbones, the full lips, the subtle mystery of that lovely face.

"Stunning, isn't she?" said a voice behind him.

He spun around to find his agent, Toby, helping himself from a bowl of pink and blue sugared almonds.

"Toby! What on earth are you doing here?"

"Why shouldn't I be here? Dominic invited me when we met at your show. I see you are eyeing that lovely Moroccan jewel. Her name is Amina. Over from Fez. I'll introduce you, if you like."

Steven pulled him back in midstride. "No, Toby. She is busy."

"Have you seen the suites?" Toby went on. "They've got a couple for people to inspect. When you've seen all this, why would you stay anywhere else? Magical."

Steven scanned the room again. "Who *are* all these people? How would a guy from Morocco know who to invite, who the 'right' kind of people are to come to the opening of a hotel in Toronto?"

"People with money always know how to do these things, never mind what nationality they are. And there's certainly money here." Toby swept his arm in a wide arc. "Most of these good folk are in the travel business, I'd guess. Anyway, who cares? Oh, yes please," he said, taking a glass of wine from a passing waiter. He craned his neck over the crowd. "I think I spy an art collector. See you later."

Steven was left alone again. Why did Catherine think it was so important for him to be here? His presence would certainly not be missed. He was concerned about her clear obsession with Dominic. This 'fling' as she once called it, had been going on for the whole summer and showed no signs of letting up. What the hell was she going to do when the guy went back to Morocco?

He started to nudge his way through the crowd and eventually spotted his daughter and friends in the narrow arcade that flanked the courtyard on three sides. They were seated on one of the couches, its many colourful cushions tossed in a heap at their feet. Lukas was there, thumbing through what looked like a large photo book.

"There you are, Dad," said Catherine. "We thought you'd chickened out. Not even drinking? I'll get you something. Wine?"

"Sure. Anything."

"Steven, come and look at these photos," said Nigel. "Dominic put the book together in Morocco. Fez, Marrakesh, Casablanca, and lots of stunning shots in the desert. Lukas is fascinated."

Lukas was staring at a photograph of the desert under the night sky that spread over two pages. "It's the Sahara," he said. "The biggest desert in the world."

"You must come to Morocco and see it for yourself," Dominic said.

He stood to the side, in full sartorial splendour: a dark suit, a yellow tie, even cufflinks. Steven pulled at the neck of his sweater again.

"I'm serious, Lukas," Dominic said, moving to the centre of the group. "You must *all* visit. Soon. My brother and his wife are anxious to meet you."

"Do you mean it?" The boy's face showed a mixture of delight and disbelief, then settled quickly into resignation. "Uncle Robert wouldn't allow it."

"It would only be a short visit. Something tells me it is definitely going to happen."

Catherine brought Steven his glass of wine. He thought he saw her exchange a look with Dominic, a slight nod. She took Steven's arm and moved him away from the others. "Come with me a minute, Dad. Something I have to tell you."

"What is it? Not your mom?"

"No. Well, yes. I'll explain. Need a quiet place. We'll go in the office."

She led him away from the courtyard and down through the business area of the hotel. Coming towards them was the young woman he had seen earlier, Amina. She was about to slide by them, when Catherine stopped her.

"Amina. I don't think you've met my father, Steven Farrow. Dad, Amina is from the Riad Capella in Fez. No way Dominic could have coped these last few weeks without her."

Steven inclined his head and raised his wine glass. "Delighted to meet you."

"Dominic has told me you are a painter, and your work is beautiful," Amina said.

"That's very kind of him."

She moved on quickly. Steven thought she looked troubled, but maybe it was the cast of those dark eyes. "God, she's quite something, eh?" he said when they were out of earshot.

"Dad! She's barely twenty."

"So? I can still admire beautiful women, I hope, even when they're a little younger than my own beautiful daughter." He looked for the eye-rolling shake of her head but caught a slight frown instead. Maybe he was being politically incorrect or insensitive. *You've got to be so damned careful these days.*

Catherine opened the door to one of the offices and motioned for him to sit on the leather swivel chair at the desk. She took a deep breath. "So, Dad. I'm moving to Morocco."

Steven sputtered out the sip of wine he had just taken. He put the glass on the desk, leaned back in the chair and blew out a long breath. *Holy shit.* He had to take a moment or two to collect his thoughts. "*Moving?* Seriously? Are you sure, Catherine?"

"Sure as I'll ever be."

"But. . .giving up a secure job? Not something you should do lightly."

"Look who's talking. Painting is a secure job?"

"Exactly. I know what it's like to be poor. I'm lucky I made some money, but I'll never forget having to worry about the rent."

"If it makes you feel any better, I'm not giving up the idea of teaching. I'm delaying it for a year. We might move back and forth. We don't know yet."

"But what are you going to do in Fez? Dominic will be busy with his work there. It's a pretty hectic business, from what I gather."

"I don't care what I do. Teach English, be a receptionist, run errands. I just want to be there, see life, have some fun, take a risk or too. I speak French, so I'll get along fine."

"Where do you get this 'seize the day' attitude? Not from me, and certainly not from your mother."

"Watching the two of you live your pale and peaceful lives, maybe that's what's driving me."

Pale and peaceful lives. He squirmed at the uncomfortable truth of the words, opened his mouth to protest, and then thought better of it.

"Sorry, but you asked for it," said Catherine. "And now you can do something exciting too. We're leaving in a week. Everything will be done here by then. This hotel will be in good shape and in good hands. And you have to come too. To Morocco."

"*I* have to come? No, Catherine. Put that out of your head."

"Thing is though, Dad, you must."

There was something in her tone that made Steven pause. "Meaning…?"

"We're getting married. In Fez."

Steven stared at his daughter. She was smiling and wincing at the same time and put both hands to her mouth, biting down on her fingertips.

"You're getting married! Oh my God, Catherine." He leapt up and embraced her, trying hard to put joy and enthusiasm into his voice, to quell his deep misgivings. "So that's what Dominic was leading up to back there?"

"It's going to be amazing, Dad. You've all got to come. You were the one who brought us together, and our friends are now Dominic's friends. He gets on so well with Nigel and Philippe and he's grown attached to Lukas. We're going to ask Lukas to be the ring boy."

"Whoa, slow down. Let me process this." Steven sat down again and swivelled back and forth in the chair. He thought about that old, hackneyed word "glowing." But there probably wasn't a better one to describe how lovely his daughter looked at this moment. "You're going to Morocco. And you're getting *married*." He looked down at his hands, steeling himself to ask the next question. "Catherine…you're still so young. Couldn't you, like, live with him for a while…to be sure?"

"I have lived with him, Dad. And, I am sure."

"You're really happy?"

She nodded with that wide-eyed look she'd had as a small child, the one that would ensure she got her way. *Morocco*. Steven let out an inward sigh. *What the hell.*

"You think the boys are going to be up to a trip to Fez? With Lukas in tow? And his uncle would have to give formal permission. It could be a big deal."

"Fuck Uncle Robert. He's more or less abandoned Lukas."

"I understand from Nigel that his wife is dying, Catherine. Don't be too hard on him."

"I'm sorry but…how can it be an issue? Lukas would be thrilled to bits to get over there. You saw his face. And it wouldn't be for long."

Steven put his hands to his head. "Shit. I haven't even asked you. What does your mother think about all this? Will she and Rich go over too?"

"You're kidding, right? Might as well ask her to leave the planet. She's gone apeshit. Blathering on about Arabian Nights and Ali Baba. Probably thinks I'll be traded for camels. I wanted Dominic to meet them, but Rich came on the phone and said Mom was 'too upset to talk right now.'"

Steven sighed and shook his head. He often wondered how Catherine's stepfather coped with the histrionics of her mother. He had only met the guy a couple of times. A placid, low key sort. Maybe he ignored all the drama.

"So, you see, Dad, I've got to have *one* of you there and you're it. Big role to play. Father of the bride."

Chapter 30

From the balcony of the mezzanine that overhung the courtyard, Amina watched Lukas. The large book with the photos of Morocco was open on the table in front of him, the one that she had rushed to get printed and brought over with her. Nigel and Philippe were leaning over his shoulder. Beside him, Dominic turned the pages, explaining different scenes.

Catherine and her father were walking back along the pillared walkway to rejoin them. And then it all changed: shaking hands, hugging, kissing, slapping each other on the back; Lukas looked in shock from one to the other. Dominic pulled him to his feet and whispered something in his ear. The boy's mouth fell open. He looked close to tears. "Really?" Amina heard him say. More hugging, more laughter.

So, they've heard the news.

Guests began to wander over to them as word got around. Liam, one of the kitchen staff, wheeled a trolley into the courtyard with champagne; glasses were filled, clinked, and refilled.

The painter was the only one who did not look happy. He stood apart from the others with a pinched, faraway look on his face.

Dominic had told her just yesterday, spilling it out in a rush: the engagement, the wedding they planned, their hope that his new friends would come to Morocco to be part of it—and that they wanted Lukas to be there too. There was a pent-up excitement about him, like a schoolboy who had acted on a dare and was desperate for approval. Amina had imagined a day like this, dreaded it every time another woman turned up in Fez. In the past, the thought had made her reel with the pain of envy and loss. But now, faced with the real thing, with Dominic standing opposite, seeking approbation, a coldness settled inside her, an unexpected feeling of detachment. Her heart did not beat faster, her hands did not shake, her eyes did not tear up. She heard herself congratulate him and felt his arms around her, but it was all distant, detached. It was liberating, this new, icy sense of composure. As he chattered on, describing the shock and pleasure of Hadir and Sophie, the plans already in place, the role he hoped she would play, the people who would be invited, his voice grew fainter and fainter until she could barely hear it. None of it was real.

"There you are, Amina." Joel waved at her from the noisy crowd below, his face beaming. Others turned their heads and looked up. "Where did you get to? Come and join us."

She made her way down and was swallowed up in the heave and swell of congratulations, raised glasses, hugs, and handshakes.

Catherine approached and seized her hand. "Amina, this is all so amazing. And there's so much I need to learn. Dominic says you know *everything*, how the hotel works, how the family works. I hope you'll help me out, show me around a bit."

So, *she* wants me to be useful, too, Amina thought. "There is nothing to worry about. The hotel runs like clockwork. I think that is the saying, yes? I hope you will like Fez. It is very different from your life here."

A shadow of concern skittered across Catherine's face as she moved away.

At last, the guests began to leave. Amina stood with Dominic and the rest of the staff, bidding them farewell, handing out gift bags she had worked hard to get ready the previous night, helping retrieve coats, telling them to call if they had any questions, anything at all. After the last few guests wandered out, some clearly light-headed, the two of them returned to the courtyard. Nigel, Philippe, Lukas, Steven, and Catherine joined them, everyone sinking into the low leather couches. The Fan Club, that's what she would call them. That's how they acted. Except for the painter. He still had that strained look, as though wrestling with warring thoughts. She wondered how he had taken the news. Surely, he would be pleased. Dominic was considered a good catch back home. He was wealthy, young, handsome, well-travelled. But a Canadian father may have a different point of view.

They had started to discuss the preparations already. Nigel would call that Uncle Robert person tomorrow but insisted there would be no problem taking Lukas. Philippe fretted about a family commitment that would be hard to get out of.

There were a few legal matters to take care of, but it would be a civil marriage, with "no fuss," Catherine insisted. Apparently, Sophie was pushing for the wedding to be on the roof of the hotel. It could accommodate the twenty or thirty people invited and would be decorated magnificently. How was Sophie feeling, Amina wondered? They had not had a chance to speak since the news was announced. Was she excited? Relieved? Nervous?

Amina looked over at Lukas, alone now, sitting on the couch and looking through the photobook. Something about the way he stared at the photos, the way his small hands fumbled with the pages, trying to separate them, filled her with a rush of warmth and sorrow. She went and sat beside him.

"You will be going to Morocco," she said. "Are you excited?"

"Do you think it's true, for real?"

"Well, everyone wants it to be true."

"Have you been here?" He pointed to a photo of sweeping sand dunes.

"That's Merzouga. Dominic has friends who live there. I have been not far from there…a place called Ouarzazate." She found it for him and told him that many films were made there.

He lingered over each of the pages and kept turning his clear grey eyes toward her, as though doubting that such magical places could really exist.

Amina became aware that the discussion had moved away from the wedding, and got up to rejoin the group. Dominic wanted feedback on the evening, what they might have heard from the different guests.

"A big success," Joel said. "For which you must credit the hard work and ingenuity of the lovely Amina…and the lovely me, too." Joel planted a kiss on her cheek and there was a round of applause and more clinking of glasses.

"I heard nothing but praise," said Philippe. "People are calling it 'boutique,' a nice change from the antiseptic atmosphere of the competition."

"We are not going to attract the mega business types," Joel said. "They need bigger presentation rooms, bigger everything. But we're not looking for them anyway."

"Excuse me," said Lukas. Everyone turned to him. "Can I look around a bit?"

"Of course, you can," said Dominic. "I'll go and find Liam. He'll give you the grand—"

Amina raised her hand to stop him. "Liam is tied up in the kitchen. I will be happy to take him. Come on, Lukas. What would you like to see first?"

"Amina…" Dominic hesitated, halfway up from the couch. "Are you sure?"

She couldn't miss the thinly veiled warning. "I'm sure."

She took Lukas to see "behind the scenes" at the reception area and the bar, up to some of the suites, through the offices and, finally, to the kitchen which served both the adjacent restaurant and the café in the hotel. The boy had an intense curiosity about how everything worked, what each person did. She found it strange, this curiosity. Most kids were loud and rambunctious and into sports and video games. Sometimes Lukas did have a fleeting, mischievous look about him, but most of the time he was like a wise adult trapped in the body of a small boy.

In the kitchen, a few of the staff were clearing up. Liam brought over a plate of warmed-up, leftover appetizers and a bowl of the sugared almonds. Lukas was obviously hungry and munched away.

"I would like to see Italy one day," Amina said. "I think it must be beautiful."

He nodded vigorously, his mouth full. "It's sunny, and you can swim in the sea. Our house was right near the beach."

"Your Uncle Robert. . .he is your mother's brother, yes?"

"I live with his family. In England. Well. . ." A darkness passed over his face. "I'm not sure anymore."

"I'm sorry about your parents."

Lukas took a spiced meatball from the plate and looked away.

"Your father," Amina persisted. "He was an. . . *astronome*? I'm sorry, I don't know the English word."

"It's kind of the same. Astronomer."

"He did horoscopes for people. Is that right?" It was noisy in the kitchen, with all the plates being stacked and rinsed, and the dishwashers running. She doubted anyone could hear or would be interested in their conversation.

"My father was clever. He knew lots about Egypt too."

"What was your mother like? You said she also loved the stars."

He gave her that lingering stare, and her pulse quickened. Dominic would be so upset with her. She cast a look behind her towards the kitchen door.

"Mostly," he said, between bites, "she loved art and paintings. But she knew lots about planets and stars. She learned before she even met my dad."

"Where did they meet?"

"In Cairo, I think."

"I'm sorry to ask so many questions. I hope I am not rude."

"It's okay," Lukas said. He finished chewing on a small wedge of avocado toast and gave her a big smile. "I know who you are. I knew you would come. My dad said."

Chapter 31

Dominic paced outside Amina's door. He called her mobile, and the phone in her room, and got voice mail. He knocked on her door—no answer. *What happened? Why did she leave without saying goodnight? Lukas.* His throat went dry. *What were they talking about, what did she tell him?*

They had been gone for nearly an hour, and it was Liam who brought Lukas back to the courtyard. There was a strange, excited look about the boy. His face was flushed. "Awesome," he said, as he started telling Nigel and Philippe what he had seen.

Amina was tired, Liam had said, and decided to call it a night. Only twenty minutes had passed since then. She couldn't be in a dead sleep already. *Could she be ill?* But the more likely explanation, Dominic realized, stopping his pacing and leaning his head against the wall by her door: she was angry.

He was sweating now and yanked at his tie to loosen the knot. He knocked again, more firmly this time. "Please, Amina. Open the door. I want to talk for a minute. I know you can't be asleep." He put his ear against the door and heard, faintly, the sound of her voice.

The door swung back suddenly. She stood before him, one hand holding it open, the other resting on her hip. Her hair had fallen forward, loose and tangled, the knot in her white silk blouse was undone; her feet were bare, her body tense, the eyes dark and cold.

He took a step back. "I'm sorry. I was worried."

"You had better come in."

He sat on the edge of the armchair by the window. Some of Amina's clothes lay on the bed, her suitcase open beside them. She began to fold the clothes, neatly, methodically.

Dominic waited, not daring to speak. Finally, she took the folded clothes, pushed them roughly into the case and slumped on the end of the bed.

"It's crazy. It's all madness. Do you know what he said to me? That my name is on a 'star map' his father did. Amina Gamel, written in English with Arabic underneath, and my birth date. And there is another chart stapled to this. Dominic, he has exactly the same two charts as the ones Da'ud gave you. He described them…the circle with twelve sections, the symbols, the hieroglyphics. That's how he knew he'd meet me. That's why he asked me to write my name both ways in his notebook when we met at the lunch. To be sure it was me."

Dominic froze on the edge of the chair. He felt dizzy and there was a ringing noise in his ears. "But how does he know you are the Amina on the chart? He knows nothing about you."

"Believe me, Dominic, he knows. I took him to my room to show him my own charts—"

"You brought them with you?"

"I wanted to try and understand them better, go over what I learned in Ouarzazate. He went crazy when I showed him, excited, his eyes all wild. 'It's true, it's true, it's true,' he kept saying. He knew I must be the Amina on the chart because we both came to Canada, and it was here that he got his father's notebook and all the star maps. We are both *supposed* to be here, supposed to meet."

Dominic wanted to reach out, grab onto something to steady himself. He gripped the edge of the table. "But why? Why does he think you are supposed to meet?"

"He said that we'll know one day. Dominic, I feel sorry for him. I really do. He scares me. And yet he is only a child. What is going on? What am I in the middle of? It's not right, it's not fair." She put her head in her hands, clearly fighting tears.

"Amina…you are not in the middle of any—"

"I want to go home." She raised her head to look at him. Her eyes were smudged with mascara.

He felt a strong urge to pull her towards him and wrap his arms around her. "We *are* going home. In just a week. Our flights are booked. The others will follow later."

"I want to go now. You don't need me here anymore."

She went back to folding her clothes. She looked strangely out of place in this hotel room, an exotic flower uprooted and blown by the wind to an alien landscape. He had assigned her the suite with a framed, panoramic photograph of Fez on one of the walls, thinking it might make her feel at home. Perhaps it only made her homesick. He suddenly ached to be back there himself.

"There's something else isn't there, Amina? Please tell me."

"He knows my father's name. His aunt talked a lot on the phone about his parents and the fire. She never knew he was listening. So, Dominic, I told him the truth. I said no matter what he'd heard, my father was a good man, he was wrongly accused, he would never kill."

Dominic slumped in the chair, incapable of cohesive thought.

"I asked him exactly what he'd heard about my father and all he would say is 'it doesn't matter, I can't remember, I know *you* are a good person.' Amina paused and drew breath. "Finally, he turned away from me. Very quietly he said: 'I heard there are lots of different stories.'" She turned to face him again. "*Lots of different stories,* Dominic. Well, I want to know what they are."

At that moment her cell phone pinged. It was on the table beside Dominic. He picked it up and read the message to her: "*It is arranged. I will come to Fez as soon as you are home.* That's Masoud, isn't it?"

"How dare you! It's personal." She grabbed the phone from him and held it against her chest.

"What do you want with him? He is no good for you."

"And what is good for me, Dominic? To ignore everything that is happening? To smile and be happy and carry on with your new friends, and with poor Lukas who probably thinks my father was a murderer? How dare you say anything about Masoud? You have never even met him."

She was no longer struggling with tears, no longer the compliant young woman he had always known. She was fierce and angry, and would make her own decisions. She swept her hair back and stood before him, hands on hips, mouth drawn in a hard line. He felt another flush of jealousy at the thought of this Egyptian texting her in the middle of the night.

"If you want to go home earlier, Amina, we will get your flight changed. But please tell me…what you have 'arranged' with Masoud? I am worried for you."

"I am going to see Da'ud. He knew my father in Cairo and in Fez. He knows more than he lets on. I'm sure of it. And I want Masoud to go with me."

PART IV – THE CLOSING OF THE CIRCLE

Chapter 32

Nigel shielded his eyes from the lowering sun that squeezed into the narrow alleyway in the heart of the Fez medina and bathed their corner café table in an amber glow. He watched Steven wrestling with the pot of mint tea, trying to imitate the sweeping up and down pour that the waiter accomplished effortlessly.

"Please stop doing that, Steven," said Nigel. "You'll never get the hang of it, and you look positively dangerous. If only Philippe could have been here. He'd have mastered it in under two minutes. Pass me that last yummy thing if you don't want it."

"They're called *fekkas*, those yummy things. I looked it up on my iPad," said Lukas. He was leaning on the iron railing beside them, peering into one of the narrow, cobbled alleyways that ran off the street.

"I do beg your pardon." Nigel lowered his voice. "For heaven's sake, he'll have gone native by the end of the week. What are you staring at Lukas?"

"See that man behind the counter in that store?" Lukas pointed. "All kinds of cats have come. They sit and look up at him and he throws them a scrap of something. See, there's another one."

"It's a butcher shop. What a kind man. There are too many skinny, feral cats here."

"I wish I could have a cat. But Uncle Robert says Aunt Melinda is allergic."

Of course, Nigel thought, and then remembered he should check how the poor woman was faring. Robert had raised no objections to this trip, even suggesting it would be "educational" for Lukas.

"My dad had a cat. One was called Copernicus, but that was a long time ago, Mom said. Then Hermes came."

"Goodness me. Very intelligent cats, no doubt."

The three of them had ventured out on their own because Dominic and Catherine were needed at the hotel to nail down wedding preparations. They had a map of the medina, and phone numbers in case they got lost.

What a wonderful place to get lost, Nigel thought, taking in the hustle of the neighbourhood. Two men led a mule with wicker baskets full of pots and pans hanging on both its sides; a young man pulled down brightly coloured bolts of material with the help of a hook on a long wooden pole; a woman remonstrated with her three children as she tried to buy onions and beans from the overflowing barrels in front of a store.

From one of the tiny alleyways came loud chattering, high-pitched shouts and yelps. A group of young boys in school uniform emerged, dark pants and blue shirts, laughing, pushing, and tripping over each other. One of them lost his balance and knocked into a trestle table, dislodging an arrangement of kitchen utensils that cascaded to the ground with a noisy crash. The merchant leapt from his chair and grabbed the unlucky one by the collar. The boys stopped, immediately humble and apologetic, and tried unsuccessfully to put the items back. The merchant shooed them away, but Nigel could see he was smiling.

"They are lucky," Lukas turned to Nigel.

Nigel felt a wave of pity as he thought about what the boy might be facing on his return.

"Well, Steven," he said, pouring himself another tea. "What do you think of all this? We haven't had a chance to talk in private since the great announcement."

"Depends what you mean by 'all this'…the fact that my daughter is getting married and moving to Morocco, or the fact that I am actually here. All I can say is that I'm well and truly down that rabbit hole."

"You're not worried about Catherine, are you? She's more capable of looking after herself than you are."

Steven ran his tongue across his teeth. "She's so young. Early twenties is no time to get married. I have this niggling feeling. But what do I know? Too late, anyway."

"Must be the protective father thing. She looks happy to me. I mean, *le monsieur* is quite the dish. You do like the man, I hope?"

"He's terrific. Great guy. And Hadir and Sophie…Christ, what a reception we got."

Hadir and Sophie and several members of staff had been lined up near the fountain in the courtyard when they arrived, and all had burst out clapping and cheering. Dominic had his arms around Catherine and her father while he made all the introductions. Nigel smiled, remembering Steven's discomfort. This unfamiliar environment in a foreign country, as father of the bride, clearly required a Herculean effort. Finally, Dominic spirited Catherine away, and neither was seen again until the following morning.

"Ahh, the delicious Sophie," Nigel said. "If I were playing for the other team, there's a woman who could spirit me away."

Steven rolled his eyes. "Snowball's chance in hell, my friend. They're great people. They treat Catherine like a princess."

"What's the matter, then? Come on, spit it out?"

"I can't put my finger on it. Dominic seems preoccupied. They both do."

"Of course, they're preoccupied. They're getting married."

"But it's all been such a rush. Her best friend wanted to come, but couldn't get away that fast. She begged Catherine to delay a couple of weeks."

"I swear, if you don't have something to worry about, you're not happy. What time is it? We should probably make a move."

As if on cue, the sunset call to prayer began.

"What's that one called?" said Lukas, still watching the butcher and the cats.

"Don't ask me. I'm afraid I haven't a clue."

"It's *Salat al Maghrib*," said the waiter.

"Thank you. Lukas, did you catch that?"

"Salat al Maghrib," Lukas repeated carefully, to the waiter's delight.

For a while, the three of them lingered to watch life on the tiny, narrow streets before them and listen to the echoing wave of the muezzin's chant. Such an eerie, soulful sound, Nigel thought, especially while the sky turned blue and mauve with stubborn streaks of fiery orange, as though the sun were not ready to call it a day.

***

After a traditional tagine supper in the hotel's restaurant, Hadir suggested they go up to the roof for a nightcap. Walking up the stone steps behind him, Nigel was struck by the elegance of this man. A well-cut cream linen jacket, khaki drawstring pants, suede low-top sneakers—Brunello Cucinelli from top to bottom, he guessed. Dominic had told them his brother was very "budget-conscious," but clearly not when it came to fashion.

They emerged from the steep stairwell with various exclamations of wonder and surprise. A few other hotel guests were seated at the bar that was strung with multi-coloured teardrop lamps. They waved a greeting. "Stunning, isn't it?"

Nigel twisted full circle to take in the panoramic view. On all sides, sweeping jumbles of the cream and white buildings of the medina fell over each other as though someone had tipped them from a large box. Many were topped with clusters of satellite dishes, their cables twisting and looping in all directions. His eye was drawn to the numerous domes and square-shafted minarets of mosques. Dominic pointed out the famous Mosque of al-Qarawiyyin, the oldest, nearby. Clustered randomly were stands of cypress that grew profusely as the city spilled into surrounding hills. The light was a beautiful soft gold, Nigel thought, not like the hard white electric glare of modern cities.

"Lukas, come, check this out," Dominic led Lukas away from two cats who had sized him up as a soft touch, and onto a platform to the side.

"This is my telescope. I found it in the storage room. It's not like anything your father had, I'm afraid, but we can give it a try."

Lukas ran his hands over the telescope. "It's a good one."

Dominic laughed. "Probably fine for beginners like me. We won't see much because there's too much light here. But maybe we'll take it into the desert one night before you return."

Nigel and the others sprawled out on the daybeds and watched the two of them.

Dominic was determined to find Capella, the star that inspired the name of the Riad. "This time of year, it's low, in the northeast, I think."

Nigel noticed that Catherine watched them with an anxious look. An awful lot for her to be thinking about, he reasoned. Her phone rang, and she jumped up and walked a few paces away to take the call. He nudged Steven and inclined his head in her direction.

"She okay?"

Steven shrugged. "You're asking *me?*"

Catherine was back in a few moments. "Was that your mom?" Steven asked. "You have talked to her, right?"

"No, it was not, and yes, I have," Catherine said.

"Has she settled down about all this?"

Catherine gave him one of her "who knows-who cares?" looks.

Nigel turned to Sophie and Hadir. "By the way, we haven't seen that young woman who was over in Toronto. Amina, right? She came back shortly before us, I think."

"Well, you see, she is—" Hadir began.

"She is staying with a friend," Sophie interrupted. "It has been such a busy time here, getting everything ready for the wedding and running the hotel at the same time. We wanted her to enjoy a few days off before the big event."

"Have either of you heard from her?" Dominic called over.

Sophie raised both hands in a 'back off' gesture. "No, and we don't expect to. That's what taking a break is all about."

"Young Lukas took a shine to her," Nigel said. "I know he's looking forward to seeing her again."

Hadir got to his feet. "I believe our glasses are empty. Will you all have another?"

Chapter 33

Amina's friend, Tabani, paced back and forth across her living room. "Why are you going to see this old man, Amina? An antiques dealer? My mother is fretting. She says you look ill."

"I'm not ill. I'm sorry, Tabani. I can't explain it now."

"Did something happen in Canada? You were so excited to be there. I was jealous."

"It's…it's about my father. I'll tell you once it's straight in my head."

"But this man you're waiting for, Masoud. What has he to do with it all?

"He helped me understand those charts, remember? Da'ud—the antiques dealer I told you about—he recommended Masoud. They've worked together on films about Ancient Egypt."

"But why must you meet here and not at the Capella? My father called Hadir about him. He is not happy that you are driving with this man who is not your husband, not even a relative. He wanted to be sure the man could be trusted."

Amina winced. "Tabani, your father is traditional. I'm so sorry to cause trouble. Hadir has met Masoud. He is a good person."

Amina reassured her friend she would tell her the whole story when everything was finally out in the open. Dominic had tried to dismiss some of Lukas's words as a young boy's imagination, but she knew he was only trying to calm her down. He promised that after the wedding he would tell his Canadian friends about the crazy coincidence, and the truth about her father. It would be another reason to celebrate, a way for all the pieces of the puzzle to come together. But she was troubled about Lukas, about what went on in the mind of that little boy, and what might she learn from Da'ud.

"Do you like him, this Masoud?" Tabani asked.

Amina blushed and looked down.

"Ah," Tabani said. "No need to answer, my friend."

Her father came into the room. "He is here. I am going out to speak to him."

Masoud waited until they were out of sight of Tabani's home, then pulled over to the side of the road and drew Amina into his arms. "You are here, finally. I have not stopped thinking about you." She lay her head on his shoulder. He was strong, solid, comforting—everything she needed.

They parked as close as possible to Nejarine Square, and walked the last short stretch, Masoud trying not to limp.

"Does it hurt when you walk?" she asked him.

"Not when I walk with you." He looked both ways, then kissed the top of her head.

She *did* like this man, with his Cairene accent that reminded her of childhood, and his gentle ways. Eventually, they came to the store where Da'ud was waiting. He greeted them warmly and ushered them through to the rooms at the back. The living area was small and sparsely furnished with low banquette-style couches. In the centre was an oversized wooden coffee table with a teapot and glasses, and a plate of almond macaroons. Amina paused in front of a shelf unit filled with ancient Egyptian artifacts ranging from a bronze bust of Nefertiti and a stone replica of the Sphinx to copper urns and canopic jars.

"You are interested in these beautiful things from your homeland?" Da'ud asked. "I am fond of them. I brought them here from my store in Cairo."

He gestured for them to sit, poured the tea, and settled his heavy frame into a big leather chair. Amina noticed his jacket and pants were baggy and well worn, his white shirt was grey at the collar.

"Masoud tells me that you have been to Canada," he said, "and that you met the son of Karl Gustav, the man your father worked for. And that the boy is in Morocco. This is most unusual. Please, let me know what is worrying you."

Amina had rehearsed for this moment. "I want to know about the fire. You were in Cairo at that time. The boy said 'there are all kinds of stories.' What could that mean? I know he was talking about my father. I don't want to be protected or lied to. I want the truth."

Masoud took her hand. Da'ud's eyes slid over and clearly took note of this. She pulled her hand away. Da'ud shifted in his chair and nodded slowly. On the table before them was a case of cigarettes. "Do you mind?" he said, pointing to it.

She shook her head.

He fished about in several pockets for a lighter. Finally, the cigarette was lit. He leaned back in the chair again. "Truth is elusive, Amina. We can never be sure that we have fully grasped it. But I don't believe your father set that fire."

Even though she was sure of this, Amina felt a hot flush of relief.

"It was possibly an accident, a candle, an incense burner." Da'ud went on. "But the flames spread quickly, blocking all chance of escape, so it was assumed to be deliberate. Earlier, Abdul, the baker who lived opposite, and Fadoul—he owns a restaurant nearby—were talking on the street and heard an argument through the upstairs window of Karl's study. They recognized Karl's voice but not the other, and could not make out what was being said, only that it was some kind of confrontation. They saw no one leave."

"My father was there often. If it was him, they would have recognized his voice."

"About twenty minutes later, from inside the bakery, they saw your father arrive with a package for Karl. Karl had apparently told him he would be out, and to leave it downstairs in the store. Your father was inside for only seconds and came out screaming that there was a fire up in the study. They ran over and began to climb the stairs, but your father pulled them back. They thought they should check, but your father said, no, no, Karl was out, they should leave, call the fire department."

"So? He was scared," Amina said. "That's not a crime. He didn't want the others to be in danger. The man who was arguing, wasn't *he* the suspect. Why didn't they find *him*, arrest *him*?"

"Indeed. The other man. If the boy heard stories, it was likely about this other man. Who was he really? Did he even exist? They began to doubt the testimony of Abdul and Fadoul."

"What do you mean. Why?"

Da'ud shifted his weight again. "Your father was superstitious. He was always fearful of the *ifrit*, the evil spirits. The witnesses were taken to the police station, to be questioned. I was there because they needed statements from anyone who knew Karl well." He tapped the drooping ash from his cigarette into the ashtray. "Amina, this may be hard to hear, but you wanted the truth. Your father began to…to rant, I suppose, talking in riddles, saying crazy things. We tried to calm him down. He went quiet and then shouted out: 'I thought *she* was up there alone. It was she who should have died, not Karl.' The police were listening. They were hard on him. Who knows what he confessed. He was not in his right mind."

Amina bowed her head and felt a hot flush creep all over her body. *That can't possibly be true. Poor Baba. The police must have made him scared and confused.* The word 'superstitious' rankled, but it brought back snippets of family conversations she had overheard as a child. "Something is on Ahmed's conscience if you ask me. The *ifrit* are plaguing his dreams."

"Who is this 'she' he was shouting about?" Masoud asked.

"Rachel," said Da'ud. "The boy's mother, an interesting woman. I never understood why Ahmed didn't like her. Brought bad luck, apparently."

"I don't care how much he disliked her. If he thought anyone was there, he'd never have left them to die."

"He was released because the evidence against him was not…conclusive." Da'ud extinguished his cigarette and pushed the ashtray aside. "I hope it helps you to know these details."

While it felt good to hear what had happened from a person who knew her father, who was there in Cairo at the time, Amina began to regret her quest for the truth and wished she had never heard what her father told the police. He must have been so upset. Perhaps he was angry with the woman, Rachel, for some reason. Perhaps he only wished it could have been her instead of Karl. The fact is, he was innocent. He had found the place already on fire and ran, like anyone would have. *"Lots of different stories"*…that was gossip and innuendo. She would make sure Lukas knew the truth, that a confession had been *forced* out of her father, and he had suffered greatly for it.

"Thank you. I won't take up any more of your time. Masoud, we should—"

"Not so fast." Da'ud rose to his feet. "There is something more you need to know."

Chapter 34

Da'ud led them to a café across the square and chose a table off to one side, the few troughs of plants around it providing a little privacy. He and Masoud adjusted the chairs, Masoud bending down with some difficulty to wedge a scrap of paper under one of the legs.

They ordered a mezze platter with hummus, fava bean dip, almonds, lavash bread, and roasted vegetables. There was something about the manner of the two men, a kind of silent communication between them, an exchange of sympathetic looks. But perhaps it was only a shared feeling of compassion for her. What did this man want to talk about, she wondered? Regardless, he obviously intended to eat first.

Da'ud asked Masoud about the film he consulted for, when it would be released, and what other projects were on the horizon.

"I am very glad, Amina, that your family took me up on this referral," Da'ud said. "You have learned, I'm sure, that this man has an excellent background and is an expert in his field."

Masoud put his hands together at his chest and smiled at the compliment. In a few minutes, he finished eating and rose to leave. "Amina, when I arranged this meeting, Da'ud told me there was something personal he needed to discuss with you. I am going to leave the two of you for a while."

Amina tried to protest, but Masoud was already walking away.

"I won't be far. Call me when you are ready to leave."

Da'ud asked the waiter for a fresh jug of water and continued to eat for a few minutes. "So," he said finally, leaning back and appraising her, his hands clasped in his lap. "What are plans for your future, Amina?"

"My future?"

"What I have to tell you will affect your future. In a positive way. But you have some thinking to do." He wiped his mouth with a paper napkin.

"Your happiness was always Ahmed's chief concern. I'm sure you know that. He worried about what would happen to you when he died. The brothers, Hadir and Dominic, assured him you would always have a home with the family, but what if something should happen *to them?* What if the hotel was sold? He took nothing for granted. Some years ago, he came to me for counsel and financial advice."

"Financial advice? He had no money…I mean, he had only his salary."

"Well, that's just it, Amina. He did have money. Not a fortune, but enough to provide some security. He set up a trust for you and asked me to be the executor. This money was to come to you when you became an adult or wished to marry. I believe he would be happy for you to have it now. You have turned twenty, I think?"

Amina felt her heart would burst. That her father would find a way to do this was unbelievable. "How much money? Surely not a great deal?"

"Eighty-five thousand U.S. dollars. Eight hundred thousand dirham. Thereabouts."

"That is not possible."

"I assure you it is so. A good American fund, gaining interest for over five years."

"But how—"

"It is a sensitive subject. Let me explain." He looked her straight in the eye for a moment, as though weighing his words. "Of course, you will remember the accident. You and your father were sitting on the side of the road at the market, not far from here. A man was hit by a car. He was carrying—"

Amina felt a sharp, cold stab in her spine. "No. This is all wrong. That was Hadir. Hadir's money. We walked to the hospital. My father gave it back to him."

Da'ud tore off a piece of flatbread and dipped it into the hummus. "Not all of it."

The ground dropped beneath her and there was a loud roar in her ears. It blotted out the clatter of pots and pans in the café's kitchen, the shouts of small children playing on the street, the raised voices of customers at the clothing store opposite. She balled her fists and pushed herself away from the table, straining against the back of the chair.

A perfect explanation fought its way through the chaos in her head. "Hadir gave him some money. That's what you mean?"

He shook his head slowly. "Please relax, Amina. What you need to understand is that this money came from a dubious source, a loan shark. It was being used to pay off someone connected to the hotel the family used to have in Casablanca. An old debt. We found this out much later, of course. The transaction was…what shall I say? Risky. It was a great deal of money Hadir was carrying. As you may recall, people were fighting each other, scooping up the notes. Your father told me that when he saw the bag, sitting there in your lap, he thought of it as a sign, a gift from the gods, a way of making things right for all the wrong you had both suffered. He went into a back alley with you and stuffed notes into his shirt, his pockets, the waistband of his pants, clutching the bag to his chest."

Amina's stomach compressed into a tight knot. She wanted to hit him, this old man who told her that her father was a thief. She wanted to grab the pitcher of water and throw it at him as he sat there, picking his teeth with his grubby fingernails.

"He told me he walked around with you aimlessly," Da'ud continued, "not knowing what to think, what to do."

"I know. I was there." Her own voice was shrill in her ears. "We walked all day to the Ghassani hospital to give Hadir the money."

"Think, Amina," Da'ud raised his eyes with a shrewd smile. "The Ghassani hospital is not so far. Your father needed time. His conscience weighed heavy. In the end, he struck a compromise."

She pushed her plate to the side and looked away.

"At the hospital, he tried to hand the bag with the leftover money to the nurses. He wanted to get out of there with what he had kept. But they insisted he see Hadir personally. Face to face with the family, who was grateful to get *any* of it back, he vacillated for a moment, but then thought about the life he *might* have, the life you might have, and could not bring himself to hand over the notes hidden in his clothes. Sophie and Dominic took you both back to the Riad Capella. You know the rest."

Amina barely made it to the bathroom before heaving up. The toilet was no more than a hole in the ground. A trickle of cold water ran from an old tap on the tiled wall, and she tried her best to clean up. Crouched in the corner, she sobbed until her body ached.

A rap on the door. Da'ud had sent a woman to check on her. She splashed a few more drops of water on her face and made her way back, holding on to the backs of chairs and clutching the sides of the table as she sat down.

"Why didn't he admit it later?" she asked. "They would have understood."

"Over the years, the compassion of the family made the idea of confessing harder and harder. He hid the money in a box in a closet in his room—didn't even know what to do with it. By chance, he learned that I came regularly to Fez. We met, and I took the money and opened an account for him. He needed to bare his soul to someone. In the end, two things made him feel better. The first was that he would never touch it. It was not for him; it was for you."

"And the second?"

Da'ud poured her some water. "Please, drink this." He looked her in the eye again. "The El Hassad brothers are wealthy. You know this. They come from money, and they have made a lot more of it. The cash your father took was assumed lost in the mêlée at the market. In the end, I doubt it was missed."

"I don't want it. I can't take it."

"But imagine what you might do with it. You need time to think, of course. For now, you can keep it invested, let it grow. But you must take it. Your father did it for you." From inside his jacket, he retrieved an envelope and put it on the table before her. "Everything is in your name. Here are the banking details…where it is, how to access it."

She rose clumsily to her feet, making the chair fall back against the railing. People turned to look. She pushed the envelope towards Da'ud.

"Don't you have any idea what this means?" Her voice sounded like a whispered shriek, not belonging to her. "You have ruined the happiness of the last five years of my life. You are telling me my father was a thief and a coward." Through the clamour in her head, a horrific thought cut through. *And could he have been a killer too?* She fought it off. "Hadir and Sophie and Dominic…they are my family. They took us in. They showed us nothing but kindness. You make them out to be criminals too. And you expect me to carry on this terrible deception. I cannot. And I can never look them in the eye again."

She grabbed her bag from the back of the chair and ran from the café.

Chapter 35

Steven walked along the dusty, pebbled trail that wove around the Merenid tombs. Dominic had brought them here to see the ruins and watch the sun set over the medina. The tombs dated back to the 14th century, he told them, final resting places for the élite of the Merenid dynasty.

They had separated at the top of the hill to explore the surrounding area before the sun went down. Nigel was studying the stucco decoration and inscriptions still visible on parts of the giant arch monument. Dominic was farther over with Lukas who jumped on and off the rocks and low stone walls, asking a million questions, as usual. The boy was beside himself with excitement because Dominic had promised they would drive into the desert the following day with the telescope to look at the stars.

Catherine had taken a pass on this excursion, needing to work with Sophie on last-minute wedding arrangements, like music and staffing. For a small affair, Steven was astonished at the preparations that were required. He could see his daughter and Sophie getting on well, but he swore there was always an "is this for real?" look in Sophie's eyes. From the offhand comments during conversations at meals, he guessed that Dominic was a classic womanizer and that a long succession of women had stayed at the Riad Capella. But Catherine was no wallflower. Perhaps they had both run the gamut and 'found each other.'

He had nearly opted out of this visit himself, preferring a lazy afternoon wandering around the neighbourhood, or relaxing on the roof of the Riad reading his book. But the others had been keen, and he didn't want to come across as lacking all sense of adventure. He was glad now for having made the effort.

Many of the nearby hills were covered with sprawling tombstones of the Bab Guissa Cemetery. To the south lay oak and cedar forests that grew into the foothills of the Middle Atlas Mountains. Strange to think of snow-capped mountains under this blazing sun, he mused. Dominic had urged them to stay longer in Morocco, to go across the Sahara to visit friends of his in the tiny village of Merzouga. He knew people who could make it all happen…they had only to ask. But Steven had more work to do for his show in Stockholm. And he was surprised at how anxious he was becoming to see Natalie again.

Turning a bend on the narrow trail, he thought about the pathway near his former home in Tuscany. He would often take that path early in the morning to stand on the edge of a steep hill and watch the sun rise over San Gimignano. Now here he was about to watch the sun *set* in a different part of the world. In Tuscany, the landscape was lush, the colours muted and gentle: the greens and tawny browns of the terraced vineyards, the pale silver shimmer of the canopies of olive trees, the smoky lavender of the sky. Here, the earth was orange and dry and dusty, the sun bleaching the colour from the sky. And yet there was a deep air of mystery about it all. He shivered, feeling an unexpected chill despite the relentless heat.

He reached into the zippered pocket at the side of his pants and drew out a small purple pouch. Inside this was a ring with the symbol of the Eye of Horus. Its black and white eye in the brilliant turquoise lapis lazuli stared back at him. He polished the silver band on his shirt sleeve and thought about the day he received it. Rachel had sent it with the letter, the letter telling him that she loved another man and was pregnant with his child. Karl had given her the ring. It symbolized protection, the idea of healing and making things whole. Steven never understood why she sent it to him; he did not subscribe to her beliefs, and had never worn it. But now he knew. It was meant for Lukas. More than that: it was meant for him to give to Lukas. He would never be able to rationalize this, but had no doubt that it must be so, a duty he must fulfil. He would give it to the boy tonight.

He took out his phone and snapped a few photos. A lone donkey farther down the hill stopped its munching of sparse grass and looked up, as if to pose. *Perfect!* He sent the shot to Natalie.

The sound of falling stones and a terrified scream came from somewhere beneath him.

"Help me. Help me. Please."

Then Dominic's voice, high above, rising in panic. "Lukas! Where are you? Oh God, please, where are you? Steven, can you see him?"

Steven ran back along the path, scouring the hillside. He saw the boy forty to fifty feet below, lying awkwardly against the steep, crumbling hillside. He had landed on a narrow shelf of rock, his legs hanging over the edge. *What the hell is he holding on to?* "Lukas. I'm right here. Stay still. We'll get you."

Lukas twisted his neck to look up. "I can't move. I don't want to die."

"You're not going to die. Hold on, stay still."

A thousand memories flooded Steven's brain. *No, no, no.* He looked up at the sky. *You're not taking this one.* "Dominic," he yelled. "I see him, I'm getting him." Turning sideways, crouching, he began to edge down the steep slope, hanging on to shrubs and rocks, his feet sliding on the loose stones. *Christ. I'm not going to make it.*

"For God's sake be careful, man." Nigel shouted, on the crest of the overhanging ridge above, a clutch of strangers at his side. "Dominic is getting help. Tell Lukas not to panic."

Directly below him, close to where Lukas was hanging, was a low, crumbling brick wall, but the slope leading to it was far too steep to climb down. He lay flat on his back and started to manoeuvre downwards, clutching at low-growing shrubs on both sides. One of these came out by the roots and his body swung sideways. *Oh God, what a fucking stupid thing to do. I won't make it. I was never meant to make it.* He grabbed at bushes, rocks, anything to try to slow his speed. But his hands could not grip them. He slid faster and faster, seeing only the vastness of the sky and the glowering sun above him, and feeing the bite of the sharp stones on his back as he hurtled over them. He raised his head and saw the wall looming up directly beneath him. He braced his feet and slammed into it, pebbles and sand spraying in all directions.

Fuck. A sharp pain shot up from his ankle, and the breath ripped right out of him. Think, breathe, he told himself. *If you feel pain, you must be alive.* He tried to stand, using the wall for leverage. But his left foot would not take the weight, and he fell backwards.

"Lukas." His voice was hoarse. "I'm right here, I'll get you." Not trusting his ankle, Steven lay flat on his stomach and dragged himself across the hill, broken bricks cutting into his chest, to where Lukas was clinging. One of the boy's hands was clasped around a half-buried tree root, the other clutching the ledge of rock.

"I can't hold on anymore," Lukas cried.

"Yes, you can. You're right below me. You need to grab my hand then pull yourself up. I'll hold you. Not yet. Wait." He stretched out his arm. "Okay. Slowly. Look at me."

Lukas looked up, his face red with sand and streaks of blood. "I'm scared."

"You *will* do it. Do exactly what I say. After three. Look at me. Don't take your eyes off me. One…two…"

The boy let go and in one motion Steven seized his hand and jerked upwards with all his strength. For a moment he felt his body tilt and feared they would both plunge to the bottom together. But Lukas managed to claw and scramble his way to more solid ground.

How they ended up wedged together behind the wall, he would not remember. Steven's breath came in big, ragged gasps and his relief was so consuming that his body went limp and began to shake violently.

He stared up at the steep hill. "No way am I going to make it back. And I'm not letting you climb on your own. Dominic's getting help." With no warning, he began to sob.

Lukas leaned on his shoulder. "It's okay. We're not going to die now. Right?"

Chapter 36

"The break is not serious?" Dominic said. "God help me, it could have ended so differently. They could have died. If we'd lost the boy—I can't bear to think about it. And Steven. This will be his memory of Fez."

They were in Hadir's office. Hadir had returned from the hospital with Steven and Lukas.

"Calm down, brother. First, Lukas is safe. A few scratches, a bandage on his hand…and a great story to tell. And Steven will be fine. He's on crutches. His ankle should really be in a cast, but you can't fly with a cast, so they've given him an adjustable ankle brace. It will do for a few days, the doctor said, and he can fly home wearing it, right after the wedding. He has medication for the pain. Nothing is going to interfere with the wedding, except that he won't be able to stand up. Come on…" He slapped Dominic on the back. "Let's go and join them."

Dominic hesitated and put a hand on Hadir's arm. "Wait. I have to know this. Are you happy for me, brother? I mean, honestly. You and Sophie?"

Hadir gave him a worried look, his head to one side. "What's brought this on? You're upset, you've had a shock. You need to get some rest."

"Answer my question."

"Dominic…we are happy when you are happy. Catherine is a wonderful woman. All we have ever wanted is that you are true to yourself, that you follow your heart. If you promise me that is what you are doing, we want nothing more for you. Come, our friends are waiting."

As Hadir gave him a gentle push along the corridor, Dominic wrestled with the thorn of discontent that persisted despite his brother's cheery reassurance.

"What some people will do to get attention." Nigel gestured to Steven as the two brothers approached. "He's complaining that he's not allowed to drink."

Steven was ensconced on a cushioned chair, his foot resting on a leather pouffe.

"I am deeply sorry," Dominic took one of Steven's hands in both of his. "I should have kept a closer eye on Lukas."

"Yes, you should have," said Sophie. "Head in the Clouds, literally this time."

"Please don't be cross with Dominic," said Lukas. "He told me to be careful. It was my fault." His face was crumpled up, on the point of tears.

Dominic sat beside him on the couch. "Sophie's always mad at me, Lukas. Don't take any notice. I know she secretly loves me as much as Hadir. Maybe more." He winked.

Sophie threw a chocolate almond at him.

Nigel's phone pinged. "Text from Philippe. Expressions of horror and sympathy. And that terrified screaming emoji."

"Why did you start down the hill, Dad? Why didn't you wait for the emergency people? They had ropes and proper equipment. They came quickly, Nigel said."

All heads turned to Catherine.

"How can you ask me that?" said Steven. "Lukas was in danger."

"They would have reached him in time."

A silence fell over the group, everyone clearly uncomfortable.

"Well, maybe not," said Nigel. "Your dad did the right thing. Might even be on the local news I hear. We are famous."

"I had to do it, Catherine," Steven said. "You know why. And it was the right thing."

"What are you saying?" said Dominic, alarmed by the change in her voice. "Your dad is a hero. He's certainly my hero, and Lukas's."

"It's a long story and a long time ago," said Steven. "Something I expected Catherine to understand in silence. Not make a scene about."

Sophie put a hand on Steven's shoulder. "Catherine nearly lost you. Relief often makes us angry."

"But the ring worked," said Lukas, pulling it from his pocket. "Can I show them?" Steven nodded. "It's called the Eye of Horus. It's so cool. It was my mom's. Steven gave it me at the hospital. It means I'm protected."

"I didn't know you had that, Dad. Another long story?" said Catherine.

At least she was smiling this time, Dominic noted with some relief.

"Well," said Hadir, getting to his feet and summoning one of the young staff. "I didn't do a single noteworthy thing today except drive our guests from the hospital, but I need another drink. Anyone else?"

Dominic would always remember the scene: the cosy room off the courtyard, a quarter moon in the high window on one wall, the smell of sandalwood from lit candles. The hotel was busy, staff scurrying about, attending to guests, with nothing pressing. His brother and sister-in-law and these new friends lounged in various relaxed positions around the room, smiling and teasing each other. He thought how lucky he was, living in this wonderful hotel in a city and a country he loved, with barely a worry in the world, soon to marry an extraordinary woman. He put his arm around her shoulders. Everyone clinked glasses and toasted Steven and Lukas, making them pose for photographs and embarrassing them.

Eventually, Steven declared himself ready for bed, and others also shuffled about and began to retire.

Then Lukas asked the innocent question: "Is Amina coming back for the wedding?"

"Amina? Yes, of course," said Sophie. "She's still at her friend's for a couple more days."

"Only she looked like she was leaving."

Everyone stopped and stared at him.

"But you haven't seen her," said Hadir. "What do you mean?"

"Last night, I heard her in her room next door."

"But she's not here," Dominic said. "Maybe it was a noise farther down the corridor."

"No. I got up. I wanted to see her. She said not to make a noise. She had come back for some things." He clearly did not understand the alarm he was causing. "She told me to go back to my room and go to bed. So I went."

"What things did she come for, Lukas? Did she say?" Hadir asked.

"She had a big bag and was holding something. I think it looked like a passport."

Chapter 37

The room warped and pitched. Dominic leaned against the wall. "Someone, call her."

Sophie punched in Amina's number and got voicemail.

"Call her friend. Tabani."

"Do you have Tabani's number?" Sophie snapped. "Why do you expect *me* to have it? Wait. Hadir, Tabani's father called you. About Masoud."

Hadir pulled out his phone. She snatched it from him, found the number, and made the call, struggling to keep her voice calm. "You mean, she is not there?" She held the phone away from her ear, eyes widening at the angry tone of the man on the other end. "I'm sure there's a good explanation. I wonder if I may speak to your daughter."

"What's he saying?" said Dominic.

"Going on about Masoud, telling me we are *'irresponsible.'* He's getting Tabani." Sophie held up her hand to silence interruptions. "Tabani, I'm sorry to call so late. I think we might be mistaken about Amina's plans. We thought she was still with you." She screwed up her face and turned away. "Last night?" She put her hand to her mouth and shook her head. "No, no, I'm sure there's no reason to worry. Of course. We will ask her to call you immediately."

"What?" said Dominic. "For God's sake, what happened?"

"She said Amina had packed her things and left—to come back here. Masoud picked her up there last night."

"So why the hell did you say there was no reason to worry? I can't believe you trusted that guy. Both of you. Smart, decent—a gentleman, you said. Goddammit."

"Don't you dare use that tone with me, Dominic. We may have a serious problem here and I don't want it broadcast all over town." She strode off toward the reception.

"Where are you going?"

"To get the key to her room. One of you call Masoud. His card must be in the office."

Hadir went to search for it.

Dominic looked at the shocked faces of his friends. They would have to be told at least part of the story. They had met Amina. They'd be concerned. But he could barely think straight. "I'm sorry. This day is getting worse," he said. "Amina was upset about something to do with her past. She went to see a man who had known her father, someone in the antiques business here. I won't go into it. We are worried about where she could be."

"But, a passport," Nigel said. "Lukas, are you sure it was a passport?"

"It had like a big gold eagle on it."

"Does she have relatives or friends in another country?" Nigel asked.

Dominic tore his hands through his hair. "No. Not anymore."

Hadir came back and threw a business card on the table. "This number is in Ouarzazate. Recorded message about a film production being completed. No longer in service."

"Jesus, Hadir…could she…I mean is it even possible that she could have gone somewhere with *him?*"

Nigel picked up the card. "*Masoud Burhan. Egyptologist. Art Direction for Stage, Film and Television,*" he read. "Boyfriend?"

"I don't know what he *thinks* he is, but if he's got anything to do with this, he's a dead man," said Dominic. "Hadir—the Egyptian. Da'ud. He must have told her something. Something that really upset her."

"What could have upset her enough to leave the country? This is crazy." Hadir looked across the courtyard. "Sophie? What's wrong? Did you find anything?"

"Her clothes are gone. This was on the bed." Sophie held up a small handwritten note.

Dominic took it from her. *Please forgive me. I am safe. I need time. I will explain everything,* he read. He punched the wall.

Hadir raised both hands and addressed the others. "I'm so sorry, everyone. This is a terrible thing to be happening. It should be such a happy time. This is a family matter. We need to get to the bottom of it."

"Don't apologize," said Steven. He pulled his crutches over and made a clumsy attempt to stand. "Let us get out of your way. I wish there was something useful we could do."

"Pardon my curiosity," Nigel said, helping Steven to his feet. "The antiques man—what did you say his name was?"

"Da'ud," said Hadir. "His relatives have a store here. He knew Amina's father when they lived in Cairo. Why?"

"Well, that's strange," said Nigel. "I knew a Da'ud who had an antiques store in Cairo. It's a common name, of course. Anyway, I'm sure it's of no consequence."

Dominic felt as though he were looking at the room through binoculars, trying to bring it into focus. "When did you know this man, Nigel?"

"Many moons ago. We're talking the early nineties. The Da'ud I knew was a Middle Eastern contact for Philippe and me. It was through him that I learned about Lukas's father and got the introduction for Rachel. I'm sure it's not the same person."

Dominic and Hadir exchanged a frozen stare. Dominic slid his eyes over to Lukas. The boy rocked back and forth, his arms crossed, his hands gripping his shoulders.

"What was the last name of that man you knew?" Hadir asked.

"Karaoui. I may not be pronouncing it right. But what made me wonder is the other man—Masoud. I seem to remember the Da'ud I knew had a son—no, no, a nephew I think, called Masoud. . .just a small boy when we were in touch. He used to like hanging about in the store, messing with all the ancient Egyptian paraphernalia."

Sophie drew her breath in sharply.

Nigel looked from one to the other of them, his face a shock of concern. "Oh dear, what have I said?"

Dominic slid down the wall to a crouching position, his head in his hands. Lukas scrambled over to his side. "Is Amina going to be all right? I'm scared." He pulled the boy into his arms and gripped him tightly.

"Get off the floor, for God's sake," said Sophie, leaping to her feet. "Hadir, both of you. Go and drag that man out of bed and put a knife to his throat if you have to."

Dominic looked across Lukas's shoulder to Catherine who had not said a word during this whole drama. She was lying back on the couch, her arms spread over the plush cushions.

Now she leaned forward, took a last slug of wine, and slammed her glass onto the table. "Would somebody *please* tell me what the FUCK is going on here?"

Chapter 38

Catherine's words hung in the silence. Steven wanted to snatch them from the air before they fell and shattered on the floor.

It was Lukas who spoke first, still buried in Dominic's shoulder. "Did I do something wrong?"

"No." Dominic raised himself off the floor and eased Lukas away, taking care not to touch his bandaged hand. "You did nothing wrong, Lukas. Nothing at all. But things have become complicated, and I need to explain to our friends. Come on, sit with me on the couch."

"I think Lukas is tired. We don't need to keep him up." Nigel made a move, but Dominic shook his head.

"It's okay. Let him stay." Dominic pulled the boy to his side as though to draw strength from him. "I'm so sorry, everyone. I don't even know where to start. You see, there is something I have known from the night I met you all, the night of your exhibition in Toronto, Steven. I still can't believe the twist of fate that brought us together. We met by accident, and yet it could not have been an accident. I don't know how to explain it."

"For God's sake, Dominic, what the hell are you talking about?" said Catherine.

Steven put his hand on his daughter's arm, not sure why he felt compelled to do this. Was it to stop her from talking, or was it a sudden need to protect her from what Dominic might say next, even though he had no idea what this could be?

"I will explain," said Hadir. "You have all met Amina. But you know little about her and there was no reason to tell you more. Now, we must. Amina's father, Ahmed, used to work with Lukas's father, Karl, in Cairo. When Karl died in the fire, Ahmed was falsely accused of setting it. He was released, but had to live with the shame of the accusation and the constant suspicion from both family and friends. When his wife died, he fled with Amina back to Fez, where he was born."

Nigel put his hand to his throat. "Oh my God, are you telling us…her father was Ahmed Gamel? But we understood—"

Steven's throat went dry. *Don't, Nigel. Don't say any more.* Nigel had told him about Ahmed, that he had been accused of setting the fire, thinking it was Rachel up there in the study that day, not Karl. He didn't like her because he thought she had "negative energy." *Don't say any of this in front of the boy.*

Nigel faltered, as though coming to the same conclusion. "But wait a minute. Everything I learned about that terrible day, everything I had to tell Rachel when she was in the hospital, sick, pregnant with Lukas…I heard all of it from that man we just talked about. Da'ud Karoui. Are you telling me this is indeed the same man? That he is here, in Fez?"

Catherine withdrew her arm from under Steven's hand and looked from one of the other of them, her face rigid with fury and disbelief. "Just hold on a minute. Why the big fucking secret, Dominic? I'm thinking about that day in Niagara Falls. That lunch. Nigel and I were telling you about Lukas's background, and you mean to say you already knew? Even then?" Her voice was rising with every question. "And you said nothing? Not even to me? What the fuck?"

"Catherine…language," Steven said, realizing too late how it didn't matter anymore. The boy had probably heard worse.

Dominic stroked the boy's head and squeezed him closer, his face tight with anguish.

"I'm lost, I'm afraid," said Nigel. His hands were shaking, and he had gone pale. "Where could Amina be and what has it all got to do with Da'ud?"

"Look, everyone," Sophie interrupted, "I'm sorry, but Dominic and Hadir must go. I will do my best to explain everything."

"We will find Amina," Dominic said into Lukas's shoulder. "You don't have to worry."

"I want to come with you," Lukas said.

"Much better if you wait here with the others. We will be back as soon as we can."

Steven watched the boy fighting his emotions. *Jesus, he's far too young to have to deal with whatever the hell is going on here.*

"Catherine, I'll explain when I get back. I promise." Dominic came over to kiss her, but she shrank back.

"Go," Sophie said. "And be careful, for God's sake."

When they left, Sophie called for one of the bellboys to bring them hot ginger tea. It was a long story, she said. Steven noticed her hair had come loose from the clip at her neck and her lipstick was smudged, betraying the turmoil in this elegant woman.

She told them about Hadir's accident, how Ahmed and Amina became part of the family; she told them about Da'ud, coming so suddenly into their lives, about the charts, how Dominic had phoned in disbelief from Canada. She told them about the trip to Ouarzazate to seek the interpretation of the Egyptologist.

"Amina is a good person," Lukas said, his eyes welling up. "I told her that in Canada, but she was very cross, and sad about everything."

"We know, Lukas. She always worried people would think bad things about her father. Now I think we should all have something to eat. None of us has had any proper supper. Why don't you go and ask Henri to come and see us?"

With Lukas gone, she told them that Nigel's revelation about Masoud being related to Da'ud was a terrible shock. Masoud had come across as a good, honourable man, but something had changed, something must have gone seriously wrong. What had Amina learned from Da'ud? They were worried sick about her. She had dual Egyptian-Moroccan citizenship and if, indeed, it was a passport she had last night, then she might have already left the country.

As he listened, Steven wondered what Rachel would make of all this, what reasonable-sounding but bewildering explanation she might give.

Some fucking rabbit hole. He moved his leg and felt a jolt of pain in his ankle.

"Are you okay, Dad?" His daughter looked shell-shocked and still angry. He nodded, not feeling at all okay. "And Amina and Lukas?" she said. "Do they each know who the other is?"

"We told Amina before she left for Canada. But here is where the story gets even stranger. When she returned from Toronto, earlier than we expected, she was upset, wanting to stay with her friend, Tabani, for a while, wanting to see this man, Da'ud, and learn more about her father. She was reluctant to explain, but I kept pressing, and she finally blurted it out. You see, Lukas told her he knew they would meet. He had the very same chart, that synastry or whatever they call it, in the box that had belonged to his father."

"Oh, dear Lord," said Nigel, collapsing back into his chair. "That bloody box and that bloody notebook. We should never have let him have it."

"But he can't read that stuff," Steven protested. "He's barely five years old."

"He reads more than you know."

"If Dominic were here, he'd tell you that the Amina and Lukas meeting was fated, a way for old wounds to heal. That he should meet you, Catherine, the same night that he met Lukas, and fall in love with you, that confirmed it all to him. As I'm sure you know, their mother had Roma blood. She was a bit of a mystic, and Dominic has got more than his fair share of those genes."

Steven adjusted his leg on the pouffe and grimaced again with the pain. He leaned back and closed his eyes. *Dammit, Rachel. Will this convoluted story never end?* When he opened his eyes, Lukas was at the entrance to the room, holding Henri's hand.

"Amina is my friend," he said. "I'm really frightened."

Chapter 39

On the flight from Casablanca to Cairo, Dominic could not sit still. He asked for food and then didn't touch it; he put his seat into the sleeping position and then sat up, his nose against the window, staring into the blue void.

Hadir, beside him, was increasingly irritated. "For God's sake. Your outrage and impatience are not going to make the damn plane go any faster."

"What if he has warned them?"

"You keep saying that. You threatened the man with his life, you threatened to ruin the business of every member of his family. You rammed his head against the wall. Shit. He's probably had a heart attack. We might be arrested when we land."

"I did not ram his head. He fell backwards."

"Right. He fell."

"I can't believe my own stupidity. He already tried to dupe Sophie and me that day in Nejarine Square with his damned family connections—God curse the lot of them. I bet he's been watching us, watching Amina, figuring out how to set his nasty little trap—and we walk right into it. I had lunch with the old guy, listened to his meanderings over those charts. And Sophie actually drove Amina to Ouarzazate. Christ. Straight into the lion's mouth."

"I tried to stop them. You know that. It's what Amina wanted."

"You've met him, this Masoud. What's he like? Is he a religious man?"

"Western dress, dark sunglasses, drinking wine. Sophie insisted he was polite, 'gentlemanly,' intelligent on their visit. What the hell are you trying to ask me, brother?"

"You know what I'm asking."

Hadir pulled out his phone, then put it back again in frustration. "Look, we know where she is. That's all that matters for now."

Dominic went to the bathroom and splashed water on his face, alarmed at how haggard he looked. He sank onto the toilet, clutching his arms around his chest. That Amina was humiliated and couldn't face them…that cut him to the quick. She was innocent of everything; she had been manipulated and lied to, even by her own father. He stood up to lean over the sink, wanting to retch. Ahmed. That was hard to take. When they told Sophie the whole distressing story about the money, she had urged them to forgive him—a poor man, wretched, starving. Of course, he would keep the money and then, when he was taken in and had built a good life with their help, he was too embarrassed.

"It was cowardly," Hadir said. "We expected better."

"We have all done things we are ashamed of," Sophie countered. "Look at where that money came from. You were dealing with loan sharks, criminals."

"We had few options, Sophie. You know that. We inherited that whole nightmare."

"You could have gone to the police."

"And none of us would be standing here today, would we?"

"Then we are all cowards."

Hadir had stormed off and slammed the door of his office. Dominic tried to comfort his sister-in-law, but she pushed him away.

The pilot's voice came through the speaker. Twenty minutes to landing.

***

Their hotel was in Giza, south of Cairo. Dominic wanted to go straight to Abu Sir where Masoud's family had a horse farm and where, Da'ud told them reluctantly, Amina was staying. She was at the house of Masoud's cousin, on the same property, he stressed, clearly frightened, saying things like "nothing improper," "never trespass on her virtue," and a bunch of other pretentious crap. Dominic had wanted to smash his face in.

Hadir insisted they stay in Giza overnight. They'd go first thing in the morning. Amina was safe. Anyway, it was far too late. They both needed sleep and would have to think clearly tomorrow. He drove the rental car from the airport.

Dominic stared through the window across the sands, anticipating that first view of the pyramids. He had been here many times and was sad to see more and more buildings springing up around them. But nothing could detract from that sense of awe when they first came into view. What a pity to be here on such ugly business, he thought, with no time or inclination to take in the ancient splendour of this most fascinating city of secrets. He made a sudden resolution: he would bring Lukas here. When, how, under what possible circumstances, he could not imagine. But the idea fixed itself in his mind. Having to put off their trip into the desert to look at the stars was a bitter disappointment to both of them. Well, one day they would come to *this* part of the desert, with so many mysteries beneath its sands, so many stories to tell. He would help Lukas discover the city his parents loved so much. This resolution made him feel better. It was something positive to hang on to.

"You have to call Catherine the minute we get to the hotel," Hadir said. "What have you decided? You can't keep Sophie hanging like this. Too many things to arrange."

"I don't know. Jesus, Hadir, I can't read her. I think she'll feel better if we postpone by a few days. It will give me time to explain things properly, make her understand there's nothing sinister in all this, no 'questionable motives' as she keeps saying."

Hadir turned away with a shake of the head, and they drove the rest of the way in silence.

Catherine had been in such a foul mood the previous night. When they got back from the vicious and nearly violent shouting match with Da'ud, well past midnight, both shaking with pent-up rage, all Dominic wanted to do was collapse into bed and offer explanations in the morning. But she was still awake, a generous whisky in hand, sitting in the armchair waiting for him, her eyes filled with condemnation.

He started to tell her what they had discovered about Masoud, and the money but she exploded. "I can't believe it. And I can't believe you encouraged us to be friends, knowing all this time that the father of one of your staff may have killed Lukas's father. It is so goddamn deceitful, it's almost malicious. And why? What was the harm in telling the truth?"

All his efforts to apologize, explain, to take her in his arms were in vain. She pushed him away and strode around the room. In the end, worn out by her own anger, she fell into a whiskey-fuelled sleep, still fully clothed. But for him, the night had no mercy, and he slept little.

In the morning, the warmth of the sun at the window, the breakfast tray he had ordered to the room, and a pot of strong coffee put her in a better mood. She had kissed him passionately before he left for Cairo. *Forgiveness, maybe?*

His brother looked straight ahead, driving with silent concentration. Hadir too was angry with him, but why? Dominic got the strong sense he was holding something back.

Here at last was the hotel, one of those imposing modern fortresses with cascading palm trees, turquoise pools and fountains, and fine dining under the stars. A young attendant in a smart uniform rushed out to relieve them of the car and their luggage.

Dominic ordered a brandy in his room and sat on the balcony overlooking the river, plucking up the courage to call Catherine. *What is she thinking in the cold light of day?*

Minutes later, there was a knock on his door. Hadir. "The decision is out of our hands." He flopped down full length on the bed. "I talked to Sophie. Steven had a terrible night. Lots of pain. Another x-ray. They're now saying surgery."

"Oh fuck." Dominic sank into the armchair and swallowed the remainder of his brandy in one gulp. "What now?"

"He can't have it done in Morocco. Surgery means a cast. He wouldn't be able to fly and couldn't get home for weeks. They've put a stronger brace on his foot which is okay for the flight, as long as his leg is kept raised. He will have the surgery in Toronto. They're on their way to the airport, he and Catherine."

"*What?* They've already left? Back to Canada?"

"He can't travel alone. She insisted. She'll call you when they get home, and it's all taken care of."

"Jesus Christ, Hadir. When is she coming back?"

"A week, ten days. Sophie has put everything on hold. Steven sent his apologies, his profuse thanks. Catherine said 'tell him I love him'."

Dominic gulped. *Tell him I love him.* Something about the way that sounded didn't feel right. "But what about Nigel and Lukas? Can they wait? Will they still be here for the wedding?"

"Depends when it is. Nigel's looking into a later flight back. Apparently, Lukas is really upset, crying, saying everything is his fault, everyone is leaving, and he is scared they are going to die. Sophie got him together with Zahra's son, Sadiq, to try to distract him. They're about the same age. They're teaching each other Arabic and English."

"Oh God, poor kid. He was so happy. I hope this hasn't spoiled everything for him."

"Leaving sooner would upset him even more," Sophie said.

"It's good…good they're staying," said Dominic. It was comforting to think of Nigel and Lukas still in Fez, waiting for them, waiting for everything to turn out well again. He hunched over in the chair, helpless under the burden of guilt.

Hadir rose and sat on the end of the bed, looking at his brother.

"What?" said Dominic.

But Hadir only shook his head and got up to leave. "Get some sleep. You'll need it."

Chapter 40

Masoud took Amina to a room in the house of his cousin, Ibrahim and Ibrahim's wife Layla, which was connected to the main one in which Masoud lived, by long, arched corridors on two levels. It was a room of pale colours: creamy stucco walls with paint peeling at the corners, a simple framed mirror on one wall, a bleached, well-worn chest of drawers, white shutters at the window. A tray of tea and sweets had been prepared for her, towels laid out on the bed. This was her room, her space, Masoud said. If she needed anything at all, she was simply to say. He took both her hands and looked at her with great tenderness. "When you can see the world again with clear eyes and a lighter heart, then we will plan our future."

She had blurted out the whole story to him as soon as she fled from Da'ud at the café, her body racked with sobs, her voice incoherent with disbelief and panic. He drove them to the *Jnan sbil* gardens where they walked for over an hour along the stone pathways, through the rows of palm trees, past the ponds, fountains, and geometric gardens until she was finally calm. He insisted she do nothing, that she had plenty of time to decide, that she should not assume the guilt of her father nor take any action she might regret. But she told him she could never go back; she could not even tell her friend Tabani. She wanted only to get away—from the family, the city, the past; she wanted to start all over. They walked in silence for a while, then he stopped and turned to face her. "Then come with me to Egypt," he said. "You will have peace there, you will have time to think, to heal."

He had left her alone in the room on the night they arrived in Abu Sir. It was late and she was exhausted from the journey, from her racing heart, the tightness in her lungs, the deep burn of shame.

But she could not sleep; her head was filled with thoughts of her father and what he did, his desperation and his willingness to deceive. In the dark fissures of her imagination, he pleaded with her to understand. It was only *her* life, *her* future he had in mind. If only she could dwell on that, on his goodness and his love. But not only must she mourn the loss of that perfect father, but also of the family that had given her a new life. They would have expected more than the short cryptic note she left, but words had failed her. She would call them soon and tell them the truth. Then they would understand her need to leave. But they would always think of her differently afterwards, and she could not bear the shame of their new appraisal.

A little later, she heard a soft rapping and Masoud's whispered voice. For a few moments she lay there, undecided. She could pretend to be asleep. But she craved the comfort of his arms around her, the roughness of his beard against her face, the reassurance of his love.

He was gentle to begin with, easing her back on to the bed, slowly undressing himself and her, gazing at her naked body and running his hands all over it, exploring, covering her with kisses. She arched her back and drew him closer, her hands damp with the sweat on his shoulders, her face hot from his quickening breath. In the dim light of the oil lamp, she watched the look on his face change. He closed his eyes and grimaced as though in pain, fumbling to move into her abruptly, forcefully. She moved with him, knowing he could not hold back. At the end, he cried out and collapsed onto her, his face turned away, his hands still gripping her shoulders. In a whisper she could barely hear, he told her he had imagined this since the day they met, but could never, ever have imagined the feelings he had now.

This man was her strength and her freedom. He would help her forget about the past, about her father...about Dominic. And this was her new life; she would surrender to it.

In the morning, he took her to meet the rest of his family and walked her around the property: stables, barns, paddocks and fields. Everyone was solicitous, asking whether she would like to eat, or drink tea, or rest a little more. In one of the barns, he showed her their Arabian horses and asked if she would like to learn to ride. She had never thought about this. The only horses she had ever seen were those in the souks and markets, thin and heavily burdened. "Some of these are Egyptian Arabians, the purest of the breed. See the dish shaped, chiselled face, the wide-set eyes, the way the tail carriage is arched high. That's how you can tell an Arabian horse. Look at that one—" he pointed to a grey at the far end of the barn. "His name is Khamsin, like our desert wind." He whistled and called the horse by name. It trotted over and nuzzled against him. Amina stroked him, squeezing her eyes against the brimming tears.

Masoud gathered her into his arms and covered her face and neck with kisses, rubbing the small of her back. "Amina, come with me, please...please," he said, his hands more urgent now. "I will make love to you until every tear has dried, every worry has left you."

But she wanted to be alone now. He understood. She was grateful that he understood.

Layla brought a light supper and *karkade* tea to her room. "Everything will feel different in a few days," she assured Amina. "You will find peace and happiness here."

Well before the sun was up, she heard a tentative knock on the door once more. This time, she did not hesitate, yearning for the intensity of his dark eyes, the grip of his hands on her breasts, the coarse brush of his beard as he kissed his way down to her thighs. He was slow, gentle, teasing, holding back, and it was she who grew more eager and urgent with mounting need. Finally, her breath quick and shallow, every muscle taut with anticipation, the heat flared through her, making her dig her fingernails into his back and cry out with the sharp thrill of pleasure and relief.

They lay for a while and watched the light seep through the edges of the shutters.

"Will you make the call today, Amina? Are you still sure about this?" he said, cradling her head on his shoulder. "You need only tell them that you wanted to start a new life with me, that you knew they would try to stop you, that's why you had to leave. They have long forgotten about the money. Why must you be your father's confessor?"

"I could never live with such a painful secret, Masoud."

He was quiet for several minutes and she wondered if he had drifted into sleep. "So be it," he said finally, leaning over to kiss her. "They will shrug it off. They have other things to think about with the marriage of the youngest, and another successor to their little empire before long. And you and I…we will build our life together here."

She flinched at the sarcasm, but he made the future sound calm and safe, far from her past life and past longings. He left, urging her to rest more, and she fell into a troubled sleep.

Waking with a start a few hours later, she could already feel the heat of the sun pushing into the room. She opened the shutters and one of the windows. The lemon scent from the oil lamp at her bedside competed with the deep earthiness of the farm, the pungent horse manure from the stables, the sweet, grassy scent of alfalfa that two young boys stacked in bins by the barn. At the far end of the driveway, a car pulled over and parked. More people coming for riding lessons, she thought. In the paddock across the courtyard, a small group on horseback was already assembled, listening to their instructor, Ibrahim, who wielded a lunge whip.

It was strange to have nothing to do. Back in Fez, the arrangements for the wedding would be getting more urgent. The thought of Lukas, looking anxious, in the dark in the corridor outside his room crept into her mind, unbidden. *What will become of him?* A wave of sadness and regret passed through her.

As she dressed, she heard Layla calling for Masoud downstairs, her voice angry…something about two men outside. Amina went back to the window.

Her heart leapt into her chest. She stepped backwards, falling clumsily against the bed. A hundred thoughts crashed through her head with one clear, razor-sharp realization: *They know everything. They have come for the money.*

The brothers stood a few feet from the front door. Even with their jeans and plain white shirts, they looked wealthy, tailored, urban, and out of place on this rugged farm. They turned, scanning the house, the stables, the paddocks. Her body trembling, Amina got as close to the window as she dared, and pressed herself to the wall beside it. They were right beneath her. Layla came out, Masoud behind her. Masoud stopped in his tracks.

"You and I have met," Hadir said. "This is my brother, Dominic. You know why we are here. Tell Amina Gamel we want to see her. Immediately."

"Amina does not want to see you," Masoud said. "She has left that part of her life behind. She is going to start a new life here in Egypt."

"We know who you are." Hadir stood six inches from Masoud and stabbed at him with his forefinger. "Your uncle confessed everything. You were planning to cash in on Amina's vulnerability, her father's deception. You are disgraceful. Bring Amina here. Right now."

Layla sprang to life. "You have no rights over the life of Amina Gamel. She is free to do as she wishes, and she wishes to live here with *our* family. She has a future with my cousin. How dare you try to take that away from them?"

Masoud snapped at her to leave them alone. He would sort everything out. But she ignored him, her voice rising in condemnation. "Get off this property. I'm going to get my husband. He will call the police and charge you with trespassing. You are not welcome here."

Dominic's face was rigid with rage. "Shut up, both of you. If you don't get Amina right *now*, I'll tear this place apart." He strode toward the house.

Layla and Masoud blocked his path and began to shout at the same time. Two of the stable boys came running.

Hadir grabbed Dominic's arm and pulled him back. "If you are so sure of yourselves," he said, struggling to keep Dominic from wrenching free, "tell Amina the truth and let her decide. Go on. Tell her all you wanted was the money."

Amina tried to take deep breaths to steady herself. She gripped the windowsill for support. *What are they saying? Who is the uncle? What is happening?* Her mouth was dry. She tried to swallow but none of the muscles in her throat would work.

Masoud limped a few steps to the table and chairs under the acacia tree that cast part of the forecourt in shade. "The money is not important. Not anymore." He gestured to his cousin. "Bring her here. And you get back to work," he yelled at the stunned stable hands.

Amina stepped away from the window, took her straw hat from the hook on the door, and strode from the room. No one was going to 'bring' her. She pushed past Layla at the foot of the stairs.

The little group fell silent as she stepped through the doorway. Dominic made a move towards her, but she put both hands in the air and shook her head. "I heard everything. Don't speak. It is Masoud who must speak."

She stood in front of Masoud but, when he could not meet her eyes, she doubled over, clutching her arms around her chest. It took all her strength to remain on her feet.

"I will tell you the truth, Amina," he said finally, turning his face toward her. "I will tell you all the truth. But please, promise me you will listen, that you will take me at my word."

"Your word is not worth a damn," Dominic said.

"Hold on, brother." Hadir let go of Dominic. "We shouldn't reject the promise of truth."

Masoud gestured for them to sit at the table in the shade with him and started to pull out a chair for Amina, but Hadir took another and helped her into it.

Amina looked down at her lap, acutely aware of Dominic pacing behind her. He refused to sit. She clasped both hands tightly together and studied the pattern of her cotton skirt: tiny swirls of grey and blue and green, intersecting, weaving around each other. The skirt was long and light but already she could feel the sweat beneath its waistband. She pulled down the brim of her straw hat, blocking the others from view. A tiny lizard scurried around her sandalled feet. She forced herself to listen to what Masoud was saying.

"With this riding accident, I can no longer help with the running of the farm, the lessons, the breeding. I must rely more on my work for the film industry. It is unpredictable. And my father is ill. Keeping the farm may not be possible. We need money to—"

"What are you looking for? Sympathy?" Dominic said.

"Amina never planned to keep your dirty money."

"Is that why you think we are here? For the money? You stupid, ignorant man. We are here to force the truth out of you. To hear you admit your scheming lies to Amina."

Amina dug her nails into her palms until they hurt.

"Da'ud *is* my uncle," said Masoud, his voice now weak with the sorrow and bitterness of defeat. "He has known Amina's father for many years. He wanted to help us all. When he found the charts, it was…an opportunity. He didn't want to hurt anyone."

Dominic thumped his fist on the table. "How long did he follow Amina, look her up and down, figuring out what an asset she would be? He came to me with those charts, so deferential, all the time scheming to get you together, so your family could get their hands on the money. And you—pretending you knew him only through your film work. What a bare faced, shameful liar you are. How can you sit there and hope that telling the truth now will exonerate you? So far you haven't told us anything that your snivelling uncle hasn't already squealed."

"There is one thing he would not have told you," Masoud whispered.

"What?" Hadir said. "Spit it out."

From the corner of her eye, Amina saw Masoud reach for her hand. She shrunk back, bowing her head lower.

"Keep your hands off her," Dominic said. "One inch closer and I'll rip your—"

"Hey, hey," Hadir said. "Sit down, for God's sake. You're not helping."

Dominic backed off, but remained standing.

"At the beginning, I wanted to help my family. I hoped only that Amina and I might be content together." Amina felt his eyes boring into her. "I never expected to fall in love with her."

"Then you are a fool as well as a liar and a thief," said Dominic.

Amina raised her head, aware that the four of them were looking at her intently: Layla defiant, her arms crossed, her chin thrust forward; Dominic, swaying on his feet, fists clenched; Masoud hunched over the table, his face creased with pain. For a fleeting second, she felt sorry for him.

Hadir, trim and cool despite the merciless sun, hands clasped together on the table, eyes narrowed with concern, said in his gentle voice, "Amina, will you come home with us?"

At that moment, what she thought was an unendurable burden began to slide from her shoulders. It was over. Not just this new deceit of Masoud's betrayal and the shame of being so easily led astray, but all the guilt and fear and humiliation of the last few months. It was *all* over. Hadir's question was an awakening, a realization that the shame was not hers to bear, that she need not be defined as part of someone else's life; she was not her father's daughter; not the rescued woman for Masoud to claim; not the grateful member of the El Hassan family. She was Amina Gamel, a whole person. Hadir and Dominic already knew the truth. They had not come here for the money; they had not come here to berate her for leaving. They had come to take her home.

"I will get my things.".

Walking toward the house, all she could hear was the sound of her feet crunching on the gravel, and the distant whinny of a horse in the far paddock, and all she could feel was the intoxicating pitch and swell of release.

Chapter 41

On the flight back to Canada, Steven tried to get comfortable in his pod-shaped business class seat. The brace on his lower leg and foot was tight and restrictive. Once the seat belt sign was off, Catherine loosened it for him and fussed around, getting his jacket hung, his iPad out of his bag, the seat tilted back, the leg rest fully raised and extended, a pillow under his knees. She clearly enjoyed his helplessness.

"No drinking, Dad. Not with that medication you're on. Doctor's orders. Okay?"

God, what I would give for a stiff whisky.

Catherine went marching to the front then, telling the flight attendants her father was in considerable pain and would like to have a black coffee and something to eat right away. "Well, you're paying enough," she said, when he tried to object. "They should spoil you."

After an hour of watching what Catherine called "a dick flick," the pain reared up again, and he popped another pill. He swore there must be some kind of hallucinogen in these pills because, after a while, his mind would veer pleasantly off course.

What a bummer this is. There was still at least one more painting to do for the Stockholm show. Toby had practically imploded when he heard the news and only settled down when Steven promised to get home immediately. "We're going to have to plan this," he said. "I'll get something set up for you, so you can paint, or we'll move you to a studio...whatever, whatever. Just get here."

Steven had considered going back to Vancouver for the surgery, but Catherine and Natalie convinced him to stay in Toronto. His condo was close to the hospital, he was set up to finish the paintings there, Catherine would be close by, Toby was on hand, and Philippe had offered to do "absolutely anything." Steven could tell Philippe was dying to be asked for help, so he could come round and demand every single detail of the visit to Fez, the hotel, the people, the food, and all the other things he'd had to miss out on. Natalie would fly in as soon as he was released from the hospital. She had insisted on this. She would cook for him, run errands, whatever. His daughter needed to get back to Morocco, she said, and she would be happy to work remotely while Steven recovered and started painting again.

Natalie. He missed her, and this surprised him again. Few women had stirred any serious emotion in him over the last few years, perhaps because he really did shut himself off, too absorbed in his own "claustrophobic world," as one of them claimed. Nigel labelled the women who gravitated to him as "socialite wannabees"… women who fancied themselves as collectors or who were connected to art or music or charitable foundations, or all three. *Maybe a successful artist is a badge, some kind of trophy.* He shook his head at this bizarre thought, considering himself nothing more than an average Canadian who loved the natural world and liked to paint it. He was still amazed that his work was appreciated and well-known.

Not long ago, he and Natalie had attended a charitable function in Vancouver where he donated one of his paintings for auction. The first thing that struck him is that she made no comment about what either of them should wear. In the past there had been so many "what on earth shall I wear," "I've got nothing, I can't be seen in that again," "so-and-so is bound to do black," or "Steven, you need a jacket, you can't do the podium thing in a sweater. Get real," kind of admonishing. When he picked Natalie up, she was wearing a long, sleeveless summer shift, white with swirls of bright colour at the hem. Her light brown hair was brushed back off her face and showed off funky, red and yellow dangling earrings from a local craft store. She looked lovely, he thought, and noticed with some satisfaction that it was she who drew the covert, appreciative looks and not the socialites, squeezed into their spangled cocktail attire.

He turned off the "dick flick" and manoeuvred to a prone position to try to sleep. In his half dream, he saw Rachel, sitting across from him on the terrace of his home in Tuscany, the lowering sun making the water in the fountain sparkle, the evening breeze stirring canopies of olive trees. She was drinking a glass of white wine and gazing over the wall at the terraced vineyards, the lilac sky, and the distant hills of San Gimignano. How perfect he thought his life was then, how little he knew of this woman who had been deeply in love with another man for the last ten years.

The image of Lukas clinging to the rock at the Merenid Tombs nudged to the front of his mind—her son, the other man's son. For the last few years, the very thought of the boy would bring back that old pain. But he had plucked the child from the side of the hill, might have even saved his life. And he had given him the Eye of Horus ring. That felt good. Rachel would say it was meant to be. Perhaps he *had* forgiven her.

Then it was Natalie's body caught in a shaft of early sunlight on his bed. She was asleep, lying on her back, one arm behind her head; the sheet pushed down, twisted between her legs. He kissed her, moving along her neck, down to her breasts, pulling the sheet away. She smiled, opened her eyes, squinting in the light, and raised both hands to—

The sudden dip and lurch of turbulence woke him with a start.

"You all right, Dad? You look flushed," Catherine said. "You haven't taken too many of the pills, have you?"

There was a loud ping. The seat belt sign lit up. The pilot said something. Steven struggled to find the right controls and bring himself to a sitting position. "Give me a break, Catherine. You're not my nurse."

"Yes, I am."

He tightened his seatbelt and gripped the arms of his seat as the plane pitched and shuddered. Catherine read her iPad, clearly unconcerned.

"What?" she said, looking over at him again. "If we're going down there's nothing we can do about it."

"Thanks. I feel so much better."

"All excited about seeing Natalie again? Is that why you're flushed? Come on, fess up."

Steven turned to look out of the window. Nothing but blue and shimmering whiteness. "I am," he said. "Very much. And I want you to meet her. I think you'll like her. I hope so anyway."

"Holy shit. My father's giving away his feelings." She looked genuinely shocked. "Is this because you think we're going down, Dad? Really, you mustn't worry."

Steven smiled to himself. He had made a decision or two in his half slumber and there were several things he was going to do when he got home. He looked across to Catherine and felt a swell of intense love for her. She was young and bright and optimistic; she had the world by the tail.

And there was something important he needed to tell her…about the romantic dream she was chasing. He was quite sure now that Fate had a different ending in mind.

Chapter 42

Over the next few days, Dominic felt nothing but the pleasure of returning home, mission accomplished. He revelled in Sophie's joy as she burst into tears at the sight of Amina, the slap on the back from Nigel, the secretive wink from Hadir as he called Tabani's father and said it had all been an 'unfortunate misunderstanding.' Lukas had run into Dominic's arms and then, shyly but willingly, submitted to a big hug and kiss from Amina. "Thank God, thank God," Dominic kept saying to himself, thinking that this was surely enough to turn him into a religious man.

But now, as he sat with Sophie and his brother at the bar on the roof, enjoying the cool of the evening after a hot day, a new anxiety began to hover at the edge of his thoughts. He kept checking his phone. No text from Catherine today.

"Why don't you call her," Sophie asked him in frustration. "We need to know when she's coming back. Nigel and Lukas will not want to hang around here forever, no matter how welcome they are."

"I will, I will. Steven should be out of hospital tomorrow. His girlfriend is flying in from Vancouver to stay with him. Catherine doesn't want to leave until Steven is looked after. It won't be long."

"Look what I've found in this freezer," said Hadir, from behind the bar. "Did Henri get these for the wedding?" He pulled out an elaborately swirled chocolate and vanilla ice cream and tore off its cellophane wrapping. "They'll go bad if they're not eaten."

"You are the worst," said Sophie. "Never mind. Eat the damn thing. We'll get more."

"May I join you?"

They looked up to see Nigel emerge from the stairwell.

"Come on over here, Nigel. Want one of these?" Hadir offered him an ice cream.

"I really shouldn't." Nigel patted his stomach and sat on one of the high stools. "But what the heck. I just spoke to Philippe. He went to see Steven today and found him bright and breezy…well, as breezy as Steven ever gets. The cast should be off in time for his Stockholm show. His agent has rigged up some sort of high, swivelling stool that allows him to keep his foot off the floor and paint. He'll be home tomorrow."

"What a relief," said Sophie.

"I have to tell you, the person most relieved is Lukas," Nigel said. "He kept saying it was all his fault. He is learning, far too young, that the world can be harsh and complicated." He looked around. "Where is he, by the way? I thought he might be up here with you."

"With Sadiq in the kitchen," said Dominic. "Henri and Amina are teaching them to make *chebakia*. What a mess. Sticky fingers. Overpowering smell of cinnamon everywhere."

"And what were *you* doing in the kitchen?" Sophie asked, eyebrows raised.

"Looking for something to eat. Why else would I be there?"

Ah, Sophie, you can read me like a book. The truth was that he felt uneasy if he didn't know the whereabouts of Amina or Lukas. He hoped it was just the 'coming down' impact from the recent stress and that it would go away when Catherine returned. His heart skipped. Did all men about to be married feel the same, he wondered: excitement laced with a *frisson* of terror.

"I asked Amina to join us, but she wanted to stay with Henri and the boys," he said.

"We must give her time," said Sophie.

"Maybe she loved that guy," said Hadir. "She could be heartbroken."

Dominic caught Sophie giving her husband a warning look. *What is that about?*

"Did you ask her?" Hadir persisted.

"She's still anxious about her father," he said, ignoring Hadir's question, "What he might have been capable of. Nigel, did Lukas's mother ever say anything about Ahmed?"

Nigel let out a long breath. "She couldn't believe Ahmed had been charged, but it's true he didn't like her. Let's just say things started going terribly wrong. She left and was gone for ten years, then one day showed up again. Too much for Ahmed. But surely not enough to try to kill her."

"I believe she was a good friend of yours?" said Sophie.

"Yes, and a good person but…complicated. I think Steven would tell you that she had a wonderful influence on his life and his work. As I've mentioned, we hoped they would stay together but it was not to be. She loved Egypt, the desert, the stars and she was deeply in love with Lukas's father." Nigel blew out his breath. "You know, I made her a promise I haven't fulfilled yet. She wanted her ashes scattered in the desert, the same as she and Lukas did for Karl. Her Uncle Vanni in Italy has them still. Well, one day." He finished the ice cream and wiped his hands on a napkin. "She and Karl…that relationship really concerned me. It was as though they were both under a spell, bewitched in some way."

"She was gone ten years?" said Sophie. "Why go back after such a long time away?"

"That, my friends, is a long story. Another night perhaps." Nigel took off his glasses and polished them on the napkin. "As for Amina, I hope she comes to believe her father was seized with panic when he saw the fire."

"We must talk about the money at some point," said Sophie. "Amina has made it clear that she wants nothing to do with it. She's pushing for us to go to the bank immediately and transfer it back to us. I finally persuaded her to let it rest. We will discuss it as a family."

"There's no hurry is there?" said Dominic.

"No, of course not," said Hadir. "But, for Amina's sake we should make a decision soon. Why? Do you have something in mind?"

"I've got an idea. But I want to think about it."

"An idea he wants to *think* about first. That I should see the day!" Hadir said, arms raised heavenwards.

"At least I *have* ideas. Give me one of those ice creams. Then I'm off to bed."

As Dominic passed Lukas's room on the way to his own, he heard voices. He knocked. "Lukas, it's me. Just saying goodnight."

"I'm learning songs in Arabic," Lukas shouted through the door. "Come and listen."

Stepping inside, Dominic stopped in surprise to find both Lukas and Amina sitting on the floor with their backs against the bed.

"Listen, listen," said Lukas. *"A ram sam sam, a ram sam sam. Guli guli guli guli ram sam sam. A rafiq, a rafiq.* Amina says it's famous."

"It is. I used to sing it when I was a kid."

"And I know another one. About being an artist. *Arsomo baba, Arsomo mama, Bil alwan, Bil alwan. Arsomo…* Wait a minute, I forget. *Fog* – something."

"Arsomo alami. Foq alqemani," said Amina.

"It means I draw my dad and my mom with all the colours, and I draw a flag. And I know the end. *Ana fanan. Ana fanan.* I'm an artist."

"You certainly are an artist, Lukas." Dominic wanted to gather them up and squeeze them tight. But something his mother once told him came to mind: *If life is going well, leave it alone. You might spoil it.*

"Okay you two, see you in the morning."

"Dominic…can Amina come with us when we go to the desert?"

"Well of course—"

"No, no," Amina jumped in. "I'd rather not. Lukas may not get this chance again. You two go together. Please."

The reminder that Lukas would be leaving before long cast a shadow into the room. Dominic tried to make light of it. "You'll come visit us again, though, won't you, Lukas?"

The boy bit his lip. "I don't know."

***

At seven the next morning, Dominic lay in bed and tried to bring cohesion to his wild ideas. The world beyond his window was scurrying about the business of the day, but he felt no immediate urgency to join it.

Nigel had chatted with him the night before about the possibility of visiting again. Philippe was anxious to see Morocco after all that Nigel had told him, and they both assumed there would be lots of 'family festivities' with Steven, and possibly Catherine's mother, one day, on both sides of the Atlantic. But as for Lukas, that was a big question mark. "Who knows what's going to happen over there," Nigel said. "I'll know more, of course, when I take him back."

Dominic wondered if the boy was already awake, helping Henri in the kitchen. Henri was usually gruff and impatient with everyone, but he indulged Lukas, letting him roll pastry or take cookies off the racks and put them in baskets and jars. What was it about this boy that made his heart constrict in his chest, Dominic wondered? Some errant thread in the tapestry of life had snagged and drawn them both inextricably together. Every time he saw him, he wanted to pick him up and squeeze him tight. Seeing him smile, clasping his hand, made Dominic feel more alert and alive.

He stared at the mosaic glass swag lamp hanging from the ceiling, its tiny turquoise, red and yellow panes reflected in pale shards on the opposite wall with light from the window. Time to get up. A lot of work had been put on hold. And he needed to talk to Catherine about what was on his mind. And Nigel. And then the others. Or he must put the whole idea out of his mind. It was probably crazy, "Head in the Clouds" again.

The ring of his phone jolted him out of this reverie. He groped for it in the bed covers. "Catherine. Hey. What time is it there? Is everything okay?"

"I couldn't sleep."

"Something wrong?"

"I was scared I wouldn't have the courage later."

"What do you mean?"

A long pause. "I'm so sorry, Dominic. It isn't happening. I'm not coming back."

It took him several seconds to take this in. "What are you saying? Is it your dad? Nigel said he was much better."

Catherine said nothing. He could hear her breathing. He swung his legs out of bed and stood by the window. "Catherine. Don't. Please. What's wrong?"

"I can't do it. I can't marry you."

"But…why? What have I done? What's happened?"

"You know as well as I do. We had a hell of a good time. But it's not going to work out."

"Yes, it is. Catherine, I thought we were both happy. Is it all because of the trouble here? I'm sorry I was so secretive. I was only trying to protect—"

"It's not that. Not *only* that."

"Is there someone else? That guy…Gavin? The one you were seeing when we met?"

"No way. He's toast. It's not that."

Toast. The word felt like a knife in his back. He swallowed hard. "Guess that's both of us, then. At least, you're efficient."

"You're pissed, I know. But you'll thank me one day."

"Come on, Catherine, what's going on? This is a real shock."

"Okay, I'll say it. That whole business with Amina. It's so fucking obvious. To everyone."

Dominic's hand holding the phone felt numb. He feared he would drop it. "What's obvious? Nothing is fucking obvious to me."

"Oh please. I could tell the moment I saw the two of you at breakfast here in the hotel. Those dewy eyes gazing up at you like you're some kind of deity. Too much already."

"Catherine, Amina has always looked up to me. I'm like a big brother."

"Sure, you are. But, Dominic, the problem is not the way she looks at you."

"What then?"

"It's the way you look at her."

Chapter 43

Every morning since her return, Amina awoke feeling light and buoyant, as though she could float out of bed without moving a muscle. She was home. *Home* – a word with wide open arms. The family had been so understanding. If only she had come to them, they said…that was what upset them most, the thought of her suffering embarrassment and humiliation when nothing was her fault.

Sophie took her aside one morning. "Amina, you have said very little about Cairo. I want you to know that if there is anything on your mind, you must tell me. For what it's worth, I believe that Masoud did love you. I could tell he was stricken from the moment you met. It is a tragic story. Do you want to talk about him?"

Amina turned away, wondering how much Sophie would have surmised. "I was fooled Sophie, by my own heart, too. I thought we…" She shook her head. "I want to forget it. It's all in the past."

"Then it will stay there," said Sophie.

Now, only the thought of the money gnawed at her. They should go to the bank and get it back right away so her conscience might finally be clear.

***

The news about Dominic and Catherine did not surprise Amina. The idea had always been hard to believe. She wondered what had driven the decision to marry. Catherine had a mind of her own and did not fawn over him—maybe that kind of independence appealed to him. Regardless, she thought with renewed resignation, it won't be long before the next one comes along.

Dominic had not been around much since their return and was not present at any of the family meals. He was out often with Nigel or tied up on the phone in his office. She dropped by to tell him she was sorry about

Catherine. There were a lot of papers on his desk which he quickly covered with a file folder. "Wasn't meant to be," he said, turning away. She wondered if he was embarrassed or just irritated by the interruption.

Much to the delight of Lukas, Nigel had decided to stay longer, despite the cancellation of the wedding. There was so much to see and do, he said, and he wanted to give Lukas the best possible time before the reality of his new life had to be faced. Lukas made the most of every day. His French was improving and, with Amina's encouragement and the help of Sadiq, he was speaking Arabic phrases, to the delight of everyone.

Each morning, he sought her out, wanting to help with small tasks or errands. Nigel asked if he was becoming a nuisance, but Amina insisted she loved his company. In the corner of her office was a big cosy chair where he would curl up, absorbed in his star books or on his tablet, while she worked. If several guests arrived at the same time and the bellboys could barely keep up, they would get Lukas to take napkins or a basket of nuts, dates, and sugared almonds to the conversation rooms for them, and sometimes he would run between the offices of the brothers or Sophie and Amina with files or papers. When Amina took a break, he'd go to the kitchen to bring her something from Henri, and then bombard her with questions: *How many guests are here today? What countries do they come from? When is the next prayer time? Can I buy one of the Fez hats? How old are Dominic and Hadir? How old is Henri?* There was no end to his desire for information.

The previous day, she had taken him to the market. It was very busy, and they had to jostle their way through different stands. Amina was anxious not to let Lukas out of her sight, but she noticed people gave way to him. He looked distinctly foreign, with his tangled blond hair, grown long, and pale features. When he smiled, his eyes had a mischievous glint and, in his own way, he was a charmer. Amina laughed as the merchants indulged him, urging him to try this little wedge of *ghurabia* date roll or that little bite of *baklava*. They were amazed with his attempts at Arabic, and he enjoyed himself immensely. Amina made him ask for whatever she needed—potatoes, onions, lemons, ginger, grapes, enunciating the words as clearly as she could and having him repeat them.

"Nigel loves ginger," he told her. "He eats it raw. Henri is going to make him a special ginger tart."

"What's Nigel doing today?" she asked.

"He's gone somewhere with Dominic again. He said they're very busy."

In the evening, up in his room he showed her the box of star maps and the notebook from his father that he had brought with him to Fez, and pulled out the two charts that had precipitated the events of the past few weeks. As they stood together comparing these to her own and finding that they were indeed almost identical—just a few different notations in the margins—Amina felt light-headed and had to sit for a moment on the bed. She wondered why Lukas had no sense of awe about this coincidence. On the contrary, he acted as though it was a totally natural thing. It was meant to happen, and so it did.

"And I think it means I can be your friend," he said, looking at her with a big smile.

Amina had to fight the sudden sting of tears. *To think that I once feared this little boy.*

She told Nigel about this when he asked to join her at breakfast this morning. Nigel had been considerate, never asking her questions about her disappearance, concerned only for her wellbeing.

"Perhaps Lukas is too young to realize how strange all this is, Nigel. I know it sounds crazy but it's like there is something deeper, some kind of force we can't explain, at work."

"I'm quite sure you're right, Amina," said Nigel. "Something is going on that binds us all together. I don't understand it one bit and, to tell you the truth, it makes me feel uneasy. But here we all are. And we all seem to like each other so where's the harm in that?"

He told her about his friendship with Rachel, the kind of work she did, the kind of person she was. "I think you would have liked her. She and Karl had something very special, something I could frankly never understand. Karl believed strongly in this unseen force that you say you feel. He claimed that each of us has a path mapped out for us and that we should seek this path, discover our destiny." He paused, biting his lip and looking off into the distance.

Amina felt a strong need to squeeze his shoulder but was too shy. Everyone is haunted by sad memories, she thought. No one escapes.

He turned back. "You know…even though Lukas never knew his father, I believe he is deeply influenced by him. Ah, speak of the devil—here's the little busybody coming over."

Lukas ran up to the table. "Are you coming with Henri and me to the bazaar? We are going to buy me a Fez hat. It's all right. It's from my allowance."

"Goodness me, what a brave soul Henri is. No, I've got things to do, people to see. Off you go now."

After breakfast, as Amina crossed the courtyard on the way to her office, she saw Dominic sitting on a couch in the hallway, a file folder and a phone on his lap. He was leaning back and staring at the ceiling, his feet stretched out in front of him, his hands clenched under his chin, his forehead creased in concentration.

What on earth is wrong? She stepped behind one of the palm trees so he would not sense her presence. *Is he angry, is he grieving?* She longed to go to him, to hold him close, tell him everything was going to be all right.

Chapter 44

The two brothers and Sophie sat on the roof of the Riad enjoying a communal shisha pipe. The hotel was full, but most guests were out and about, enjoying the warm but pleasant late afternoon air, so they had the roof to themselves. Dominic looked over the top of his sunglasses at his brother and sister-in-law. They were such an anchor in his life, patient, wise, tolerant and, over these past few days, such a safe haven as he wrestled with his wild, erratic moods, his inability to sort out his feelings.

"Henri wants to know what food we want," said a voice behind them.

They looked over to see Lukas at the top of the stairwell.

"Ah, Lukas," Hadir said. "Tonight's the night. Finally, off to the desert. Look at that sky—totally clear and forecast to stay that way. You won't get much sleep, I'm afraid."

"I don't need any sleep, ever."

"Tell him to give us some chicken pieces and fruit and nuts and something sweet, that's all we'll need," said Dominic.

Lukas ran back down the stairs.

"Does he know it's a long drive?" Hadir asked.

"The drive is all part of the fun. I've booked a place for us to stay on the way back."

"He's so excited. What a sweetheart," said Sophie.

"I love him to bits," Dominic said. "I think he's a kindred spirit."

"He loves you too, that's clear," said Sophie. "And I have a very strong feeling that what you are planning is the best idea you have ever had. Where's Nigel by the way?"

"Another phone call to make, a few more emails."

"When are you going to tell Lukas?"

"Soon."

They fell silent. Dominic leaned back and closed his eyes, enjoying the smell of the apple and molasses tobacco from the shisha pipe, and the chatter of people in the streets below.

A hand on his shoulder startled him. He opened his eyes to see both Hadir and Sophie leaning towards him. "Brother, look at me," said Hadir. "We won't stay quiet any longer."

Dominic froze.

"What, Hadir? What's wrong?"

"Come on. I think you know what I am going to say."

Dominic widened his eyes and gave a slight shake of his head.

Hadir took his wife's hand. "Sophie and I are sure that Lukas is not the only one who has stolen your heart. When are you going to have the courage to admit that other love?"

The sentence stretched out in Dominic's head, the end of it such a long way from the beginning, as though he had smoked some potent weed. He put both hands to his head, elbows on the table. "I don't know what you mean."

"Yes, you do," Sophie whispered.

All his thoughts collided and fused in his head and no words would come out of his mouth. He waited in vain for one of them to fill the gaping silence. "It can't be," he finally managed. "I've blown it."

"For all your experience with women, you are such an amateur," said Sophie. "Useless. You really do not understand us. You don't even understand your *own* feelings. All this sleeping around with other women, falling in and out of love and lust, nearly getting married…while the woman you really love, and who loves you too, is right in front of your nose. You have been running away, denying your own heart."

"I don't—"

"Dominic…you were mesmerized by Amina from the moment you saw her at Hadir's bedside in the hospital all those years ago, sitting with her father."

"*Sophie*, she was fifteen years old. A beautiful lost soul, a street angel. That's all." He sank lower on to the table.

"Well, she grew up, didn't she?"

He tried to swallow, but his throat was parched. "All this time…if you believed this, why haven't you said anything?"

"We were hoping *you* would grow up. It is taking forever."

"*Are* you in love with her?" said Hadir.

"She wouldn't want me, couldn't trust me. I don't know what to say," he muttered into his chest, not daring to bring that stifled longing into the open, let it finally breathe.

"Is that a yes?"

"Of course, it's a yes," said Sophie. "You men take so long to process the simplest information."

Dominic continued to stare down at the table, tugging at fists full of his hair until his scalp burned. "I love her so much I want to curl up and die with this feeling."

"Well, that's a brilliant idea," said Sophie. "Another idea might be to go and tell her."

Chapter 45

Dominic paced his room. A shutter in his mind, closed and bolted for years, had been wrenched open and flung back, the light flooding in, nearly blinding him. His heart was laid open, the truth of his feelings exposed. Everything was bright and raw, and his whole body felt bruised. He was a fool, he had lost his chance, if ever he'd had one. Amina had been manipulated and betrayed and wouldn't trust *any* man.

He kicked the wall and spun around, striding back to the other end. *The whole business with Catherine. What does she think of all that? And what about Masoud? Had she loved him? Had he been manipulated by his uncle too, and were his feelings genuine? Would she have married him and spent the rest of her life in Egypt?* A lump of bile rose in his throat. He slumped onto the bed.

Lukas would be waiting for him. He packed the telescope, threw some clothes into his overnight bag, took several deep breaths, and knocked on the boy's door.

Nigel answered, Lukas right behind him. "All ready? He's practically airborne with excitement."

"Thanks for everything, Nigel. I will never forget—"

"No need. Nothing to thank me for." Nigel patted him on the shoulder, then drew him into a hug. "Right. Off you go, you two. I'm heading up to the roof." He handed over Lukas's backpack and walked down the corridor, waving over his shoulder. "Be good," he called back.

"Lukas." Dominic dropped to a crouch and spoke quickly, scared to lose his courage. "Remember, you asked if Amina could come with us? Maybe *you* could persuade her. She won't be able to resist your charm."

Lukas spun around and jumped in the air. "I knew it."

"Whoa, what do you mean, what do you think you knew?"

"Nothing." He ran next door to Amina's room.

"Hey," Dominic whispered loudly. "Take it easy, okay?" He stood back against the wall and listened, feeling like an anxious schoolboy.

"Please Amina. We want you to come ever so much. *I* want you to come. It will be so cool," Lukas said. "But I think you have to pack some clothes."

Amina stepped into the corridor. "Dominic? Is this right? No arm-twisting?"

"No, no. Come with us. It'll be fun. And Henri has packed enough food for an army."

"You'll have to give me a few minutes."

I will give you whatever you want for the rest of your life.

Eventually she joined them in the corridor. She was dressed in layers: cream linen pants and a shirt, a long sleeveless wine-coloured vest over these, a cream and gold scarf hanging loosely around her shoulders. On her arm she carried a small bag with a sweater looped through the handles.

"See, Lukas, Amina has a warm sweater and scarf. And you are in shorts and a shirt. Has Nigel packed you something warm too? The desert can fool you. One minute you're toasty warm and the next you're shivering." He spent a few minutes double-checking the boy's backpack, glad of the excuse not to have to look at Amina.

They had been driving for over an hour, Lukas chatting away, asking his usual string of questions. "What's that town over there?," "What's a wadi?," "Do Berbers speak the same Arabic?," "Will we see camels?," "What does that sign say?" And so on. He and Amina answered them as best they could.

She had insisted on taking the back seat and Dominic tried to keep his eyes from the rear-view mirror. When he did sneak a look, he was struck by how calm she looked. *Was* she happy or simply relieved to be home? And was it even possible that she loved him, really loved him, not just cared for him? He tried to push away the thoughts of Masoud and what probably happened on the nights she spent in Cairo, but his imagination gave him no peace. He squeezed his eyes shut and had to swerve sharply back into lane. What right did he have to question this anyway? *All those women. They meant nothing, nothing.* When he told Sophie and Hadir about Catherine's call, they admitted they'd been shocked about the marriage, then fleetingly happy and then eventually concerned. But at last, Sophie said, he had met his match. Catherine was no fool.

Twisting the steering wheel around a sharp bend, he saw the leather bracelet on his right hand, the trigger that had set in motion events that would transform his life. *The Tower: your beliefs, your habits, your day-to-day routines turned on their heads. No kidding. And Amina?* Please God, he thought, let Amina be a happy part of this devious plot, this never-ending twist of fate.

Another quick look in the mirror. She was staring through the window at the dark sweep of desert, the lights of small towns less and less frequent now. What he would give to know her thoughts. The prickle of intense jealousy and self-doubt crept over his skin again. She would never accept him. She might even laugh at him.

Eventually, up ahead, the road became little more than a gravel track. He parked the car off to the side and unloaded the telescope and the bags. Lukas pulled out his warm sweater and tied it around his waist.

"We should leave our shoes here," Dominic said. "Much easier to walk barefoot."

As his eyes adjusted to the darkness, he saw a high dune and some rocky patches in the near distance and no sign of any people. That's where they'd go. It would be tough to climb, and it might be hard to secure the telescope, but it would be worth trying. He walked ahead of them and told them to stay close behind him.

Lukas had gone quiet.

"You okay, Lukas?"

"I can't believe the stars."

Dominic heard a catch in the boy's voice. He turned to see him leaning way back, his mouth open, staring at the sky.

"We'll be taking a long rest at the top of the dune. And it's not even fully dark yet. You'll see more stars soon."

Am I crazy, he wondered for the thousandth time. *How is this little kid going to react to the plans all these adults have put in motion? And Amina…what if she's doubtful, uncertain?*

At the foot of the dune, Dominic gazed at the dazzling sky above him, not finding any of the easily recognizable constellations. There were just too many stars, great clusters and bands and scatterings of them. Climbing the slope was hard work, his feet sinking and sliding into the soft sand, the backpack cutting into his shoulders. He looked back to the other two, who were making much slower progress. Amina held Lukas's arm to steady him. "Don't try to keep up with me," he called to them. "Just follow where I'm going. Slow and steady."

Stumbling hand over hand, sometimes sinking to his knees, Dominic climbed as fast as his breath would allow him, overcome with the need to get to the top, the very top, to lie on his back and soar into the milky way, wallow in that great bowl of stars and promise these two people he loved so dearly, that they would never have another care in this world.

Finally, he made it, dizzy with the effort, crawling on hands and knees during the final stretch. He took the rolled blanket from under his backpack and spread it out, then climbed a little way back down, to help pull the other two to the top. They collapsed together and for several minutes lay on their backs, panting, astonished into silence by the dense, shimmering splendour above them.

"That's where my dad lives," Lukas said after a little while.

Amina raised herself on one elbow. "You mean in heaven?"

"Kind of. We took his ashes in the desert, my mom and me, near Cairo where she said they always went. I made them fly up in the sky. I remember. My mom said he went home to the stars. I wish I could see him." He wiped at his eyes with his knuckles.

Amina took his hand. "You can't see him, but I think he can see you. And I bet he's really happy there. How could you not be happy with all those magical stars around you?"

Dominic tousled Lukas's hair. The boy's shirt collar was open, and the Eye of Horus ring hung at his neck. Sophie had found a chain for him. Good of Steven to give it to him, he thought, and so right. "You know, Lukas. I would love to have met your father and mother. From everything I've heard, they were very special people. And so are you. Imagine how your dad must be feeling now, seeing you down here. He'd be proud of you. And so would your mom."

He sat up. "Okay, time to take a closer look. I'll get the telescope and a few things organized but we should eat first. Lukas, can you find a place and unpack what Henri's given us? There are a few rocky patches over there, flatter bits." He pointed the flashlight. "Don't forget your own flashlight and don't go any farther. Call if you need help."

"I won't need help." Lukas scrambled to his feet and dragged the bag behind him, his flashlight bobbing and weaving with his staggered steps.

Dominic lit a small kerosene lamp and wedged it in the sand. Amina's face was solemn in its half light. The vast canyons of the desert spread out on all sides. He took a handful of sand and squeezed, trying to stop the grains from sliding away, trying to take deeper breaths.

"Amina, there something I want to tell you. But there is another thing you need to know first. A decision I want you to be happy about." He paused. "It's to do with the money."

Her hand flew to her mouth, and she shrank back. "Please. No. I've said already. I want nothing to do with it. It's not mine."

"You are right. It's not yours. But it's not Hadir's or mine either." He looked over to where Lukas was, absorbed with unpacking the food. "It's for Lukas. We will put it in a trust for him, for his education, for his future. But here's the important thing. I want him, we all want him, to stay here, to live with us, with the family, at the Riad Capella. He doesn't know this yet. I hope so much he will agree. And I am praying that you will too."

"Oh my God," Amina got clumsily to her knees and threw her arms around him. He didn't dare to move. "Oh my God. It's a wonderful, perfect idea. Of course, I agree. How could you even ask me? It's the best thing that could happen to that money." She pushed herself away from him and the distance between them opened again like a gaping wound. "He will be thrilled. Look how he's learning Arabic, look how he wants to help at the hotel. He knows he can't stay with Nigel and Philippe forever and he's so unhappy in England. He told me that. But what about his uncle, how will you make it all happen?"

The surge of relief nearly felled him, but he yearned for the feel of her body against him again, and had to force himself to slow down. "It's what Nigel and I have been so busy working out these last few days. If he says yes, everything is prepared. Philippe will fly over from Canada with the rest of his things and help him settle in. Nigel and I will fly to England to see his uncle, Robert. Robert has provisionally agreed but obviously he wants to talk to Lukas and to us. And there'll be endless paperwork to set in motion."

"So…would it be forever? He would stay here, live here always?"

"That's up to him."

Amina let out a stifled sob. "He was right. We will find out why we were supposed to meet. That's what he said. He loves you so much, Dominic. He will want to stay. I'm sure of it."

"I hope so. You see, this *is* a time of healing. Your father knew his father. Who knows what happened that day, but the fact is Karl died tragically and never knew his son. And then his mother, Rachel,…she died too. It is such a sad story. Amina, I believe the money came into your father's hands, not for your sake, but for Lukas's. It was fate's way of eventually making things right. And you…you were the beautiful, wise messenger of fate."

She leaned back on her hands and turned away, shaking her head. "I've been foolish, Dominic. I'm not wise."

"Look at me. I am the foolish one. I love you so much. I have always loved you. I've never had the courage to admit it to myself, to tell you. I've been so stupid. Can you ever forgive me, Amina? Can I…can I hope that you love me too?"

His words hung sharp and clear in the night air, escaped now, irretrievable. He held his breath, half wishing that the greedy darkness of the desert would swallow them whole and the silence would return, but still they hovered, and he swore that a whole age would pass as he waited, bracing himself for her response, staring across the sand, and hearing only the echo of his own voice.

She untied the knot in her scarf, and he watched in disbelief as she slid it from her shoulders, got to her knees and wrapped it around his neck, still holding both ends. "You are a crazy, wonderful and impossible man," she whispered, pulling him close. "Of course, I love you. And I have been waiting far, far too long."

He slumped into her arms, overwhelmed, his head buried in her chest, his body heaving with supressed joy. He breathed in the smell of her skin, her hair, the jasmine perfume she loved. Every inch of him ached to make love to her, but for the first time in his life, he was nervous at the thought. So often he had imagined it in the dark and secret corners of his mind, before shutting down and chasing away the fantasy with clumsy and meaningless affairs. Now, he could feel that foolish self falling away like the grains of sand from his clenched fist. With each new breath, he felt vital, serious, and tender. He wanted only to hold on to Amina, feel the press of his fingers against her back, in case she slip from his grasp again. He felt no urgency. He would *earn* the love of this woman. The future nights of his life spiralled endlessly forward like the loops and strings of stars above him.

He kissed her, scarcely believing this, pulling her so close that she gasped for breath. "Can you truly forgive me, Amina?"

She lay back on the blanket and pulled him down beside her. "Maybe the past could not have been any different," she said. "Maybe there were strange reasons why we had to wait. Many things needed to fall into place." She leaned her head on his shoulder. "Perhaps, after all, it was fate—so there is nothing to forgive."

"You can kiss some more," Lukas shouted over to them. "I knew you were going to."

"Well, aren't you the clever one?" Dominic called back.

He and Amina sat up, side by side on the blanket, digging their bare feet into the cold sand. Below them, the smaller dunes cascaded over each other like the cresting waves of a dark sea. They looked up at the thousand flickering stars, at the thin wedge of the waxing moon, and over to the young boy who was waving his flashlight back and forth as he danced and stumbled about in the sand, acting the fool, singing to himself.

"He belongs here," Amina whispered. "When are you going to tell him?"

Dominic gently pulled away from her and got to his feet, struggling to keep his balance in the deep sand. He took both her hands and helped her up. "Come on," he said. "Let's tell him now."

EPILOGUE – SIX MONTHS LATER

Tearing the last sheet of brown paper from the huge package propped against a pillar in the courtyard, they took several steps back in disbelief.

"I *can't* believe it," Dominic whispered, squeezing Amina to his side. "I can't believe he'd do this."

He opened the letter.

Dominic,

Please forgive my long silence. I am not a good communicator.

This is my painting 'Aphelion' that you admired at Nigel and Philippe's. I hope you can find a place for it and that it makes you think about the strange connection you and I forged and the tremendous good that has come from it. What a weird, magical world this is, despite our many flaws and failings.

I think often of Lukas and your beautiful Amina. It was always very clear to me that the three of you were meant to be together.

Steven

Amina looked at the man standing on the edge of the steep slope, the clusters of cypress trees and terraced vineyards falling away beneath him, his arms raised to greet the rising sun. She could feel the promised warmth of that sun and the soaring spirit of the man himself.

She placed her hands on her swollen belly and sent up a silent prayer.

-End-

Acknowledgements

My first thanks must go to Brahim K. who introduced me to Morocco and its wonderful people, driving my husband and me and two friends across the desert from Marrakech to Merzouga and to the magical city of Fez, all of which inspired the main setting for this novel.

Over the past two years, I have been very grateful for the ongoing support of my talented friends at First Page Writers: Tina Tzatzanis, Josée Siguoin and Michelle Alfano whose terrific suggestions and tireless, thoughtful critique made such a difference to the final edit of the novel; to Arif Anwar, Justine Mazin and Michelle Boone whose advice and enthusiasm I could always rely on; and to Linda Rui-Feng who joined us recently and who, in such a short time, made razor-sharp and very helpful observations.

Thanks also to all those who read and enjoyed my first novel, The Way Things Fall, who felt strongly that the story left tantalizing "open doors" and encouraged me to venture through one of them in this new direction.

I am greatly indebted to Shane Joseph, my editor and publisher who believed in the idea behind this novel, and its predecessor, and once again wielded his brilliant editorial pen to hone and sharpen it.

And, finally, I want to thank my wonderful husband Jürgen, who has always been my patient sounding board, my shoulder to lean on through thick and thin.

Author Bio

Liz Torlée lived and worked in England and Germany before emigrating to Canada. She has always been fascinated by the idea of fate and the way it makes all our lives intersect in strange and far-reaching ways. She and her husband are avid travellers, especially through the Middle East…or any country with a desert! They live in midtown Toronto. *In Love With The Night* is Liz's second novel.